THE PROBABILITY OF MURDER

J.D. BARKER
PATRICK LOGAN

The Probability of Murder

Published by:
Hampton Creek Press
P.O. Box 177
New Castle, NH 03854

Worldwide Print, Sales, and Distribution by Simon & Schuster

For information about special discounts for bulk purchases, please contact Simon & Schuster Special Sales at 1-866-506-1949 or business@simonandschuster.com

Cover Design by Domanza
Book design and formatting by Domanza

Manufactured in the United States of America

ALSO BY J.D. BARKER

Forsaken

She Has A Broken Thing Where Her Heart Should Be

A Caller's Game

Behind A Closed Door

Something I Keep Upstairs

4MK THRILLER SERIES

The Fourth Monkey

The Fifth To Die

The Sixth Wicked Child

WITH JAMES PATTERSON

The Coast to Coast Murders

The Noise

Death of the Black Widow

Confessions of the Dead

The Writer

WITH OTHERS

Dracul

Heavy Are The Stones

We Don't Talk About Emma

The Lies We Tell

The Finer Things

The Quiet Neighbor

To stay on top of J.D. Barker news and releases, sign up for the newsletter at *www.masterofsuspense.com*

CHAPTER 1

AARON TREADMAN HAD never been good with numbers. Not as a kid, not in school, and definitely not now, as an adult.

If it weren't for his fingers and toes, he would have had difficulty counting his fingers and toes.

But there was one number he did understand: 78,000.

$78,000 . . . the current going rate for one Bitcoin. And that was what he was going to get. He *was* going to get that Bitcoin—they all were.

Who gave a fuck about the other numbers, anyway?

The game seemed simple enough: ten different boxes, ten different numbers inside. Open five, find your assigned number in one of these, and you can move to the next room. If all ten contestants find their numbers in the first five boxes they open, closing them before the next player enters the room, they all win one Bitcoin each.

Simple.

Fifty-fifty—had to be. He understood those numbers, too, and knew that these weren't bad odds.

Aaron was contestant eight, which meant that the first seven had already found their numbers. But it was an all-or-nothing game—the voice over the loudspeaker had told them so.

If even one contestant failed to find their number in the first five boxes they chose, they all lost.

Left with nothing.

Aaron wasn't planning on losing—this was his chance to finally get ahead.

It didn't matter that the numbers themselves were all fucked up and random: two, three, seventeen, nineteen.

And thirteen.

That was the number that he'd stuck to his chest, as per the instructions.

The fucking instructions, spoken by some random voice over a wireless speaker.

Aaron had already opened four boxes, none of which contained his lucky number thirteen. He had one more to go.

He moved in front of the box marked seven.

Stared at it, squinted, tried to see through the wooden top to the number inside, the one that really mattered.

He shook his head.

No. Not this one.

Aaron slid to his left—Box Eleven.

Yes. This is it.

He took a deep breath, held it. Reached for the lid, pulled his hand back.

Licked his lips.

It was warm in the small, ten by ten-foot room. Sweat formed on his brow, and he swiped at it with the palm of his hand.

Last chance.

Fuck it.

Aaron opened the box.

Like the other four boxes he'd already looked inside, there was a number within, printed in a large font on a crisp sheet of paper.

Fuck.

"Fuck!"

Number eleven.

Close, but not number thirteen.

Aaron expected the harsh incandescent lights above him to turn red, an alarm to sound. The voice on the speaker to announce: "Sorry, better luck next time!"

Nothing.

Aaron slammed the lid closed, moved to another unopened box.

Twenty-nine inside.

Another: nineteen.

Aaron finally found his number—thirteen—in the second to last box. He snatched the piece of paper, gripped it tightly in one hand.

"Found it! I found thirteen!"

Still nothing.

Aaron noticed a small camera mounted in one corner of the room.

"I found it!" he shouted again, shaking the piece of paper high above his head. "*Hey!* I found it! Thirteen! That's my number!" He pointed at his chest, jumped up to make sure the camera got a good shot at the two pieces of paper.

"See?"

No voice, no lights, no alarm.

Aaron took the paper and walked to the door on the right, the winner's exit. Tried the knob but it didn't turn.

"Hey! I won!"

Aaron gripped the knob in his calloused hand.

"Hey!"

He tried again, even used his foot to brace himself against the wall for leverage.

"Open the fucking door!"

One last attempt and Aaron dropped the sheet of paper.

Anger swelled.

He reached for one of the small boxes and grabbed it by a spindle-like leg. He swung it against the doorknob. The box shattered while the knob remained intact.

Aaron hoisted another box, smashed it against the knob, too.

His whole body had broken out in sweat now.

Something was wrong. Win or lose, this wasn't right. Panic welled inside him.

"Open the door! Let me the fuck out! I won! *I won!*"

Aaron launched the third box at the camera, had to actually throw it to get it high enough. The camera exploded. Glass and plastic rained down.

"Open the—"

Aaron stopped mid-sentence.

He finally heard something.

Not an alarm, but a hiss.

What the fuck is that?

He searched for the source of the sound, realized it was coming from a rectangular vent halfway up the wall. The air around the vent warped his sight lines.

Something was leaking out of it.

"What the—"

Aaron gagged as he was hit by an awful smell, like rotten eggs.

Covering his nose and mouth with the sleeve of his shirt, Aaron stepped over the broken wood and glass and tried the doorknob again.

It *still* wouldn't open.

Aaron's stomach lurched and he coughed. His eyes watered and his chest burned. A fire ignited in his lungs.

"Let me the fuck out!"

Aaron gagged again, and this time, he wasn't able to hold down the vomit that rose in his gorge. He was dizzy, nauseous.

He reached for the door, but missed and staggered forward.

His shoulder struck the wall and he rebounded, collapsing to his knees. He was coughing violently now, every inhale like breathing underwater. Every breath flooded his throat, but this did little to douse the intense burning he felt deep inside his core.

Aaron vomited a second time, and then darkness closed in on him.

CHAPTER 2

Ivy Reeves glanced up at the students seated at their desks. She was only a few years older than most of them, but they all looked so young.

And lost. God, they all looked lost.

Ivy decided to go over it again, starting from the beginning.

"Bayesian statistics really isn't that complicated. In essence, it's the interpretation of probability."

Blank, glassy-eyed stares.

Ivy sighed.

"You know how frequentist statistics relies on long-term frequencies and data?" She pointed at the digital display behind her, where the second of two peaks was bisected by a single line marked, "New Estimate."

"Well, Bayesian statistics differs because it incorporates additional data into the data set to form new beliefs."

She moved her finger to the first peak now.

"See how the estimate changes based on these new data or beliefs?"

Ivy's eyes returned to her class, expecting to see arched eyebrows and slight smiles indicative of understanding.

She saw neither.

Instead, she was met with the same glossed over expressions that had graced the faces of the twenty-three members of Fundamentals of Statistics since she'd started the lecture.

Fundamentals . . .

If the students couldn't grasp the fundamentals, how could they ever be expected to understand complex concepts like regression analysis? Clustering? Dimensionality Reduction?

Ivy shot a glance at her TA sitting behind the desk at the front of the class.

Tristan Coates stared back.

He understood, at least.

But when the young man just shrugged, Ivy knew that she wasn't going to get any help from him. Tristan may be the teaching assistant, but the teaching part was all up to her.

She enjoyed teaching and was good at it . . . *usually.*

Ivy exhaled.

"Okay, let's start again. Tristan, pull up the original data set."

The peaks disappeared and a table took its place.

"Using frequentist statistics, we can—"

Ivy's pocket started to vibrate and she frowned. Then it made a sound: two beeps followed by one beep.

Now the class seemed to come alive. Someone snickered. Someone else muttered under their breath.

Beep, beep. Beep.

"I'm sorry, but this is an emergency."

Ivy slipped her hand into her pocket and grasped her phone, but didn't pull it out yet.

"Tristan," she said quietly. "Think you can take it from here?"

The TA tucked his dark hair behind his ears.

"Sure, no problem."

Ivy nodded.

"Thanks. Don't forget to give them their phones back after the bell." Then to the class, she raised her voice and said, "We should have last week's tests marked for next class. As a reminder—"

Beep, beep. Beep.

Ivy spoke more quickly now.

"—the test isn't going to count toward your final grade. It's just to help me figure out where you all are, where you're starting from. The next test *will* count, however. If you need extra help, I'm keeping regular office hours all week."

The students groaned as Ivy moved to the door and opened it.

"Enjoy the rest of your day."

Ivy nodded at Tristan, who had since moved to take her spot in front of the digital screen. Sure, teaching was her job, but she didn't think that the TA finishing the last few minutes of class was a big deal. After all, assistants assisted, didn't they?

She left the room, closed the door softly behind her. Only now did she remove her phone from her pocket.

Sucked in another breath.

Ivy wasn't surprised by the caller ID. The ring—*beep, beep,* pause, *beep*—was a dead giveaway.

Her students weren't allowed phones in class—she confiscated them and put them in her desk drawer prior to the start of a lecture—and Ivy was extremely reluctant to use hers. She almost never did. It stayed on silent.

Except for one number.

Lecture, midnight, even in the middle of a meeting with the department head—it didn't matter. If that number rang, Ivy answered.

Always.

"Is he okay? Please tell me my father's okay."

CHAPTER 3

As a detective with the Princeton Police Department, Vaughn Ryan knew better than to enter a private residence without either just cause or a warrant.

He presently had neither.

Vaughn reached for the handle anyway.

It was unlocked, and he opened the door. Leaning inside, the first thing that struck him was the smell: a distinct musk, a combination of acrid sweat and sour alcohol.

Jesus.

Vaughn turned his head and took in a mouthful of outside air, holding it as he entered.

The place was a disaster. Fast food containers on the counter making friends with more empty and half-crushed beer cans than Vaughn could count.

Shaking his head, he moved deeper into the home, using the sound of thick, wet snores as his guide.

The bedroom door hung open a few inches, and Vaughn pushed it all the way with his foot.

The reek of sweat now overpowered the stink of alcohol.

Surprising, considering that the number of opened beer cans in the room rivaled those in the kitchen.

They littered the bedside table where a black belt (complete with a gun holster, the weapon still safely tucked inside) dangled over the edge.

A man lay on the bed. Large belly, mostly white underwear. A bottle of Jack Daniels tucked under one arm.

The man snored, hiccupped—*you can hiccup in your sleep?*—then rolled over, showing Vaughn the crack of his ass.

"Hey, wake up," Vaughn snapped.

No answer.

"Wake up."

A snort.

Vaughn reached out and grasped the man by the shoulder, gave him a little shake. His skin was warm to the touch.

"Darnell, get your ass up."

The man farted and flipped over once more.

"Darnell!"

The man's eyes finally opened and he blinked rapidly.

"Vaughn?"

The lids closed.

"C'mon, get the fuck up. It's time to go."

"I'm—" Darnell cleared his throat, swallowed a wad of phlegm. "I'm up."

No, you're not.

"Get dressed."

Vaughn backed out of the room, grateful for a lungful of moderately less foul air. He picked up a couple of beer cans, tossed them in the garbage under the sink.

Now able to access the coffee maker, Vaughn opened the

cupboard and pulled out a can of grounds. Filled the filter. Took the carafe and moved to the sink, which was so full of spent cans that he had to angle it to fill it.

Jesus, Darnell . . .

Vaughn started the coffee.

"Vaughn?"

"Can't you get one of those instant coffee makers like a normal person?" Vaughn asked, his back to Darnell.

"I don't know if you can tell, but I'm not exactly normal."

Vaughn turned.

Darnell was still in his underwear, but now his gun hung loosely from one hip. His large, dark belly hung over the belt, hiding most of the glossy nylon.

Darnell scratched his balls.

"Yeah, I got that. Go get dressed—we're running late."

"Yes, boss."

Mock salute before returning to the bedroom, closing the door behind him.

With the coffee now percolating, the bitter aroma slowly starting to cut through the funk, Vaughn heard Darnell's radio come to life.

Heard the man clear his throat again, spitting this time—*where?*—before answering.

Vaughn couldn't make out the words.

You can't keep going like this, Darnell. You're going to give yourself cirrhosis before your fifty-third birthday.

The bedroom door flew open.

"Vaughn? We got a case." The thick grooves around Darnell's mouth grew even deeper. "And fair warning, it's a nasty one."

CHAPTER 4

Ivy slowed, her eyes locked on the field of Queen Anne's lace to her right. It stretched for miles. This time of year, the thousands of white flowers that form the lacy, flat clusters were thick and heavy. The thigh-high stems sagged under their weight.

The lacy canopy also provided exceptional cover, if someone was so inclined to sit or lie in the field.

Ivy put on her hazards and pulled over. Turned off her car and got out.

The high-pitched whine of cicadas filled her ears and she felt a trickle of sweat make its way down the hollow of her lower back. It was hot for this time of year and at this early hour.

Using her hands, Ivy carefully parted the flowers as she stepped into the field. After just a few paces, she gave up trying not to snap any stems.

She pressed forward, her eyes scanning in all directions.

A honeybee buzzed close to her face and she gently swatted it away. Her movements stirred up dozens of tiny hoverflies.

Come on, where are you?

The bugs, the heat, the noise. Any one of them could have unsettled her. Yet calm washed over Ivy. The field held some of her best memories.

She kept moving.

"Hello?" she said softly.

A grasshopper replied with a raspy rattle.

"Hello?"

Her movements left a trail of bent flowers in her wake. She spotted another such trail to her right.

Ivy moved into this one, trying to limit the damage the way one might step into existing footsteps in freshly fallen snow.

Someone else was here—someone else had made this path.

She found this someone less than five minutes later.

This was Eugene Reeves's happy place—everyone knew that. When taking a break from his work, he would often come here or a place like it, sit in a field of Queen Anne's lace, hold one of the flowers in his mangled hand.

Stare at it while he spun it ever so slightly.

A perfect radiating fractal. The florets start from a central stalk, then spread outward. Here, hold it close to your face, Ivy. Now pull it away a little. A little more. More. See? It's the same pattern, repeated at every magnification. Queen Anne's lace grows following a Lindenmayer systems pattern—predictive, recursive geometry at its finest.

How old had Ivy been when Gene first explained fractals to her?

Nine? Ten?

It didn't matter. She might have been as young as four.

Gene never used age as an excuse or a limiting factor. He

was the one who had explained to her that learning anything was a process from A (not known) to B (known). The path between these two points was different for everyone, for every subject—loops, backtracking, precipitous drops.

Peaks and valleys.

But no matter the route, this process had one singular name: frustration. And the only thing holding you back from learning something new, at any age, was your inability to remain in a frustrated state for a prolonged period of time.

Ivy didn't want to break the serenity of the scene that opened up before her.

Was remiss to do so.

But she had no other choice.

She took one step, then another, before dropping down to his level.

"Hey." Her voice was barely above a whisper.

He didn't answer. Just spun that fractal in his perfectly smooth and pink hands. His fingers were shorter than normal, the tips having been too badly burnt to save.

Ivy reached out, gently caressed his cheek. Didn't flinch at the roughness of his mottled skin.

The entirety of the man's face was covered in patchwork sections. Most of his left ear was missing.

The doctors had done their best trying to graft skin to his ruined face, make him look as normal as possible.

They'd failed.

Ivy had learned that autografts from the postauricular region—the area behind the ear—were best for facial reconstruction.

The extent of the damage made this impossible in his case.

They'd gone over the options—allografts from donors, even xenografts from pigs—but these all seemed too garish. The plastic surgeons had settled on removing the top few layers of skin from his lower throat and collarbone region.

These had helped seal the surface, prevent infection, but they had done next to nothing to improve the man's appearance.

He was unrecognizable and, to most, resembled something out of a cheap horror film.

Not to Ivy. To Ivy, it was the *idea* of her father that mattered most. How he looked was irrelevant.

"You okay?" A silly question, but Ivy didn't know what else to say. Never did.

He didn't look at her, but he did extend the flower in her direction.

Ivy took it.

Queen Anne's lace wasn't highly allergenic, but squatting as she was, and after having disturbed the flowers on her trek, the pollen was getting to her.

As her eyes began to water, Ivy reached into her pocket and produced a thin, cream-colored, stocking-like piece of material.

A transparent facial orthosis, Ivy had learned—a TFO. She now knew as much about facial burns and reconstruction as she did polynomial equations.

After the grafts, he had been required to wear the TFO for almost a year to help him heal. Now, nearly three years in, he still sported the mask nearly around the clock. His appearance frightened the other long-term residents in the adult assisted living facility.

Ivy gently slipped the mask over the man's head, adjusted it so that the eye, nose, and mouth holes lined up.

Then she wiped wetness from her own cheeks.

Damn pollen.

This was the second time in the past month that he had snuck away from the assisted living facility.

No surprise; it was coming up on the third anniversary of the accident. Ivy was amazed that the man still recognized the timing of the traumatic incident that had taken everything from him—from *them*.

Even though he couldn't speak.

Could no longer add two and two together.

The timing couldn't be worse. His primary nurse—no, not nurse; they were called resident care aides—had already warned Ivy that the home was frustrated with her father, and thought his little outings had the potential to be problematic with their insurance policy.

More like problematic with their bottom line.

And with Ivy's lack of progress at work and her failings in getting through to her students, the idea of looking after him full-time was something she couldn't even fathom.

Ivy straightened and wrapped an arm around his waist.

"Come on then, let's get you back."

She helped him to his feet, only later noticing that the flower he'd been holding had fallen to the ground.

The stalk was broken.

CHAPTER 5

"NASTY OR NOT, you're not going anywhere like that." Darnell had only managed to add socks to his outfit that consisted of underwear and police belt. "Get dressed."

Darnell nodded.

"Yes, boss."

Vaughn hated when Darnell called him that. His partner was nearly double his age, which meant double the experience.

Double the baggage, too.

Vaughn watched Darnell retreat to his bedroom as the man's previous words echoed inside his head: *We got a case . . . a nasty one.*

It was too soon for another nasty one.

Their previous case involving the Princeton Pervert had taken a lot out of both of them.

A rather benign moniker, given what Armand Reese had eventually confessed to. But the media loved their alliterations nearly as much as they loved sensationalism.

The Princeton Pervert, PP, Armand Reese—call him what you want, the man was an absolute sadist. Abducted six girls, aged nine to eleven, and kept them shackled in the back of his van for upwards of a week.

Raped them repeatedly.

Manually strangled them before tossing their tiny bodies into an abandoned gravel pit.

They'd tracked Armand Reese for nearly six months without making any progress. If it hadn't been for one of Darnell's hunches, he might still be out there terrorizing young girls.

Darnell's hunches . . . the thought made Vaughn shake his head. Darnell was old-school, still believed in those sorts of things. Vaughn did not.

Yet he couldn't deny their effectiveness. In retrospect, Vaughn came up with tangible evidence that would have indicated where Armand was keeping the bodies—fine gravel dust at the scenes from where the victims were abducted, the sighting of a pickup truck that was lower on the rear axles, indicative of wear from carrying heavy loads. But in the moment, he'd missed those clues.

Hunch or no hunch, Darnell was right: it was too soon for another nasty one.

Vaughn poured himself a cup of coffee, then set about tidying the place up. Mostly just tossed out spent beer cans.

The shower came on.

Vaughn considered using a cloth he found in the sink to clean the counters, but decided against it. He was Darnell's partner, not his fucking maid.

He tried not to count the cans. Told himself that these could have been accumulating for weeks, even though he knew they hadn't.

Vaughn's cleanup efforts led him to the front hall. Two cans on the table by the entrance.

He scooped these and then stopped.

There were four framed photos sitting on the table. The first, Darnell in police uniform, smiling. Holding a diploma. Second: Darnell in a suit, arms wrapped around a pretty Black woman in a white dress—their wedding. The third, Darnell and three buddies at a football game. Vaughn didn't recognize the friends.

The final frame had been placed face down. Even before Vaughn righted it, he knew what it would show: Darnell, his wife, and a smiling kid with unruly hair missing a front tooth.

"Thanks for cleaning up. Maid's on vacation."

Startled, Vaughn put the photo back the way it was. He crushed one of the cans as he turned.

"Darnell . . ."

"What?"

In a clean suit, somehow shaved even though Vaughn didn't know how that was possible given the short time frame, Detective Darnell Sacker was a different man. And with most of the beer cans in the garbage, the detective projected a different air entirely.

That of a bachelor—a bachelor detective who likes to drink. Name one who didn't? If he worked hard enough, Vaughn could convince himself that his senior partner was normal.

Almost normal, anyway.

"You keep staring at me like that and I'm going to get back into my skivvies."

Vaughn tossed the cans into the garbage. It was overflowing and the lid refused to close.

"Let's get out of here. It stinks. And don't forget to lock up—door was open this morning."

Darnell shrugged. "Don't have anything left to steal."

They got into Vaughn's unmarked car and he started the engine. "Well? What've we got?"

"Let me ask you something: one person killed is a homicide. Two, a double homicide. Three, a triple." Vaughn pulled out of the driveway. "What do you call ten homicides?"

"*Ten*?" Vaughn's eyes bulged.

"Ten."

"I don't . . . I don't know."

"Ten*uple*? Double quintuple?"

"No idea."

But he did. Vaughn knew what it was called because Darnell had already said it.

A nasty one. A *fucking* nasty one.

It was too soon for another nasty one.

CHAPTER 6

"Everything okay?"

Ivy didn't immediately answer her TA. She exhaled as she took a seat behind her desk.

"Yeah."

Not really.

When Tristan didn't say anything else, she shot a glance in his direction.

He quickly looked away, red pen in hand, his attention focused on the stack of papers on his desk—a much smaller version of hers.

Ivy logged into her computer and checked her emails. There were only three. Well, only three that mattered. The rest were spam, countless spam.

She opened the one from the ACM Conference on Economics and Computation.

EC '25 cordially invites you to present at our upcoming conference. As a Clay Research Fellow . . .

Ivy stopped reading. She couldn't focus, couldn't concentrate.

How many times had her father presented at the EC? Six? Eight? A *dozen*?

Keynote, guest lecturer, career achievement award. You name it, Eugene Reeves had done it.

Ivy closed the email and continued to scroll.

Found one called "Anniversary" from an unknown email address. Normally, Ivy wouldn't open such a thing, but she needed a distraction.

The moment she did, her eyes narrowed. She'd expected to see a block of text or colorful graphics advertising a casino or a dating service, but saw nothing of the sort. Instead, Ivy read something that seemed like a macabre poem.

> *1092—three days to the date.*
>
> *Twenty-nine minutes, why were you late?*
>
> *Thirteen will fall, if their problem is unsolved,*
>
> *Reduced to a constant, your death is involved.*

Ivy shuddered. Spam, no doubt. Still, it was ominous and disturbing.

Your death is involved?

Ivy quickly deleted the email. So much for taking her mind off things.

"Hey, Dr. Reeves?"

"Hmm?"

Tristan slashed at a page with his red pen.

"The students' grades are pretty bad."

"How bad?"

"Not quite done yet, but . . . seventy-six average? Maybe lower?" Tristan raised an eyebrow and Ivy made a face.

"You sure?"

As soon as the words were out of her mouth, she regretted them. Of course Tristan was sure. Like her, math was what the TA did. What he knew.

Would she be pissed if someone asked her if she'd made a simple arithmetic mistake?

Well . . . no, probably not. But Tristan Coates was a year older than her, in his second year as a PhD student in the Applied Mathematics department while Ivy was a tenure-track professor, the youngest in Princeton's long, esteemed history. She was also a Clay Research Fellow, a Sloan Research Fellow, a finalist for the Fields Medal, *blah, blah, blah*.

Tristan had something to prove.

Ivy didn't.

"Sorry."

Ivy pulled up the reports from the previous ORF 145 Fundamentals of Statistics class and did some quick calculations.

The historical mean for this particular test—one that didn't actually count—was 86 percent. Standard deviation ±3 percent.

This year? 76 percent, which was a 4σ deviation. Like Tristan had said, pretty bad. If this was just a one-off, Ivy wouldn't be too concerned.

But it wasn't—it was a trend.

Ivy's strategy when introducing a new topic was to give the students a test early into her teachings. Gage how well they were grasping the material.

Well, here was her answer.

"Hey, maybe this year the students are just—"

"No," Ivy said sharply. "I'm not getting through to them."

Ivy wasn't one for external validation, but she wouldn't have minded a comment from Tristan now. Something positive, reassuring. But Tristan just went back to marking, saying nothing.

"Tristan," she hesitated. "You have any advice? A way to explain Bayesian stats more on their . . . level?"

A half smile crossed the man's lips, and he tucked his hair behind his ears.

Tristan was older than her, but he was also more in tune with today's students. Had taken a more or less traditional route to his current position. Hadn't skipped countless grades and countless more social events to reach the highest levels of the profession in record time.

"I mean, what do kids their age—what do first-year students—think about?"

Drinking and sex. And drugs.

"Drinking and sex," Tristan said, his half smile growing into a full grin.

You forgot drugs.

Ivy cocked her head and Tristan shifted uncomfortably in his seat. His smile faded.

"But I doubt the department would go for something like that," he added quickly.

"You're probably right."

Tristan lowered his eyes to the tests and then immediately raised them again. "Hey, the marks are generally bad, but Rebecca did well. Ninety-three."

A glimmer of hope. Not surprising, though—Rebecca Quinn was one of the brightest students in the class. Pretty, too. Red hair, green eyes, freckles. Interested and interesting. A good combination. Reminded Ivy of somebody, minus the red hair and freckles. Blue eyes instead of green, but still.

"Zeke, too," Tristan added hesitantly.

"Zeke?"

"Zeke."

This was a surprise, and not a welcome one.

"Huh. What did he get?"

"Ninety-three."

Alarm bells rang.

"The *same* ninety-three?"

"Yep."

Tristan flipped through the tests, found Rebecca's and Zeke's, and held them up.

Ivy took them and looked them over to confirm what Tristan was implying.

This wasn't the first time that Ivy had suspected Zeke of cheating. She'd reported him once before for copying off Rebecca, no less. This was the last thing Ivy needed right now.

Or maybe not.

A close second to thinking about her father and her own project, on which she'd made zero progress over the past few months.

EC '25 cordially invites you to present at our upcoming conference. As a Clay Research Fellow . . .

Third, then.

Ivy glanced at the tests again. Zeke didn't even try to hide it. The tests weren't just close to the same—they were identical.

If they'd both gotten perfect marks, there would be no way to tell that he was cheating. The proof, however, was in the wrong answers. It always was.

"What do you want to do about it?" Tristan asked.

Ivy stood.

"Only one thing I can do."

CHAPTER 7

THEY WERE SIX miles from the Princeton PD headquarters. Farmland. A narrow, secluded, one lane access road.

Seven Princeton PD cruisers were already on the scene—no, make that eight. A blacked-out Crime Scene Unit cargo van was also parked off to the right.

Darnell hadn't told Vaughn anything about the crime other than his eloquent description. Vaughn preferred it this way. A clear head, no bias.

Beyond the cars, a red barn. Not ancient, but definitely not a new build.

Vaughn and Darnell got out. A couple of the uniforms recognized them, nodded.

Vaughn nodded back.

Only one came over.

"Detective Ryan." A smile. "Detective Darnell." No smile.

"Officer Delaney."

Vaughn and Darnell continued toward the barn and Delaney followed.

"Got here about an hour ago," Delaney offered. "Anonymous call came in the middle of the night."

"Who owns the building?"

"An old LLC. Hasn't been used in at least a year. Probably longer."

"Anybody notice anything? Cars coming and going?"

"No. There are a couple of farms around here. Plants, fruit. Early to bed, early to rise, that sort of thing. I have my men asking around, but so far nobody reported noticing anything unusual. There's also the Cedar Ridge Preserve not too far from here—"

"The Preserve has security," Darnell interrupted.

"Coupla rent-a-cops who were probably sleeping or jerking off in the woods last night."

"Delaney, get someone to head over to the Preserve, talk to them."

Darnell made no effort to hide his dislike of the cop. Spoke quickly. Exerted his authority.

"Right."

"Now, Delaney."

"Right."

Delaney bound off.

"Don't know why you put up with that guy," Darnell said.

I put up with you.

Harsh and maybe unwarranted after what his partner had been through. Didn't make it any less true, however.

The massive front doors to the barn were in decent shape. Firmly closed. Locked via chain and padlock. Vaughn tried to peer through the wooden slats, but couldn't make anything out. Strange, given that there were gaps in the old wood.

How the hell do you get in?

A man wearing some sort of gas mask appeared from the right side of the barn through a much smaller door.

There, I guess.

Clad in a black windbreaker, with "CSU" in yellow lettering on the sleeve, the man was holding a strange-looking device in one hand.

He removed his mask, propped it on the top of his head. Red lines marked his face from where the rubber seal had pressed into his skin.

The machine in his hand beeped. He looked up, noticed them.

"You must be Detectives Ryan and Sacker."

"Sacker." Darnell pointed at his chest then at Vaughn. "Ryan."

A nod.

"CSU tech Landon. You're cleared to enter—don't need a mask. It still smells a little, but it's no longer dangerous."

Now Vaughn wished that Darnell had given him a little more background.

Gas masks? Smell? No longer dangerous to enter?

What the hell was going on here?

"Follow me."

Landon opened the door and Vaughn waited for his eyes to adjust before entering. It wasn't dark inside the barn, not really. It was just . . . different. The lighting was harsher, less natural.

Landon went first, then Vaughn, then Darnell.

The smell *was* bad. Rotten eggs. Just shy of strong enough to make Vaughn's eyes water.

Bodies at crime scenes tended to be on the floor, so he, not wanting to be distracted by death and thus miss a potentially vital piece of evidence, made sure to keep his gaze confined to the upper third of the room.

And a room, it was.

This wasn't a barn in any traditional sense. There was drywall, and a ceiling that looked much lower than the exterior of the building would have suggested. Not peaked. No exposed beams. No stalls or stables for livestock.

It was as if someone had built a modern room inside the barn. Retrofitted it. Tube lights ran along the ceiling. The construction wasn't perfect—no one had bothered mudding or taping the drywall seams. No paint, either. A rough job.

An amateur job?

There was some sort of portable speaker mounted on a cheap shelf on the back wall, the power cable exiting through a hole behind it. An air vent—new—directly above.

Vaughn took two steps. He didn't want to look down yet, but his shoes kicked up dirt, drawing his eyes. Whoever had made this room had stopped short of constructing a floor.

He saw the bodies now—two of them. Both face down, their arms and limbs posed awkwardly, but not unnaturally so. Both were male.

The face of the closest victim was aimed toward the door. His skin was pale—no, it had a bluish tinge to it—and his wide eyes were cloudy. A white substance had accumulated in the corners of his lips.

Vaughn craned his head around, looked at the door they'd just walked through. The knob was warped, the circular shape dented out of true. There were scratch or pry marks near the frame.

"The exterior door—" Darnell began.

"Locked," Landon said, predicting the detective's question.

"Like the padlock out front?" Vaughn asked absently.

"No. Digital. Fancy, expensive. Had to use a crowbar to get it open."

Vaughn took a moment, a breath—regretted it.

Goddamn eggs. What the fuck is that smell?

"Darnell? I thought you said ten bodies?"

Landon was the one who answered.

"*Yeeeeah*, we're not done yet." He made a wide berth around the corpses to a door on the other side of the room. Vaughn noted the digital lock. Landon gave the door a small push, and it slowly swung inward. "Had to pry this one open, too."

CHAPTER 8

It wasn't that Ivy didn't like Dr. Ben Moorehead. It was more that there was a divide between them. Not intellectually, not professionally, and definitely not politically.

But he was the department head; she, a tenure-track professor. One might be inclined to think that this made them aligned. But a professor, tenure-track or not, is to the department head as a widget maker is to the CEO.

Different bottom lines.

Dr. Moorehead was bald with a liver-spotted head. Round glasses. Trendy, if unironic.

"Dr. Reeves, I wasn't expecting you today. How are things?"

"Well, to be honest, I have a bit of a problem."

Ivy produced the two tests, placed them on Dr. Moorehead's desk.

Dr. Moorehead didn't like problems. He liked grants, awards, prestige.

For someone with advanced alopecia, Dr. Moorehead had an impressive set of eyebrows. Spent a considerable amount of time mastering their movements, too.

They did a little dance.

Nope; the man did not like problems.

"What is it?"

"Remember the student I mentioned a few weeks back? Zeke Godfrey?"

"Yes."

"I was concerned that he was cheating."

"Yes."

"Well, I have these tests here . . . the class as a whole did poorly, but two students did particularly well."

Dr. Moorehead glanced at the tests over the top of his glasses. Made no move to pick them up or inspect them more closely.

"Did you get around to speaking to Zeke about the last time?"

Dr. Moorehead said nothing as he finally lowered his gaze and allowed his eyes to skip across the pages.

It wasn't the department head's job to deal with cheating—not unless things required escalation. And if it had been any other student, Ivy would have spoken to them directly. But Zeke wasn't just "any other student."

Even Ivy, as a lowly widget maker, knew this.

Dr. Moorehead's eyebrows lowered. Bounced up, lowered again.

"What do you think? They both made the same mistake on questions seven and—"

"What do I think?"

Ivy frowned. She hated repeated questions. Nothing said "stall" more than repeating the words of the person you were speaking with back at them.

Where were you last night—the seventeenth of April, Mr. Criminal?

The seventeenth of April? Why, I was . . .

"I think that this is concerning," Dr. Moorehead said after a pause.

Ivy also disliked noncommittal replies such as this one. Still, she rolled with it.

"I agree. And with the department's—no, the *university's*—zero tolerance policy on cheating . . . "

'Nuff said.

Or so Ivy thought.

"It's concerning that two students are copying off each other."

The wording was off, and Ivy didn't care for the insinuation.

"Dr. Moorehead, Rebecca Quinn is one of my brighter—"

"If the two tests are mostly identical, as you say, then that's a problem. But unless you actually saw Mr. Godfrey actively cheating off Ms. Quinn, then I'll have to bring them both in for questioning."

Ivy's lips formed a thin line. She hadn't actually witnessed the infraction.

She said nothing.

"Right." Borderline smug, but not condescending. Ivy was, after all, Dr. Moorehead's golden goose. Youngest professor in mathematics department history, Clay Fellowship winner, *blah, blah, blah.* "But I'll tell you what. I'll pull Mr. Godfrey in for an informal meeting. How does that suit?"

You should have done that last time.

As usual, *zero tolerance* meant *zero tolerance for* some *people.*

Ivy still didn't say anything, just stacked the two tests and prepared to leave.

"How's your work going, Dr. Reeves? I got an email from the ACM conference. They've reserved a spot for you— not just a poster, but a talk. This is a big deal."

A big deal for whom?

"To be honest, I'm not really at a point where I'm comfortable sharing my work just yet."

If Dr. Moorehead can speak in a cipher, so can I.

Dr. Moorehead saw right through her words. But unlike Ivy, he had the authority to call her on it.

"I understand your desire to carve your own legacy, Dr. Reeves. Understandable—noble, even. But there is no shame in taking over your father's work. There's even something romantic about it, if you believe in that sort of thing."

I do not.

"He was close, you know," the man continued. "Gene kept most of his work a secret for obvious reasons. He and Dr. Neely both. But I know they were close to finding a solution. If you looked over what was left after the fire, you might—"

"Dr. Moorehead, I appreciate your advice." *How do you like being cut off, sir?* "But I'm making progress. If you think that I should present at the ACM, then I'll put something together."

Even if you discarded romanticism, the problem with Dr. Moorehead's suggestion was that only two people were smart enough to solve the Riemann hypothesis. And one of them wasn't her.

Lord knows she'd tried.

How did the old Mark Twain saying go?

Two people can keep a secret if one of them is dead?

That wasn't exactly true.

Two people could keep a secret if one of them was dead and the other mute.

She stood, a sad smile crossing her lips.

"Please speak to Zeke. And thanks for your time."

Asshole.

CHAPTER 9

No matter how many crime scenes you attend, no matter how many murders, suicides, rapes, or mutilations you encounter in your career, the first thing that comes to mind is that its all just a horrible accident.

The brain was a curious organ.

It could ignore the locked doors, the chains on the outside of the barn. The strange room within a room. The speaker, the vent.

The claw marks on the drywall.

It was all an accident. A team of men were renovating this barn when a pipe burst, leaking toxic gas into the room. By mistake, someone—the crew chief, perhaps leaving for his late dinner—locked the door behind him. Silly, but this was where Vaughn's mind went first.

The carnage in the second room made this assumption a feat of mental gymnastics—a floor routine, if you will, something even Simone Biles would have had a hard time completing.

Another body on the ground. Cloudy eyes, foamy mouth.

And . . . boxes? There were three cheap wooden boxes, all

on thin legs, standing upright. Countless others smashed to pieces on the dirt ground.

There were also numbers. Lots of numbers.

"What the hell is this?" Darnell grumbled. He was close enough that Vaughn could detect undertones of alcohol beneath a thick, minty layer of mouthwash.

There were numbers engraved on the lids of the boxes, sheets of paper with large numbers printed on them scattered throughout the room.

Vaughn read: three, nineteen, twenty-nine, and others.

The closest number to the corpse, face down on the ground, was thirteen. The way it was slightly crumpled suggested he was holding it when he died.

"We waited for you guys to arrive before we disturbed anything," CSU tech Landon informed them. "Once you give us the go-ahead, we'll document everything, make a list of the numbers."

"You guys have one of them fancy new cameras?" Darnell asked. "The kind that takes a 3D image of the entire room? Like they use for some of those expensive real estate listings in Robbinsville?"

"We do."

"Good. Use it to take photos of everything before you disturb the bodies. Any idea of what they might have died from?"

"Probably the gas."

Vaughn could almost hear Darnell roll his eyes.

"Specifically? What was that little doohickey you were holding when we got here?"

"A Dräger X-am 5000—gas detection device. Picked up trace amounts of hydrogen sulfide gas in the air."

That explained the noxious egg smell.

"Landon, can you please lead with that next time?" Darnell said.

"Sorry."

Vaughn noticed a door opposite the one he'd just come through. The doorknob was dented. He also spotted a cable dangling through a hole in the wall and plastic on the ground.

He pointed at the latter.

"I see it. Looks like it was a camera," Darnell said.

Vaughn pointed at the door next.

"Locked as well?"

"Yes. Same digital lock. Pried it open."

Vaughn trudged through the dirt, pushed the door open with his elbow. He inhaled sharply.

Seven more bodies, same as the first three. Not all were on their backs, however, and Vaughn saw numbers stuck to their shirts with tape. Straight ahead, a final door, this one likely leading to the outside. Three separate rooms, all connected, all locked, all filled with bodies.

"Looks like some sort of fucked up Squid Game."

"Delaney, I thought I told you to check with Cedar Ridge security," Darnell said.

Vaughn had been concentrating so hard on the scene that he hadn't noticed the cop join them.

"I put a coupla junior officers on it."

"What'd you say, Delaney?" Vaughn asked.

"Sent two PPD officers—"

"Before that," he clarified.

"Oh, Squid Game . . . this looks kinda like some sort of Squid Game."

When neither Vaughn nor Darnell said anything, Delaney added hesitantly, "You know, that Netflix show? Like an extreme version of *The Price is Right*?"

"The price is wrong, Bob," Darnell muttered.

Vaughn was familiar with *Squid Game*. It wasn't his cup of tea, but he understood the allure of the show. It was the subtitles that got him. Vaughn spent so much time reading the damn screen that he missed half of what was happening. And the dubbed version was just terrible. But he had to admit, with all the numbers and strange boxes inside the barn, mostly destroyed, the scene did appear to be part of some sort of deadly game show.

"How long until the medical examiner arrives?" Darnell asked.

"Put a call in about an hour ago," Delaney said. "Middlesex is sending someone over. My guess? Another thirty minutes or so before he gets here."

"Call him back. Tell him to get his ass over here now. Tell him to bring extra gurneys, too."

Ten dead. *Ten*.

The word came to Vaughn then: *decuple*. This was a decuple homicide.

Vaughn thought he still liked Darnell's term better: a nasty one.

CHAPTER 10

Ivy reluctantly accepted the invitation to present at the ACM. She went through several iterations of a title—"Emergent Cooperation in Chaotic Strategic Environments" was the sexiest option—but ended up going with the nondescript "TBD."

Considerably less sexy. Infinitely more intriguing, though.

She tried to do some actual work. Now that Tristan had left for the day, she thought that the quiet would help her concentrate.

It did not.

She kept thinking about Zeke and Rebecca.

During her undergrad, thirty thousand years ago to the day, a fellow student had copied her project, which had been worth a whopping 40 percent of their final grade. The project was also what Ivy was planning to use for her grad school application.

The student, who Ivy had actually liked, hadn't even bothered changing a single word—outside of the author name, that is.

There had been an inquiry, and both of them claimed the other had plagiarized their work.

Ivy had provided the review board with all of her reference material, thinking that this would be more than sufficient to clear her name. But the board dragged their feet, and Ivy got nervous.

Gene had heard this in her voice, knew something was wrong.

Pried the information out of her.

Ivy asked him not to step in on her behalf, but Gene did what Gene did.

The next day, the review board accepted Ivy's story and expelled the other student. But rather than feeling vindicated, Ivy felt dirty. She imagined a situation in which the roles had been reversed: her dad hadn't been Princeton's most venerated math professor, but the other student's father had. What would have happened then?

The school would have expelled Ivy.

She hadn't cheated, she knew this, but it still felt wrong to submit this work for her grad school application.

Three nights—that was all the time that Ivy had before applications were due. She slept a grand total of six hours during this interval.

Ivy finished a new project, though, and was promptly accepted into the program. No idea what happened to the other kid.

As much as Ivy knew of Zeke Godfrey and his eight-figure power broker father (or was it nine?), she knew little of Rebecca Quinn, and spent the next hour looking into the student.

Great marks—excellent. High school valedictorian. Ran track in high school, made the Princeton junior varsity team. Won a scholarship. Raised by a single mother—this much, Ivy had to intuit from the application.

If push came to shove, who would the review board side with?

Rebecca Quinn or Zeke Godfrey?

More specifically, *Devon* Godfrey, whose smiling face was plastered all over *The Daily Princetonian* for multiple seven-figure donations.

If Dr. Moorehead decided to take the cheating to the next step, Rebecca would have no one in her corner.

Except for Ivy.

That might hold some sway.

Ivy pulled back from her computer and rubbed her eyes. She'd accomplished next to nothing today.

Again.

And whatever 'sway' she might have would evaporate if Dr. Moorehead found out just how little actual work she'd completed on her project.

Clay Fellowship *blah, blah, blah* or not.

Her phone lit up.

No ring—good.

It wasn't the resident care aide Sarah Kachinski, so this wasn't about her dad.

Ivy took her phone out of silent mode and answered the call.

"Hey."

"What's up, bitch?"

"Abs—"

"Don't start with that. Don't 'Abs' me. We're still going out tonight."

Ivy frowned.

"You forgot, didn't you?"

Forgot what?

"Ivy . . . *ugh*, you always do this. We were supposed to go for drinks tonight, remember? When's the last time you went out?" Abby didn't hold back. "A month? Year?"

"Abs, I'm sorry, but I can't go out tonight. I have so much work to do. I promise—next week."

"Nope."

"What do you mean, *nope*?"

"I need to explain it to you? You're so smart, a goddamn genius, and you don't—"

"Abs—"

"—understand *nope*? Let me break it down for you, Ivy. We're. Going. Out. Tonight. Going to have some drinks. Too many, probably. Maybe meet some cute frat boys. And you're going to forget all about this nerdy math stuff."

"I can't."

"You *can*. And you better hurry, because I'm sick and tired of sitting on your steps waiting for you."

Ivy straightened.

"You're at my *house*?"

"You bet your ass I am. Been here for almost an hour. Called you but . . . anyways, you better hurry home because I'm not leaving. And you don't want me to stick around. I stick around and you're going to end up with duck lips and a BBL. And don't forget about squatter's rights," Abby droned on. "Not sure if they pertain to just staying on your porch, but I wouldn't mind living in your house. Beats the shit out of my five hundred square foot apartment. Get your ass home, *bitch*—we're going out tonight, whether you want to or not."

CHAPTER 11

THE MOMENT LANDON finished taking the 3D photos and dismantled the tripod, Darnell left the scene. The retrofitted death chamber was much smaller than the exterior of the barn, and they needed to gain access to the rest of the space.

Vaughn suggested that they unscrew the drywall and remove it, but Darnell had nixed the idea. Said it would take too long.

The medical examiner arrived before Darnell returned. Vaughn had worked beside Dr. Alex Button on several past cases. Liked the guy. Appreciated his no-nonsense approach.

"What are you thinking? Cause of death?"

Dr. Button rolled one of the victims onto his back with gloved hands. Landon helped him out.

"Won't be able to say for certain until I get these bodies back to the lab."

No-nonsense, but still a doctor. Just one rung lower on the "hesitant to make assumptions" ladder than a lawyer.

"Consistent with hydrogen sulfide poisoning?" Vaughn asked, remembering what Landon had told them about the readings on his Gas Detector 5000.

"Not inconsistent."

So, probably.

"Rough guess at time of death?"

"Again, I'll know more when I get back to the lab and check liver temp. If I was forced to hypothesize though, I'd say in the last six or eight hours."

Darnell entered the room, hardware tools in hand. He held up a reciprocating saw.

"Detective Ryan? Ready to get to work?"

"You have at it."

"Don't need to ask me twice."

Darnell revved the battery-powered saw, made a pose reminiscent of something from *The Texas Chainsaw Massacre.*

With the sound of the blade biting into drywall filling the room, Vaughn went outside to clear his head and met up with Delaney.

"What a mess in there." The cop had a bit of a twinkle in his eye as he said this.

What did Darnell like to call the young officer?

Puppy dog.

Yeah, it fit.

As much as Darnell's distaste for Delaney was without merit, Vaughn's partner was right about that part.

"Yeah. Hey, there's some sort of cable hanging from the wall in there. Probably went to a camera that was smashed. Also, a speaker. Any way to track incoming or outgoing signals?"

"I can look into it."

"Do it. What about Cedar Ridge security?"

"Like I told the grumpy old guy—"

"Delaney," Vaughn warned.

The smirk vanished.

"Sorry. There was a patrol last night, but nobody noticed anything."

Vaughn glanced around.

The dirt path that led to the barn was overrun with vehicles now. More PPD cruisers, the CSU van, the ME's car. If there had been castable tire tracks in the dirt, they'd since been obliterated.

"How the hell did they get here?" Vaughn wondered out loud.

"What do you mean?"

He turned his attention to Delaney.

"This is pretty far from any bus stop or parking lot. There are ten victims . . . did they all drive here? If so, where are their cars?"

"I mean, if it's a game show, maybe they had a bus?"

A bus?

Vaughn frowned.

"See if you can trace those signals."

He took a few gulps of fresh air before heading back inside.

Dr. Button and Landon had moved all of the bodies into the center room, lining them up like they were corpses from some sort of mass casualty circa World War II.

Vaughn supposed they were. The first part, anyway.

"As soon you can, I'm going to need the victims fingerprinted. Check their shoes, too," Vaughn said.

"Shoes?" Landon asked.

"I want to know how they got here. Check for wear, I don't know, grass, dirt. What kind of farms are around here again?"

"Fruit," Darnell answered over the whir of his saw.

"Fruit, right. If they walked here, they might have fruit in their treads."

"On it," Landon said.

Darnell used the saw again, and a large section of drywall fell inward. Bits of plaster covered his face and clung to his sweaty skin.

"I think you're supposed to wear safety glasses while using that."

"That's a Gen Z thing." Darnell set down the saw, used his phone flashlight to illuminate the space beyond the poorly constructed wall. Then he gestured toward the opening with his free hand. "Hey, isn't parkour a Gen Z thing, too?"

Vaughn grimaced.

More like you can't fit.

The hole that Darnell had made between two studs—definitely not to code, not thirty-six inches on center—was about three feet wide. Four feet tall.

"I'll do it."

"Thanks, boss."

Brandishing his cell phone, the flashlight on, Vaughn turned sideways and slipped one foot through the drywall. Felt soft ground beneath his shoe.

Put his other leg through.

This was the barn that he'd expected to find when Landon had initially led them inside. High, peaked roof. Square beams covered in cobwebs. Undertones of long-buried manure, less so of rotten eggs.

"What do you see?" Darnell asked from the other side. He peered through like Jack Nicholson in *The Shining*.

Vaughn didn't answer.

He swung his phone around. Saw where the cable from the camera and speaker went. A small, router-looking thing sitting on a table that was a carbon copy of the boxes containing the numbers.

He noticed the tank next.

About the size of a piece of scuba equipment. Silver, polished.

The top had been modified. A thick rubber nozzle bifurcated three ways, each prong heading into a separate duct that looked like the hot air exhaust from a dryer. Secured with silver tape to prevent leaks where the two different materials met.

The three ducts spiraled upward. One to each of the interior rooms.

"Vaughn?"

Vaughn stepped forward, dropped down. Sprayed light on the side of the tank.

There were stickers wrapped around the cylinder, flanked by the appropriate hazard symbols. Skull and crossbones—fatal. Flame—flammable. Red/yellow burst—explosive, reactive. Exclamation mark inside a yellow triangle—irritant.

Finally, in bold print, Vaughn read: "Hydrogen Sulfide Gas."

He leaned back to take everything in.

When Vaughn had first stepped into the barn, he'd thought that this was an amateur job. And maybe the construction of the three connected rooms was.

But *this*? This set up with the tanks and the tubes and the nozzles?

This was anything but amateur. This was pro-level shit.

And that only meant one thing: this deadly game, or whatever the hell it was, was only the beginning.

CHAPTER 12

Abby Granger was a solid six. Tall, thin by design—she spent more time in the gym than anyone else Ivy had ever known—with platinum blond hair. Face more oval than round, a nose that was just a little too long. Abby was a six the way she was now. By the time they were ready to head out, however, that would change.

"Damn, you look terrible." Abby gave Ivy a hug, crinkled her nose. "Smell bad, too."

"Gee, thanks."

"Hey, if I can't tell it to you real, who can? Anyways, you only smell this way when you're stressed. What's going on?"

"I'll tell you inside."

"Oh, it's one of those." Ivy unlocked the door. "One of those, *I'm going to need a glass of wine first.*" Abby grinned as she produced said bottle of wine from her purse. "Don't worry—I've got you covered."

They stepped inside, and Abby popped the bottle of red and poured two glasses. More than two thirds of the contents gone.

"So?" Abby handed her a glass. "What's up?"

Ivy took a healthy gulp of wine and Abby did the same.

She didn't feel like sharing, but this was Abs. She told Abs everything. The only person in the world she could fully trust, no questions asked.

Ivy told her about the call from assisted living. About the upcoming anniversary of the fire—but this, of course, Abby already knew. She was one of the few people left who had known Gene before the accident. They'd both gone through undergrad together—met in first year, instantly became friends.

Opposites attract and all that.

Ivy doing a math degree, Abby social sciences. Still, Abby wasn't an airhead—despite how she came across. Abby was smart, strong. Loyal. Incredibly skilled with computers.

Their lives had diverged dramatically since those first few years, with Ivy continuing her education while Abby had gone directly into the workforce. Abby had made some connections in school, had gotten a job at a beauty clinic, one that specialized in Botox and plastic surgery. Took advantage of the employee discount.

Her lips were plumped, falling just shy of the duck look that seemed to be all the rage these days. She'd gotten her breasts done, too, going from a large A to a small C—something that Abby had never admitted to, but having seen her in the shower countless times, Ivy would have to have been brain dead not to notice. Botox, for sure—Abs didn't have a single crease on her face.

"Shit, Ivy. I'm sorry."

"I'll be okay."

Ivy hopped in the shower while Abs occupied the mirror

and used some sort of Dyson wand to turn her thin blond hair into something spectacular.

"How about you, Abs?" Ivy asked, allowing the cool water to wash over her.

"Oh, you know, living the dream. Listening to rich New Jersey housewives bitch about their old-ass husbands."

In a way, Ivy envied her friend's simple life. But, hey, this is what you get when your father is a math prodigy and you become the *blah, blah, blah.*

"Hey, Ivy?" Abby was serious now, and she was rarely serious.

Ivy shut off the water and reached through the curtain for a towel. Wrapped it around herself, tucked it beneath her armpits.

"Yeah?"

"You know, he's no longer your responsibility. It's been three years since—"

"Almost three. And he *is* my responsibility," Ivy said flatly, putting an abrupt end to the discussion.

Abs read the room, changed the subject.

"We're going to have some fun tonight, Ivy—forget about all that stuff. Find you a man."

Ivy rolled her eyes.

"That's all I need. More trouble in my life."

"Wow."

Ivy pushed back on the fake eyelashes, ignoring Abby's comment that it would help accentuate her bright blue eyes, but other than that, she let her do her thing.

Ivy knew her limits and, when it came to gussying up, they quickly approached zero.

Honestly? Not bad. Her curly hair typically tied up in a ponytail was straight now, flowing down just past her shoulders. She was wearing a mini dress. Black. Sheer. Low cut up top, came to about midthigh.

"You ready?" Abs asked, squeezing Ivy around the waist.

"Ready as I'll ever be."

Abs had free rein—almost—on Ivy's outfit and makeup. She also had free rein on where they were going. But Abby knew Ivy.

No neon club for them tonight.

Instead, Abby chose a bar just outside the campus sphere. Classic Celtic decor, thick all wood bar, loud Irish music.

Ivy snagged a small standing table that two men had just abandoned while Abby fetched the drinks—martini glasses filled to the brim with a clear liquid. Lemon slices adorned the rims.

"Did you get some water?"

Abby rolled her eyes.

"You and your water."

She signaled toward the bar, and a young man in a black t-shirt arrived with a pitcher of water. Ivy thanked him, then wet her lips with the martini only to immediately pull back as if she'd just gotten a whiff of ammonia.

"What *is* this?"

"Martini with a twist."

"What's the twist? Kerosene?"

Abs laughed.

"Shut up and drink it."

Ivy did, alternating with sips of water.

"Hey." Abs gave her a nudge.

A duo of men—businessmen, judging by their suits, top buttons of their dress shirts undone—were not so subtly staring in their direction. One of them, handsome, blue eyes, saw her looking.

Ivy averted her gaze.

"Let's go talk to them," Abs urged.

"*Yeahhh*, I'm going to pass."

"The blond guy with the Giga Chad jaw is cute. You take the one on the left, I get right."

Abby started to move.

"What are you doing?" Ivy hissed.

"What do you mean? I'm going to talk to them."

"Abs . . ."

"What?

"I—"

"You *what*, Ivy? C'mon—you promised to have some fun."

Ivy's idea of fun wasn't talking to horny drunk men at the bar.

"Sorry, Abs. Just not in the mood."

"*Fine,* but I'm dry." Abby slurped down the rest of her drink. "You want another?"

"Sure."

Ivy finished her own drink, chased it with water. She figured the martini had three shots in it, and she made sure to down a full glass of water, her third.

Someone laughed loudly in the corner of the bar, drawing Ivy's gaze.

Oh, shit.

It was Zeke Godfrey with two buddies she didn't recognize. Their eyes met. Ivy wasn't sure if Zeke had laughed—but he wasn't laughing now.

She whipped around. Abs was returning, drinks in hand.

"We have to go," Ivy said quickly.

"What? Why?"

"One of my students is here."

The left half of Abby's upper lip curled. Just a little. Too plump for an actual whimsical grin.

"So? It's not a crime for a professor to go out and have a few drinks."

"No, it's not that. This guy, he's—"

"You gotta live a little."

Ivy glanced behind her nervously. Zeke was approaching.

"I get that, okay? But can we go somewhere else? *Please?*"

"I paid sixteen bucks for these drinks—*each!* I'm finishing my martini."

To emphasize her words, Abby slammed half her drink in one gulp. Grimaced.

"You've made your point, Abs. I—"

"Hey."

It was too late. Zeke's face was red, his eyes bloodshot.

"You ratted me out." Slurred words, minimal consonants. "You know who my father is?"

"Zeke, please. I'm just—"

"What's your problem?" Abby said, coming to Ivy's aid.

"Who the fuck are you?"

"Who the fuck are *you*?" Abby shot back.

Zeke snarled.

"I'm Zeke fucking Godfrey, that's who."

CHAPTER 13

Delaney confirmed that the camera and speaker, and probably the digital door locks, operated via WiFi—the router thing had a satellite connection, apparently—but had no luck tracing incoming connections.

Something about VPNs, mesh networks.

Who knows.

Delaney promised to pass it off to the two cops—Bowes and Caine—who acted as the unofficial PPD tech department, but made a point of telling Vaughn that he doubted they'd have any luck, either.

Delaney wasn't completely useless, though, despite Darnell's comments to the contrary; he identified the strange-looking nozzle on the top of the hydrogen sulfide tank as some sort of automatic trigger.

All signs pointed to the person behind this, their unknown subject—unsub—having set it all up to run remotely.

Death via remote control.

After Dr. Button and CSU tech Landon loaded the bodies bound for the morgue, Darnell ordered Delaney to continue processing the scene—mostly because he didn't want to do it, not because he expected to find anything of value—and then he and Vaughn headed back to the station.

"You really think this is some sick fuck trying to reenact *Squid Game*?" Darnell asked. He had his feet up on his desk. Leaned back. Acted as if seeing ten dead bodies didn't affect him.

And maybe it didn't. Maybe after you went through something like he had, nothing bothered you anymore. But if that was the case, why the heavy drinking?

"No idea."

Darnell removed his feet, grabbed a sheet of paper off his desk.

"In the show, they have, like, five hundred contestants, and each is given a number from one to five hundred."

"Didn't know you were such a big fan."

"*Meh*, not much to do after work anymore." Darnell's seriousness suddenly cut through his self-defense shield, which was constructed entirely of dad jokes. "And what can I say? The chick in the show was hot."

"Right," Vaughn said, letting his eyes drift upward in annoyance. "One to five hundred, you said?"

Vaughn was picturing the numbers he'd seen on the floor, on and inside the boxes.

Nonconsecutive. Seemingly random.

"Yeah. But . . ." Darnell read from a list that Landon had made. "I've got two, three, five, seven, eleven, thirteen, seventeen, nineteen, twenty-three, and twenty-nine, I think? Landon's writing sucks. What the hell do they mean?"

"Those were the numbers *in* the boxes?" Vaughn asked.

"Yep. One number in each box—I'm guessing, as most

were on the floor—and one number engraved on the top. Not the same number, though. Box nineteen had number three inside. Box seven, number two. Can only guess at the others. I'm thinking that the guy in the middle room lost the game or whatever and went ape shit. Smashed everything."

Seemed like a reasonable assumption.

His thoughts still on the numbers, Darnell attacked his keyboard.

Vaughn, on the other hand, was thinking about the gas. Post 9/11, whenever gas was used in some sort of crime, the first thing that came to mind was a terrorist attack. A biological weapon.

Anthrax, smallpox, the bubonic plague.

But nothing about the incident at the farm struck Vaughn as an act of terror.

Secluded, rural New Jersey. Not an airport, shopping mall, or sporting event. Nothing highly populated.

Delaney had said that the barn was owned by a defunct LLC. Darnell had added generating a more comprehensive ownership report to Delaney's growing list of things to do, which could have easily been renamed "Things Darnell Didn't Want To Do," but Vaughn doubted that this would lead anywhere.

Terrorists got off on media coverage. The media spread fear as efficiently as any airborne pathogen.

Besides, the victims had likely come to the barn of their own accord—the ME hadn't noted any defensive wounds other than minor damage to the fingers and nails of some of the victims.

Wounds that he'd hinted were conceivably, feasibly,

probably, perhaps a result of them desperately trying to get out when the gas started flowing.

The victims were all men, all between twenty and fifty, if Vaughn had to guess.

These weren't high school kids. This wasn't a 'let's find a place where we can get high and drink without our parents finding out' thing.

Maybe it *was* a game show.

But hydrogen sulfide gas? What the hell even was it, besides something that smelled like someone shit their pants?

Now it was Vaughn's turn to address his computer. He typed "Hydrogen sulfide gas, H_2S" into the search bar.

Primary industrial uses included petroleum refinement, chemical manufacturing, and various lab and research facility applications. It naturally occurred in wastewater plants. No central registry, but to use H_2S, a corporation required permits from the New Jersey Department of Environmental Protection. Surprise, surprise—no mention of *Squid Game*.

Vaughn compiled a list of local places that had or might have access to H_2S tanks: River Road Wastewater Treatment Plant, Princeton's Chemical and Biological Engineering Department (CBE), and some random ass company that offers gas solutions, whatever the hell that meant.

"Prime numbers."

Vaughn wasn't sure he'd heard Darnell correctly.

"What?"

"Prime numbers. All of the numbers in the barn are prime numbers."

"What?" Vaughn said again.

"Prime numbers," Darnell repeated a third time, his eyes

darting to his monitor. "A number that can only be divided by one and itself."

"I know what a prime number is." *Sorta*. "What does it mean?"

Darnell shrugged.

Sometimes it was hard to believe that he was the senior detective, the lead.

Why do I put up with this guy?

"Found some potential places where the gas might have come from." Vaughn got up, grabbed his coat. "Hey, let me ask you something. What do you know about construction?"

"Construction?"

"Yeah, someone had to build those rooms in the barn."

"I built a shed once. Hardest part was laying the concrete foundation. The rest? Studs, drywall? Like *that*? Easy. Can do it in a few hours."

"Great." Another dead end. "Alright, gas it is. Let's go."

CHAPTER 14

THEY STRUCK OUT at the water treatment plant. The NJEPD didn't actually use H_2S gas; it was just a byproduct of sewage decomposition.

When Vaughn had asked if they had any tanks, went as far as to inquire if any had recently gone missing, he was met with a stare that rivaled the emptiness of their victims' faces.

No dice.

The company that provided "gas solutions"—which Darnell had high hopes would be able to help him with his flatulence problem—was only slightly more fruitful.

Yes, they sold gas. No, they hadn't sold any H_2S gas in the last six months. Yes, they had to get a special import permit for that particular gas. Yes, the detectives could do an inventory of their stock. No, there wasn't any H_2S gas on the premises.

That left the Princeton CBE department.

First, a detour.

Officer Delaney called, told them that Dr. Button had an update from the morgue.

Seeing bodies in the morgue was always easier for Vaughn than coming across them at a crime scene. The temporal and physical separation from their location of death had a numbing effect, helping affirm their status as victims rather than actual people.

Callous, but a necessary coping mechanism.

Not so for Darnell, who grimaced as they approached the first victim, naked, splayed out on the table, chest opened in a classic Y cut.

Hard to make jokes in the presence of death.

"Hydrogen sulfide is extremely volatile," Dr. Button said. He was the least affected by the ten bodies, speaking in a professorial tone. Matched his appearance to a T. The only thing he was missing was a bow tie. "It dissipates rapidly. Found evidence of chemical burns in the mucosal membranes of the deceased's nose and mouth. Fluid in the lungs." He pointed at the grayish organs that were still contained within the body cavity. "Blood analysis revealed the presence of low levels of thiosulfate in his system."

"Thiosulfate?" Darnell asked. He shivered. "Also, there a reason you're doing this in a meat locker and not out there?"

Apparently, you *could* make jokes around the dead.

Dr. Button frowned at this.

"Like I said, H_2S is highly volatile. Keeping the bodies cold slows the degradation process. As for your question, thiosulfate is a metabolite of hydrogen sulfide. Smell that? That rotten egg odor?"

Vaughn inhaled. He mostly smelled cleaning chemicals, perhaps embalming fluid, but there was a distinct, albeit subtle, egg odor. He just couldn't tell if this was still lingering from the crime scene or if it was new.

He nodded anyway.

"I need to do some more tests, but I'm fairly confident that this victim died from acute H_2S exposure."

"How does that happen?" Vaughn asked. Dr. Button blinked. "I mean, what does the gas do to the body?"

"Binds to cytochrome C oxidase. Prevents the mitochondria from utilizing oxygen."

"So they suffocate?"

"In simple terms, yes."

"How long does something like this take?"

"At high concentrations, Victim Thirteen would have lost consciousness in seconds. Death occurs in less than a minute. Also, the conditions inside the barn were ideal for specimen preservation. I've officially listed the time of death at 1:30 in the morning. Plus or minus half an hour."

Vaughn nodded again, glanced at the table beside the gurney. Neatly folded atop the man's clothes—jeans, a generic t-shirt—was the piece of paper with the number thirteen on it.

"Aaron Treadman," Delaney said out of the blue.

Vaughn had forgotten that the officer was in the cold room with them. Delaney had a way of doing that, just popping up without warning.

Like herpes or gonorrhea.

"Excuse?"

Delaney smiled, showing off a mouth just a little too full of teeth.

"Ran his prints, got a hit. Victim with the number thirteen on his chest is Aaron Treadman. He was picked up about six months ago for petty theft."

"Really?"

"Yes, sir."

"Where?"

"Princeton."

Vaughn raised an eyebrow.

"The university?"

"Yep. Worked as a campus security guard. Some faculty member's laptop went missing from their office or something when he was the only one around. Cops were called and he was pulled in and printed. Never officially charged, but the uni let him go anyway."

"Address?"

"Not yet. Working on it."

Vaughn took a photo of Aaron's face with his phone. His skin looked even more blue now, but at least Dr. Button had cleaned the white foam from his nose and mouth.

"Delaney," Darnell said. "Keep printing the other victims, see if we can get names for them, too. Names and addresses."

Delaney stopped smiling.

"Do you have the 3D photos that Landon took at the scene?" Vaughn asked.

"Yeah, he sent them to me. Also let me hold onto the gas detector. Cool little thing."

Vaughn ignored this last part.

"Forward the photos to me."

"Sure thing."

Vaughn turned to Dr. Button and held out his hand, only to pull it back. The ME was wearing thick black gloves that glistened with an unknown substance.

"Thanks, Dr. Button. If you find anything else, let Delaney here know. He'll pass the message along."

"Should be another six or eight hours before I process all

the bodies, but if they're anything like Victim Thirteen, I don't expect to find anything new."

"Well, if you do, let us know. Darnell?"

CHAPTER 15

"Cool story," Abby said. "Why don't you just move along?"

"Don't tell me what to do," Zeke snarled.

"Abby, let's just go," Ivy said, tugging on her friend's arm.

Abby shrugged her off.

"No, I'm not going to let this loser ruin our—"

"There a problem here?"

It was Giga Chad. Now that the blond guy was standing beside Ivy, she realized how big he was. Six three, two-twenty. Solid.

"Yeah, there is a problem here," Zeke said. His anger had simmered a little in the presence of the much larger man. "This—"

"You want to speak to this guy?"

"No," Abby snapped. "I want him to leave us the fuck alone."

Giga Chad faced Zeke, inched forward.

"You heard the woman."

Zeke's cheeks reddened again, this time more from embarrassment than fury.

"I—"

"Let's go." One of Zeke's buddies had come up from behind. "Zeke, let's just get the fuck out of here."

Ivy didn't recognize the kid, but he had that frat boy look about him.

Zeke hesitated. The kid pulled.

Zeke eventually lost the battle, but the student kept his intense eyes locked on Ivy until the bar door closed behind him.

Ivy finally let out a breath.

"You okay?" Giga Chad asked.

"Yeah, fine. Thanks," Abby said.

"He was just drunk. Let me buy you guys a drink. I'm Blake, by the way."

"I'm Abby. This is Ivy."

Blue Eyes appeared at Blake's side.

"I'm Tony."

"Hi," Ivy said, still a little taken aback by the violence she'd seen on Zeke's face.

"We should be buying *you* a drink," Abby said with a little laugh. "Thank you."

"How about this? I flip you for it. You win, I'll buy the first round. I win, you can get me and Tony a beer."

Blake had a nice smile, but he was a little too polished for Ivy's taste. Too done up. Then again, did she even have a type after this long?

"Ivy?"

Abby had that look about her. That *c'mon, live a little, please don't mess this up* look.

"Sure, I guess."

Abby's eyes brightened as Blake pulled a quarter out of his

pocket. He rested it on the back of his thumb, lowered his arm a little as he prepared to flip it.

"You call it."

"Wait," Ivy said.

Abby shot her a sidelong look.

That look again.

Ivy smirked.

"How about this . . . we don't flip the coin once, but three times. You pick a combination of three results, and I will, too. Whoever's sequence comes up first wins, the loser buys the round."

"Ivy, let's just flip—"

"No." Blake beamed. "I like this. Tony, you have a pen?"

Tony passed him one and Blake grabbed a coaster.

"I'll go first: heads, tails, heads. Your turn."

Ivy wrote down "T-H-H."

"You wanna flip or me?"

"You can."

The game played out exactly as Ivy expected: eight total flips later, her sequence appeared.

"Alright, you win. Tony, grab a round." Blake pointed at Ivy playfully. "Let's go again. This time, I choose heads, tails, tails."

Ivy wrote down "T-T-H."

It only took six flips this time.

"My God, you're lucky. Again!" Tony returned with the drinks and Blake told him to grab two more. "I'm picking the same that you just did." There was a gleam in his eyes, as if he thought he had her. Broke the code. "Tails, tails, heads."

Ivy countered with "H-T-H."

She won again.

And again.

Ivy was having fun with this. She quickly downed two drinks, paced herself on the third.

"This is insane—I'm gonna go broke playing with you. What do you do, Ivy?"

Ivy chuckled. She was enjoying herself. Realized that she hadn't thought of Zeke, her father, or her work for the better part of an hour.

"I work at a beauty parlor."

"Seriously?"

Ivy just smiled.

Blake was in banking. Finance.

Trust fund, six foot five, blue eyes.

A stupid song she'd heard some of her students singing before class.

Blake was a little shorter than 6'5, Ivy couldn't be sure about a trust fund, and his friend Tony was the one with blue eyes. But still.

They played a few more rounds—Ivy only lost once to heads, heads, heads, by sheer luck—and she forgot about her water. Unsurprisingly, she was drunk. *Very* drunk. It was getting late, and Ivy still had three drinks lined up.

Blake leaned close.

"You're not just lucky, are you?" he whispered in her ear.

Ivy grinned.

"I know this game; Penney's game, right?"

Drunk as she was, Ivy was surprised.

"You know Penney's game?" Her words all ran together.

"Of course. I love numbers. I'm a finance guy, remember?"

There was something about the way he said this that made her uncomfortable. If he knew the game, why did he let her win?

Abby came near and Blake backed off.

"Hey, I'm staying at a hotel not far from here—the Marriott at Forrestal. We're only in town for three days. How about you and your friend come back with us? Hotel bar is open late."

Bad idea, Ivy thought. Sorta thought. Her mind was swimming. And three days? This triggered something in Ivy, but she was too drunk to place it.

"Actually, my friend has a busy morning tomorrow," Abby said. She put her arm around Ivy, propped her up.

"Busy day at the spa?"

Blake wasn't making fun of her, but he was challenging her claim.

"Yes. Lots of BBLs to do."

Blake didn't push. Neither did Tony.

"Can I get your number at least? I've spent nearly six figures—" *Trust fund, 6'5", finance* "—tonight. I need a rematch."

"I can take yours," Abby offered.

Blake didn't seem excited about this, but went along with it.

"Sure."

Abby was a good friend. She'd pushed Ivy to come out, to stay, to drink. But she also knew Ivy's limits. If she went home with Blake, she'd regret it.

"Thanks for the drinks, boys." Abby gave them both a little coquettish wave and guided Ivy out of the bar.

Ivy passed out in the cab home.

CHAPTER 16

A LITTLE RESEARCH revealed that the head of the Princeton Chemical and Biological Engineering Department was a man named Dr. Troy McGill.

Darnell was surprisingly upbeat as they navigated the interior of Sherrerd Hall, an impressive, square, all mirror glass building on the northern edge of the Princeton campus.

The detective even went as far as to crack a few jokes. Vaughn knew that his partner used humor as a defense mechanism, but it was still unnerving, Darnell joking while all he could do was picture Aaron Treadman's naked corpse.

Vaughn found the office he was looking for at the end of the hall: a corner office, befitting of a department head.

Or so he figured.

Instead of Princeton—not that this was really an option considering A, Vaughn's grades, and B, his financial status—Vaughn had attended Mercer County Community College. They didn't have department heads at MCCC.

He knocked.

"Enter."

They opened the door.

Dr. Troy McGill had thick glasses and long hair. He sat behind a desk—a desk littered with papers and energy drinks—and his slender forearms rested on the dark wood.

If Vaughn had to guess, he thought the man had probably been dozing when they'd knocked.

"Dr. McGill?"

"Yes?"

"PPD Detectives Ryan and Sacker."

Dr. McGill perked up.

Yeah, he'd been sleeping, all right.

"What can I do for you, detectives?"

"Just have a couple questions. Do you guys have hydrogen sulfide gas in the department?"

"Yes. Why?"

Vaughn ignored the question.

"You keep the tanks here in the building?"

Dr. McGill shook his head. His gray hair flopped in front of his face, and he pushed it back with the palm of one hand.

"No—outside. Locked up. What's this about?"

"Think you can show them to us?"

"Detectives—"

Darnell stepped up. He might be a drunk who made inappropriate jokes, but he was also an imposing figure.

"Dr. McGill, you're not in any trouble." *Yet.* "All we're asking is to see where you keep the hydrogen sulfide." *For now.* "If that's not something that you're capable of or willing to do, we can go above your head." *We will.*

Dr. McGill stood.

He was skinny. Almost emaciated. When he swallowed, like

he did now, Vaughn could practically see the saliva making a track down the inside of the man's throat.

"No, no. That's fine, I just—here, come with me."

They walked three abreast down the hallway.

"Do you know a man named Aaron Treadman? Used to work security here on campus?"

"Don't think so."

Vaughn pulled up the photo he'd taken from the morgue. He wasn't in the habit of shocking civilians with pictures of the dead, but he had no other options.

"This is him."

Dr. McGill stopped, lifted his glasses to his forehead.

"Jesus, what happened to him?"

When he inched closer, Vaughn put his phone away.

"You recognize him?"

"No."

They exited the building, went around back.

Dr. McGill led them to a fenced-in area filled with gas tanks. Dozens of them. Different sizes. Some white. Others chromed like the one at the barn.

"We use hydrogen sulfide for biodegradation experiments and for some pharmaceutical applications. It's very volatile. Dangerous, even. Strictly controlled."

Vaughn observed the fence. It was chain-link, but the individual steel wires were closer together than a typical yard fence. Too small to fit a hand through, let alone a tank. The top was also covered, completely boxed in. No jumping over.

Several specialized-looking vents—much more sophisticated than the dryer ducts in the barn—exited through the top of the fencing.

No cuts or breaks that Vaughn could see.

Dr. McGill produced his wallet, swiped it against a card reader. It beeped and the lock on the gate disengaged. He opened it and held it that way.

"You first," Darnell said.

Vaughn used his foot to keep the gate from closing while Dr. McGill and Darnell entered.

They wove through the cannisters, all attached to pillars with those tie-down straps with ratcheting mechanisms.

Vaughn read the thick black letters on the tanks: Ammonia. Chlorine. Oxygen.

Dr. McGill stopped abruptly.

"What the hell?"

He was staring at a pole. An *empty* pole. Tan-colored tie-down straps lay on the ground.

"Something wrong?" Darnell asked.

Dr. McGill muttered something to himself. There was a plastic-covered clipboard hooked on the pole. He grabbed it, flipped through the pages. Flipped back and forth.

"Dr. McGill?"

He turned, his eyes impossibly wide behind his magnified lenses.

"They're supposed to be here—the hydrogen sulfide gas is supposed to be *here*."

"How many canisters?" Darnell demanded.

"Four."

"You mean to tell me that four canisters . . ."

Vaughn didn't hear the rest of his partner's admonishment. The word "four" kept repeating in his head, drowning everything else out.

Four . . .

Four missing canisters.

Four potential crime scenes.

CHAPTER 17

DRESSED ALL IN black, the intruder tried the front door first.

You never know—even in today's world, some people still left their front doors unlocked.

Or forgot to lock them.

No luck.

The intruder hurried around the back of the bungalow, sticking close to the wall for cover. Tried every window. All locked.

This was supposed to be quick and easy. Get in, find the laptop, get out.

It was never quick and easy. All these years of searching but no luck. It was gone, destroyed in the fire.

But they had to keep trying.

The back door was also locked.

"Shit."

The intruder produced a lock pick kit and dropped to one knee.

Thankfully, it wasn't one of those digital ones. Those could also be picked—hacked, really—but that would take time.

Too much time.

The tension wrench—a thin, L-shaped piece of metal—slid into the base of the keyhole. It turned just a little.

Next, the pick. Looked like a cross between a screwdriver and the horrible thing that dentists used to scrape plaque from the gum line.

Into the lock with the wrench.

The intruder wiggled the pick back and forth, pressing it up against the pins. Moved it out when they heard the click.

One, two, three.

Easy.

Four was more difficult. Five was a bitch. It always was.

The mask was hot and sweat started to soak the fabric.

Why am I doing this again?

A sigh.

Tried the fifth pin again. Heard a satisfying clack. With all the pins raised, the tension wrench turned easily and the deadbolt opened.

The intruder was in.

The interior of the bungalow was dark. Quiet.

Good.

For the next hour, they searched the home from one end to the other.

It wasn't there.

The figure in black quickly checked their phone.

It was getting late—early, actually—when they came across a pantry, tucked behind the fridge. The door was sealed with both a digital lock and a padlock.

Shit.

The padlock was smaller than the deadbolt on the rear

door, which made it more difficult to pick. But it was the digital lock that was the real problem.

Sleek, black. Six digit pin. Fingerprint scanner. Not uncrackable, but time consuming. Not only that, but if unlocked, it might send a text alert to the owner's cell phone.

That was a big no-no.

The intruder inspected the door frame. It wasn't reinforced. A thousand-dollar digital lock that could be rendered useless by just a two-dollar crowbar. But that would leave evidence of the break-in. Another no-no.

Cursing again, the intruder wasn't ready to give up just yet. Tried a few six digit combinations. Common codes—696969, 42069, 123456, 999999.

Nothing worked. If the laptop was in there, they weren't getting it.

Not tonight.

The intruder performed one final look around the home, searching places that they might have overlooked on their first pass.

Nothing.

The pantry—it had to be in the pantry. Dejected, they finally gave up. Exited the way they'd come in. They'd only just closed the door when the silence of the night was broken by the unmistakable sound of a car approaching.

The intruder tried to will it to keep going. That never worked.

The car rolled into the driveway and stopped.

More sweat now, but not from the heat. Not from their own breath condensing on the thick fabric, but from stress.

The intruder worked quickly, lifting the pins again.

The front door opened just as the deadbolt on the back door slid into place, leaving it exactly the way they found it. No trace that anyone had ever been inside.

The intruder dissolved into shadow. Two streets over, one down, they slid behind the wheel of their car. A gloved finger clenched between teeth, tugged free.

Then a single text: *I couldn't find it.*

CHAPTER 18

Darnell went hard on Dr. McGill. Tore him a new one. Got the man to write down everyone who had access to the gas storage area, with a shaking hand.

It was a short list.

The man himself, a TA, a couple other department heads. And security, of course.

"Should . . . should I get a lawyer?" Dr. McGill squeaked.

"Maybe." Darnell loved playing the bad guy. Happy, funny. Mean. It was all the same to him. Seamless transition. Father, husband . . . widower, childless. "If you say anything to anyone about us coming here today? Then I'd definitely recommend it."

They left. On the way out, they heard Dr. McGill rattle energy drink cans in search of a final slurp.

"How the fuck does that happen?" Darnell mumbled, shaking his head.

"No idea. You know where the security head office is?"

"Lemme check—200 Elm. Fifteen-minute walk from here." The sun was starting to set now, but it was still warm out. Darnell was sweating. Maybe from the heat, maybe from withdrawal. "Don't even think about it. I'm not walking."

They drove. Pulled up in front of a beautiful building. Small, multicolored brick exterior. Curved, thirty-foot entryway, matching windows down the side.

Flashing their badges was enough to get them through the door. A stern conversation with a guard gained them access to the room that housed the security footage.

"Right—so you want to see the footage from outside Sherrerd Hall, 'round back. What time?"

What day?

"Dr. McGill said that the cans were still there last Tuesday."

"Cans?" The guard questioned. Neither Darnell nor Vaughn entertained this. "Okay. Last Tuesday. Day, night, what?"

Vaughn wasn't sure. Took a different approach.

"Do you know an Aaron Treadman?"

"He a security guard?"

"Was."

"Aaron . . . ?"

"Treadman," Vaughn confirmed.

"No—don't think so. Only started working here a couple of weeks ago. Haven't met everyone yet. They got me locked up in here most of the time."

Darnell appeared about to say something disparaging, Vaughn could see it in his face. His eyes. The way his mouth twitched.

He didn't give his partner a chance.

There were three tanks of hydrogen sulfide gas still out there. They didn't have time to chastise and condemn.

"Do campus security guards have access cards to all areas of the university?"

"Almost all, I think. There are some—"

"The swipe cards, are they individually coded?"

The guard raised an eyebrow. He was young, maybe late twenties. Ratty little goatee he probably thought was trendy.

"Coded?"

"What I mean is, if a security guard scans their card, does it register as campus security, or can you link it to an individual?"

"Ah, I get it—individual."

He stroked the long blond hairs on his chin.

"Can you look up Aaron Treadman's data? He was let go a few months back."

"If he was let go, then he would have had to turn in his card."

"Just look."

"Even if he didn't, all of his privileges would have been revoked. They told me this during orient—"

"Just look," Vaughn repeated sharply.

"Alright, alright."

The guard was seated in front of a computer. Judging by the size of him, he wasn't used to moving much. But at least he typed quickly. A spreadsheet appeared, the cursor jumped around.

"That's weird."

"What?"

"I see Aaron's name here. His card wasn't deactivated."

Darnell grumbled something disparaging.

"When was it last used?"

"A couple of days ago. But if he was fired, it shouldn't—"

"Pull up the video footage from the last time his card was used."

The guard muttered under his breath, something about this *not* being protocol.

Darnell was fuming, heat coming off him in waves. A manifestation of his anger.

The spreadsheet vanished, replaced by a black screen. The guard clicked furiously. Logged out, logged back in.

"What's happening?" Darnell demanded.

"The footage . . . it's all black."

"Where was the card scanned?" Vaughn asked.

"The cage behind Sherrerd Hall."

Of course it was.

"What do you mean all black?" Vaughn said, shaking his head. He was starting to heat up, just like Darnell. "Was the camera painted over?"

He pictured their unsub standing on their toes, maybe on a portable step stool, showering the camera with black spray paint. More than likely wearing a mask but before they blacked out the lens, they might be able to get an idea of the unsub's height and build.

No such luck.

"No, I have footage from today, but not the day the card was used . . . someone deleted the video. Wait—that's not right, either. It wasn't deleted. Someone replaced it with an all black video. Why would they do that?"

Vaughn thought he knew why.

A missing file might be noticed. Perhaps security did a daily or weekly audit to make sure all cameras were up and running properly. If they noticed a missing file, they might be inclined to investigate. Realize that the tanks were gone, too. Sound the alarm.

"How difficult would it be to do something like that? Get into the system?" Vaughn asked. "Delete or replace files?"

"I . . . I dunno. I just monitor the cameras. I don't—man, I just started here."

"Fucking hell," Darnell said.

"Any way to recover the lost footage?"

"I mean, if it was missing, yeah, maybe, but it's not. It's been overwritten."

"Is it on the cloud?"

"This *is* the cloud. Everything is on the cloud. No local storage."

Vaughn glanced at Darnell. The man practically had steam coming out of his ears.

"Take my card. You find out who replaced the footage or if you somehow manage to recover it, call me."

The guard looked stunned as he accepted the card. Vaughn could tell that Darnell was about to shit on this guy.

"Let's go, Darnell."

They started toward the door, Vaughn in the lead. Darnell stopped.

"Hey, it's your job to watch the cameras, right?"

"Y-yeah."

"Then watch the fucking cameras! You know what? I want to speak to your supervisor."

"M-m-my supervisor?"

"Yes, your—"

Vaughn grabbed Darnell's arm, tried to reel him in. As much as this kid had fucked up by not noticing the black video before now, he was just a kid. This was probably his first job. Besides, getting him fired would bring them no closer to the missing tanks. It would also waste time.

"What?" Darnell bared his teeth and shook free. He was on the verge of becoming unhinged, but somehow managed to regain his composure. "Fine—let's just get the fuck out of here before I strangle someone."

Vaughn believed him.

CHAPTER 19

"FUCKING USELESS."

Vaughn couldn't argue with his partner. But he also knew that they were coming at this from a different angle—in hindsight.

They knew the crime, were working backwards.

A few missing tanks that were rarely used. A keycard belonging to an ex-employee that was supposed to have been deactivated. An overwritten video file. Separately, none of these amounted to much.

Together, however . . .

"Speaking of useless," Darnell continued unprompted, "I'm gonna call Delaney again."

Vaughn was still wrapped up in the four missing gas canisters. The elaborate setup. The *Squid Gam*e or whatever the fuck it was.

Couldn't help but think: *one down, three to go.*

He shuddered involuntarily.

"Delaney!" Darnell barked. "Any update on an address for Aaron Treadman?" Pause. "No? Why not?" Pause. "Get 'em printed already. Upload them. We need to move—"

"Darnell, ask him if he has a copy of the 911 call."

Darnell relayed Vaughn's question.

"Send it. And get the other vics printed already!"

They were running out of leads. Aaron Treadman's security card had been used to gain access to the gas. Someone—probably also using Treadman's still active credentials—had overwritten the security footage. Darnell had implied that building the rooms within the barn was an easy task. Could be done in an evening or two by a non-skilled laborer.

No one noticed cars coming or going last night. No vehicles left at the scene.

It was possible that Aaron himself was behind all of this and had just lost at his own game, but Vaughn didn't put much stock in this half-brained theory.

Whoever put all this together had to have a modicum of intelligence, foresight, and planning.

Locking yourself in a room filling with hydrogen sulfide gas didn't fit this truncated profile. Nor did prime numbers. What the hell is with the prime numbers?

"Take a listen."

Darnell played the recording.

The voice on the line was clearly altered, distorted. The highs and lows condensed.

"Gas leak. Ten dead." The voice—probably male, but that too could have been changed—spat the address next. Then the call abruptly ended.

"When was the call made?"

"This morning. 1:32 a.m."

"And Dr. Button said that the victims died at 1:30," Vaughn noted.

"Plus/minus thirty minutes," Darnell said, imitating the ME's nasal voice.

"Still, the person called either right before, right after, or during the gas leak."

No, it couldn't have been Aaron Treadman. No cell phones were found at the scene.

"Let me guess, the 911 call came from a burner phone?"

"Burner phone," Darnell confirmed, staring at his screen.

Unlike their depiction in popular TV shows, burner phones could be tracked. Each phone was equipped with a unique IMEI number. Calls made from a particular cell, irrespective of a SIM card or lack thereof, could be traced back to the device. Moreover, the location of a device that dials 911 was also automatically tracked to the nearest cell phone tower and the position triangulated in case the person was in distress and unable to tell the operator their address.

"You have the data on where the 911 call was made from?"

"Delaney."

"When we find out where, we should do a drive by. I doubt—"

"Delaney."

"What about canvassing local hardware stores? See if anyone loaded up on drywall and lumb—"

"Delaney."

"Trying to find the victims' cars?"

"Delaney."

"Looking at the victims' shoes?"

"Delaney."

Vaughn sighed. Took a page out of Darnell's book.

"What about giving me a hand job?"

"Delaney."

"Good, he's got softer skin than you."

Darnell laughed. Vaughn didn't.

"What's your problem with Delaney, anyway?"

"I don't have a problem."

"Really? You've been on his ass all day."

All month. All year, actually.

Darnell shrugged, slumped deeper into the passenger seat. No chuckling now. The man's dramatic mood changes were something to be studied.

"You know why."

Yeah, I do.

Two years ago, Darnell had been on a stakeout with a different partner; Vaughn was just a rookie detective back then.

Trying to bait a child predator. Working a sting operation, pretended to be an eleven-year-old girl. Text messages were exchanged. A meet-up arranged.

The man never showed. Brass called the sting off when the suspect failed to respond to subsequent texts. He'd smelled something was up; either that or he'd never been serious in the first place. They'd been dismissed, but Darnell had decided to stick around.

The pedo never appeared.

Darnell went home.

Was confronted by an unspeakable tragedy.

Vaughn's partner was put on mandatory three-month administrative leave. Was forced to perform fitness and psych evals before returning to work.

Probably cheated on both.

Darnell hated Delaney because during his mandated leave,

Delaney had overtly expressed interest in becoming a detective. As far as Vaughn knew, Delaney just assumed, like many in the PPD, that Darnell would never return, leaving a position that needed to be occupied.

It wasn't Delaney's fault, and he'd done nothing wrong. But Darnell saw things differently.

Took it as a personal affront, projecting his fury over his family's tragedy on the ambitious puppy dog cop.

"What do you wanna do then, Darnell?"

"Go home." There was no humor in Darnell's voice.

Vaughn took his partner home.

"Take it easy tonight."

"I will."

He wouldn't.

Unlike Darnell, Vaughn wasn't ready to end his shift just yet.

He contacted dispatch himself, got the cell phone data from the anonymous 911 call.

The phone pinged three towers in Hopewell. Two in the city, one northeast in the farmlands. Not far from the barn.

Vaughn spent the next two hours driving around, not really sure what he was looking for. Maybe someone holding a sign saying, "Hey, look at me! I'm the Gasman!"

He spent about half of this time on Snydertown Road. Even visited a place called Stonybrook Meadows Farm.

Vaughn eventually decided that Darnell was right: it was time to go home.

Hell, he might even have a drink.

Unlike his partner, he deserved at least one.

CHAPTER 20

Ivy's head was pounding. Her tongue thick and rubbery.

Something was beeping.

Heart monitor, probably. She'd drunk too much and had been admitted to the hospital. Stomach pumped. IV drip installed.

No . . . she'd gone home with Mr. Finance. He'd drugged her. Him and his buddies had run a train on her. Dropped her off at the side of the road, clinging to life.

Ivy knew that neither of these were true, but she couldn't stop her hands from roaming all over her body. Gently prodding, probing.

Nope, none of that happened, and the beeping wasn't a medical device.

It was her fucking phone.

She reached for it, knocked it off the bedside table. Groaned. Rolled over. Grabbed it. Hammered blindly at the screen.

It stopped making noise.

"I hate you, Abs."

She squinted at the screen. There was a single text message

from her friend. She frowned, deleted it. Then Ivy closed her eyes.

Wait.

She had work today.

Fuck.

Ivy grabbed her phone again, opened one eye just wide enough to see the time. Paper width.

It was after eight.

Shit.

Ivy sat up. Waited for the world to stop spinning. Gagged. Swallowed. Waited some more.

When vomiting all over herself—her outfit from last night—transitioned from a certainty to a mere possibility, Ivy finally got out of bed. New data, Bayesian statistics at its Finest.

She had to get moving, had to get to work.

Ivy stumbled to the bathroom, grabbed a face cloth. Wet it and scrubbed.

One of the worst inventions in the history of mankind was waterproof makeup. In theory, it was a great idea. In practice, not so much. It was a pain in the ass to get off.

Sure, there were makeup removal chemicals, a secondary industry created from the first, but Ivy didn't have the fortitude nor the time to start rooting through her drawers.

She rubbed until her skin turned red.

Her hair was a mess. Abby had straightened it yesterday, but it had battled to return to its native curly state overnight.

Gave up somewhere halfway. It was a wavy, kinky disaster.

Ivy brushed her teeth, scooped water in her palms and drank.

Cold—so cold.

Feeling marginally better now, she quickly slipped out of her dress and into her 'uniform.' Tied her hair back.

Got the fuck to work.

"Sorry I'm late." During the short drive from her house to campus, most of the events from last night came back to her. Blake. Tony.

Flipping quarters for drinks—Penney's game.

Zeke . . .

She'd hoped that he'd slept in, too—he'd been lit at the bar. But Zeke was already in class when she arrived.

What annoyed Ivy more than the entitled kid's presence was his appearance. Sporting a sharp, crisp polo, his blond hair perfectly coiffed.

Fuck him.

"Tristan, can you pull up the graphs on Bayesian statistics again?"

Her TA, who hadn't mentioned her appearance and had a cup of hot coffee waiting for her, obliged.

Ivy turned around, glanced at the digital display. The two bell curves, one pink, one blue.

She sighed. Touched her forehead. It was burning up.

She needed a different approach.

What did Einstein famously say?

The definition of insanity is doing the same thing over and over again and expecting a different result.

Something like that.

Ivy lowered her head, closed her eyes. Opened them again and glanced over at Tristan sitting behind his desk. He stared back, a confused expression on his face. Silently urged her to get started.

"Okay, okay."

There was a podium at the front of the class, but Ivy rarely used it. It was too formal. She intended on using it now, however. With the stylus, she pressed the clear button on the embedded digital pad.

"I'm going to try something a little different today. We're going to do a deep dive into Bayes's Theorem, which is the basis of Bayesian statistics."

I hope you're right, Tristan.

A couple of groans.

Sex, alcohol, and drugs.

"Let's say that the probability of a first-year student contracting an STI is 5 percent."

The groans stopped. Replaced by a solitary uncomfortable chuckle. Ivy, worried that her resolve would fade, kept her eyes locked on the screen. She scribbled: "STI probability = 5%."

Her penmanship was horrible.

"Now, let's say you were a bit . . . concerned after a particularly eventful weekend. You decide to get tested. The test isn't perfect—they rarely are. Now, if you *have* an STI, the test is fairly accurate—95 percent of the time, it will come back positive. But if you don't actually have an STI, the false positive rate is 10 percent."

She wrote these numbers on the board, too.

No laughs now; no groans, either.

A good sign? Were they finally following along? Or just too shocked to react?

Ivy still couldn't believe that she was going through with this. The lasting effects of alcohol were still lowering her inhibitions.

Had to be.

"Hypothetically, after your weekend, the test comes back positive. What are the chances that you have an STI?"

Ivy finally raised her eyes. She was surprised to see everyone's attention locked on the display. Everyone except Zeke, because Ivy still couldn't bring herself to look at him.

"Anyone?"

"95 percent?" someone offered.

And that's why you guys bombed the first test.

"Not quite. Don't freak out just yet. Here's Bayes's formula."

$$P(A|B) = P(B|A) \cdot P(A)$$

$$P(B|\sim A) \cdot P(\sim A) + P(B|A) \cdot P(A)$$

"Where P(A) is equal to the probability that someone in first year has an STI—so 5 percent. P(B|A) is the opposite, that you *don't* have an STI—95 percent. P(~A) is the true positive rate of the test—also 95 percent. While P(B|~A) is the false positive rate—people who don't have an STI but still test positive—10 percent."

Ivy was on a roll now, writing at a rapid clip. Penmanship still awful.

"Now, to find the actual probability that you have an STI *and* tested positive, all we have to do is run the numbers."

The math was fairly simple, and Ivy had no problem performing the calculations even with her foggy brain. She wrote out all the steps, then circled the final value.

≈0.333.

"So? What's the answer?"

A beat of silence.

Ivy was worried that she'd lost them somewhere along the way. Not sure how, given how simple her example was. Simple and relatable.

Then someone said, "It means that Zeke might not have gonorrhea!"

The class erupted into laughter.

Try as she might, Ivy found it impossible to keep from smiling.

"It means that you should always double bag it in first year!"

"Yeah, I think the horse has already left that barn on that one," Ivy said.

More laughter.

"Okay, calm down. Calm down. The actual chance that you have an STD? 33 percent repeating."

There it was. The light bulbs. Bright, shining, illuminating their young, eager, horny faces.

For fuck's sake, Tristan was right. You just had to speak on their level.

Now Ivy glanced to the upper left-hand corner of the class. Saw Zeke.

His face was red, bordering on purple.

The smile on Ivy's lips grew.

Good—fuck him. He's an asshole.

Do you know who my *father is?*

CHAPTER 21

Darnell hadn't taken Vaughn's advice to lay off the booze. The smell was back—sweat and alcohol.

Or maybe it never left.

The cans had returned, though.

"Darnell, time to go."

Darnell didn't fart, snore, or hiccup. He had no reaction.

"Darnell?"

Worry set in and Vaughn shook the man's bare shoulder. He stirred. Opened his bloodshot eyes.

"Time to go, Darnell."

A simple nod.

No jokes today. No silly outfit.

Recalling Darnell in his underwear sporting only his police belt inspired Vaughn to look around for it. Like yesterday, the belt was on the side table. Except today, the holster was empty.

When Darnell slowly started to rouse, Vaughn saw the gun.

It was lying in the bed beside the mostly naked man.

Darnell noticed his partner's gaze. Didn't offer an explanation other than, "Rough night. Gimme five."

Vaughn left the room, started coffee again. Didn't bother cleaning up.

When Darnell emerged from the bedroom, Vaughn handed him a cup.

"Hey," Vaughn began, staring at the pitch-black liquid in his to-go mug. "I think—"

"I'm going to get help, Vaughn. After this case."

Things had never been this bad. Vaughn had heard stories about the type of detective that Darnell had been prior to the tragedy, but they were difficult to believe.

This man? Once a prized PPD detective?

Perhaps seeing something in his face, Darnell continued, "I get help now, the department is gonna put me on leave again. I can't do that. This is all I got, man. We wrap this up, they'll go easy on me."

Vaughn wasn't sure if it was deliberate or just habit, but Darnell's hand dropped to his holster—his service pistol was back in place—and he adjusted it slightly.

"Okay. After this case. I just want you to get better, Darnell."

"Me too."

Vaughn had his doubts. Some people lived inside their tragedy for so long that it fused to them, became their identity. Even if they wanted out—forward, backward, anywhere—it was impossible. Like telling a kleptomaniac to stop stealing. A pyromaniac to stay away from fire.

Vaughn hoped it wasn't too late for his partner.

In the car, he gave his partner an update on some of the work he'd done himself last night while nursing a bourbon, though most was Delaney's doing.

He omitted the latter, figuring that mentioning the PPD officer would only trigger Darnell.

Trigger . . . Why was his gun in bed with him?

"Got an address for Treadman," Vaughn began, then fired off the details, bullet-point style. "Have the names of three more victims, still working on the rest. Nothing remarkable about them. No links to the university. Nothing notable about the victims' footwear, either. No crushed fruits. Don't think that they walked far. I made a list of the most likely locations they would have parked and walked to the barn from." Vaughn reached into his pocket and passed Darnell a sheet of paper torn from his notepad. His partner gave it a once over. "I figure we go by these places after we finish."

"Finish with what?"

"Visiting Aaron Treadman's house."

"Delan—"

"Don't say it."

Darnell didn't.

"What about the barn?"

Vaughn shook his head.

"Nothing there. The high-tech router made everything digital untraceable. No luck contacting the owner of the LLC either. To be honest, I'm surprised someone hasn't scooped the barn up yet. Property taxes haven't been paid going on three years."

As Vaughn pulled up to the address that Delaney had provided him with after doing some social media research/doxxing he realized he had misspoken. Aaron Treadman didn't live in a house but an apartment. Not exactly in the best part of Trenton, New Jersey, either.

Low-income housing, high crime rate.

Considering that Aaron's last job on record had been as a Princeton security guard, this wasn't surprising.

They located the superintendent, a chain-smoking man who looked to be in his mid-sixties, with a shaved head. Asked about Aaron.

From the looks of it, the complex only had a couple dozen units, thirty at most. This bode well for them, and the super, who introduced himself only as Dale, knew Aaron. Didn't seem concerned that two PPD detectives were asking around, which was telling about the area.

"Never had no problems with Aaron. Was late a couple of times with rent, but always paid in the end. Can't say the same for some of the other tenants."

"Can you take us to his apartment?" Vaughn asked.

"Sure."

They technically needed a warrant to enter Aaron's apartment. But if the super let them in, then all was fair game.

Aaron's apartment was on the second floor, toward the south end of the building. It was too small to have an elevator, so they took the stairs.

Darnell made a point to indicate some drug paraphernalia—a spent syringe, a broken glass pipe, burnt sections of foil—in the stairwell, ensuring that Dale noticed this, too.

"Some tenants prop the entrance open with a brick when they go for a smoke. Forget to remove it afterward. They're not supposed to, but . . ."

Darnell gave this a disapproving, "Hmm."

Dale led them to apartment 2F and Vaughn knocked.

"He live alone?" Darnell asked.

They were fairly certain Aaron did, based on their scraping of the man's social media.

"Yeah. Quiet guy."

There was no reply from inside the apartment, and Darnell shot Vaughn a look. Then he sniffed dramatically.

"You smell that?"

Vaughn knew where his partner was headed with this and went along with it.

"Smells like rotten eggs."

The open-air hallway did have a funk to it—not eggs so much as general BO and the faint hint of stale cigarette smoke.

"I don't smell nothin'."

Even if someone had smashed a crate of eggs and left the debris in the sun for a week, Vaughn doubted Dale would have picked up the scent. The man's fingers and teeth were stained a pale brown from nicotine.

"What's this about, anyway? Aaron in some sort of trouble?"

Darnell disregarded Dale's questions. Most of being a detective amounted to just that: ignoring people's questions while posing your own. Or just listening. There were very few things more uncomfortable than an awkward silence.

"I definitely smell rotten eggs. Dale, think you can save us some time and unlock the door?"

"I'm not supposed to do that."

"Here's the deal, Dale." Darnell made himself big as he spoke, adjusted his belt, drawing eyes to his service weapon, which had shifted toward the front. "You can let us into Aaron's apartment, or we can all stand here and wait around for an hour or two while my partner here calls a judge and applies for a warrant."

Dale nodded as if he was okay with this. The man had nothing better to do. Vaughn took over.

"We do that, and then we're going to have to do some real digging." His eyes flicked to the stairwell. "You got a conference room in this place?"

Dale scoffed.

"A conference room?"

"Didn't think so. In that case, we'll probably have to use your office to interview all of your tenants. Ask a *whole* lot of questions. You know those tenants you said didn't pay on time? Didn't pay at all? I'm thinking you might never hear from or see them again."

Dale's right hand didn't move to the keyring on his belt, but it did twitch a little.

"Dale, we just want to take a look around," Vaughn pressed, changing gears slightly.

Dale shifted, sighed, and finally grabbed his keys.

"You gonna keep my name out of this, right?"

A hint of a smile graced Vaughn's lips.

"Of course."

They were in.

CHAPTER 22

Ivy was pleased with how the class had gone, unorthodox as her lesson had been. Tristan's suggestion had panned out—the students seemed to *finally* understand Bayesian statistics.

Ivy was less pleased when she stepped into the hallway after everyone had left and saw Zeke waiting for her.

Here it comes, she thought. *The apology.*

Ivy was working out what to say—slowly, on account of her head still being a little fuzzy—when the angry little shit came forward.

"What did you do?"

Okay, so no apology forthcoming.

"Mr. Godfrey—"

Zeke stepped toward her.

"You said I was cheating? I didn't cheat. Who the hell would I cheat off, anyway?"

"Mr. Godfrey, I don't know what—"

"It was Becky, wasn't it? That bitch was pissed I wouldn't go out with her, so she lied and said I cheated."

Last night, Zeke had been drunk. Sober today. But the look in his eyes was the same.

"I don't know what you're talking about."

"Yeah, you do. I don't think you understand who I am. My father donates millions to this university. *Millions*."

Ivy glanced up and down the hallway. All the other classes in Fine Hall had let out—they were alone. And Zeke was standing within two feet of her.

There was nowhere for Ivy to go.

"You think your daddy was pretty important, don't you? You think because you are his daughter, the daughter of this big math wizard, that you're safe? Because of *math*?"

Ivy had been scared at the bar; now she was terrified.

"Here's what you're going to do," Zeke continued. "You're going to go back to that weasel Dr. Moorehead and you're going to tell him that you made a mistake. You're going to tell him—"

The door opened behind Ivy and she jumped.

"Dr. Reeves?" It was Tristan. She moved aside, not realizing that she'd backed up nearly to the classroom door. "Everything okay here?"

Zeke was bigger than Tristan. Thicker through the chest and arms—barely, but still. But when their eyes met, it was Zeke who backed down first.

"Remember what I said," Zeke hissed and scurried off.

"What the hell was that all about?" Tristan asked.

Ivy was too rattled to answer.

"The cheating, right? Did you go to Dr. Moorehead?"

Still, Ivy remained silent. She was trembling. Hated the fact that she'd let the entitled brat get to her but couldn't help it. That look.

Now, a full blown shudder coursed through her.

"Hey, you gonna be okay?"

Ivy finally snapped to.

"Yeah, thanks. Thanks for that."

"Want me to walk you to your office?"

Ivy shook her head.

"No. I'll be fine."

And I'm not going to my office. I'm going back to see Dr. Moorehead.

Dr. Moorehead wasn't happy to see her. He'd just hung up the phone, and as unlikely as it might be, Ivy couldn't shake the feeling that the conversation that had left the department head ornery had been about her, courtesy of Zeke's father.

"What can I do for you, Dr. Reeves?"

He ran a hand over his bald head. It made a sound like sandpaper on rubber.

"We have to do something about Zeke Godfrey."

Dr. Moorehead raised his chin.

"I spoke to him yesterday about the allegations and just now I got a call from his father. He wasn't pleased." So it *was* about her. Ivy tried to cut in, but Dr. Moorehead continued. "The simple fact is that there's not enough evidence to do anything about it, unfortunately. Now, if there's nothing else—"

"He cornered me outside my class." Ivy tried her best to keep her voice even but a small tremor crept in.

Dr. Moorehead's eyes went dark.

"What do you mean, 'cornered you'?"

"He came up to me, accused me of speaking to you about him cheating."

"Did he threaten you?"

Ivy thought back. The interaction had certainly *felt* threatening. But she didn't think that Zeke had come out and directly threatened her. Ordered her around, intimidated her, but never actually threatened.

"Not exactly. But he was aggressive. Told me to come here and rescind the accusation."

Dr. Moorehead seemed to relax a little.

"He's angry and frustrated. If he didn't touch you or threaten you, there's not much I can do. As for rescinding the cheating—"

"I don't want to do that. Zeke cheated—I know it."

"And you of all people should also know that we work on facts here in this department," Dr. Moorehead said, quickly transitioning from concerned to annoyed. "Not intuition. There's not enough evidence against Mr. Godfrey to do anything about it. Not for this one test."

It wasn't one test, it was two, but Ivy didn't think this was the time to point this 'fact' out.

"If he says anything threatening or touches you, you let me know. I'll deal with it."

There was also the incident at the bar, and Ivy was almost certain that Zeke had threatened her then. But she'd been drunk. The only witnesses were Zeke's buddies, who would claim ignorance, and Abby and Blake. Also drunk.

Their testimonies wouldn't hold much weight with Dr. Moorehead. Not nearly as much weight as a cushy seven-figure donation, which Zeke's father had likely offered to make all this go away and to keep his son enrolled at Princeton.

"Look, Ivy, if you're really scared of this kid, I can talk to security. Get them to spend more time on your floor."

"It's fine."

"You sure?"

"It's fine," Ivy repeated harshly.

It wasn't fine.

Zeke Godfrey was a young, angry, entitled asshole.

And almost certainly dangerous.

CHAPTER 23

Aaron Treadman kept a surprisingly neat apartment. Protein powder, creatine on the counter. Not much else out in the open.

Vaughn thought about the man's naked body at the morgue. Muscular—Aaron took care of himself.

"I'll check the bedroom," Darnell said. "Clear the kitchen."

Dale waited in the apartment entrance, looking nervous. Looking like he needed a cigarette.

Vaughn wasn't sure what they were searching for. The key-card, maybe? A tie-down strap? Anything to link Aaron to the gas.

The man's phone would be nice.

Whatever had drawn Aaron to that farm in the middle of nowhere, the man had been in no rush to get there. There were no dirty dishes in the sink. No half-eaten sandwich or protein bars.

"What are you guys looking for?" Dale asked.

"Just stay outside," Darnell hollered.

Dale put his hands up, took another step back. He had a

cigarette out now, twirled it in his fingers. Put it in his mouth, removed it.

On the kitchen table, Vaughn found an open laptop. He pulled a latex glove out of his pocket and clicked one of the buttons beneath the trackpad. The laptop wasn't password protected, and an image appeared on the screen.

"Bedroom's clean," Darnell announced. "Find anything in there?"

Vaughn squinted at the image.

"Vaughn?"

"Yeah, I got something."

Darnell came over, breathing heavily. Leaned in.

"Shit."

Aaron had left his email open.

They both stared at what looked like a crudely made ad. Vaughn had seen dozens like it in his own email. A scam, most likely.

> *We are recruiting participants for a new game show to be aired on a major streaming network. The game involves simple puzzles that teammates need to complete both together and individually. Show to be aired sometime in the fourth quarter 2025. Prizes will be awarded in the form of cryptocurrency. Minimum payout: 1 Bitcoin (actual value to be determined by market price).*

There was a contact number at the bottom.

"You've got to be shitting me," Darnell said, pulling back. "You believe that, and I've got a bridge in San Francisco to sell you."

Vaughn reread the ad, then took out his phone and dialed the number. The line had been disconnected.

"People actually fall for this shit?"

Vaughn shrugged.

"No job, no money. As cheesy as the ad looks, if you got nothing to lose …"

"What email is it from?"

Vaughn clicked a button with the glove.

"Looks generic. If whoever sent this actually lured ten people out to the barn, I doubt they're going to sign up for this email using their actual name."

"You never know." Darnell gestured at the screen dismissively. "A lot of *really* stupid people out there."

"What do you want to do?"

Vaughn knew what he wanted to do. Take the laptop back to the PPD. Get Bowes and Caine to go through it. Only, they had no right to remove it from Aaron's apartment.

Darnell scratched his head. Thought for a moment, then said, "Why did Delaney say Aaron got fired?"

"Accused of stealing a laptop."

Darnell raised an eyebrow.

"Some student's, right?"

"Faculty, I think."

"Yeah, you're right. And guess what? I don't see any receipts for a laptop in the apartment, do you?"

Vaughn grinned a little. Looked around dramatically.

"I do not."

"Then this might be the very laptop in question, which makes it evidence. Pack it up."

Vaughn didn't need to be asked twice.

He slipped the glove on now, and worried that if he closed the laptop lid completely, he might be required to log in when it opened again, he kept it in its current state.

"What are you doin'? I—I said you could come in, but you can't take stuff out."

"You a lawyer now, Dale?" Darnell asked.

"No, but—"

"We have reasonable suspicion that this laptop is stolen."

"Stolen?"

"Stolen," Vaughn confirmed.

"O-okay. What if he—what if Aaron asks where it went?"

"He won't." Darnell's eyes darkened and he produced a business card. "But if anyone else comes by asking questions about Aaron, I want you to give me a call."

Dale reluctantly took the card.

"Thanks for your help, Dale. You can have that smoke now."

Delaney was waiting for them back at the station.

"What's that?" he asked, hooking a chin toward the laptop that Vaughn still clutched in his hand. On the entire ride over, he'd been moving the cursor every few seconds to make sure it didn't go into hibernation mode. Probably unnecessary, since it was sitting on Aaron's table for a whole day without being used. But you could never be too careful.

"Aaron Treadman's laptop."

Delaney's eyes widened.

"Know how to make sure it doesn't power down?" Vaughn asked.

"Sure."

Vaughn set the device on his desk, minimized the browser. He passed Delaney a glove and the officer navigated through the settings.

"So far I've identified five of the victims," Delaney informed them. He passed the computer back.

"You have addresses for them?" Vaughn flopped into his chair and brought up the ad again.

"A couple. The others are—what's that?"

Delaney was looking over his shoulder. Darnell, who had yet to say a word to the officer, retreated to make a pot of coffee.

"Found it on his computer—an ad. Not exactly *Squid Game*, but close."

Vaughn waited for Delaney to finish reading.

"Scam."

"Yeah, that's what I thought. But Aaron had no job. If he was desperate enough . . ."

"You know what, give me a second."

While Delaney got on his phone, Darnell returned with two cups of coffee, not bothering to ask Delaney if he wanted one.

Vaughn took a sip. Grimaced. It was thin and oily.

"I knew it." Delaney beamed. "Heard some of the other officers yapping this morning in the bullpen. Someone called in last night—their husband went to film some game show and never came home."

"Really?"

"Yeah, just confirmed it."

"So you bring up *Squid Game* in the barn then this

morning you hear them talking about a missing person who went to a game show and don't connect the dots?" Darnell said.

The pride on Delaney's face sloughed off.

"I didn't connect them until now. I was looking into addresses and—"

"What the fuck are you doing here, Delaney?" Darnell asked aggressively.

Delaney stiffened.

"I came looking for you guys to tell you the—"

"No, what the fuck are you doing here *now*?"

Delaney looked to Vaughn for support. Vaughn averted his eyes.

"Go! Get the fuck out of here! We have ten dead people in a barn, Delaney. Find the person who called about their husband."

Shaking his head, Delaney moved to the door.

Darnell shouted after him.

"And while you're at it, put out an APB on Aaron's car!"

CHAPTER 24

"You don't have to be such an asshole to him," Vaughn remarked after Delaney was gone. "He's a good cop."

"He's a piece of shit."

Vaughn sighed.

"Alright, well we gotta do something." Vaughn sipped his coffee. Every cop he'd ever worked with made strong, thick as tar coffee. That was the cliché; that was the calling card.

Everyone except for Darnell. His coffee was like lightly tinted water.

Tasted like piss.

"I can take the laptop to Bowes and Caine, see if they can trace the phone number and email address. Probably a job for Delaney, but you sent him away," Vaughn said.

A bit of veiled humor. A Darnell special. The man didn't so much as crack a smile.

"Let me see that ad again?"

Vaughn swiveled the laptop.

"A *major streaming network,* huh?"

"Yeah, I highly doubt that any network would air people being gassed to death."

"There was a camera," Darnell remarked as he sat, his chair squeaking under his weight. He slurped his coffee loudly and took out his phone. Started swiping.

There was a camera, sure, but it was there so that whoever set this thing up could remotely release the gas if the ten participants failed the "simple puzzle."

Now Vaughn was on his phone, his brow furrowed. He pulled up the crime scene photos. Smashed boxes, numbers on the victims' chests and numbers in the boxes.

On the dirt ground, too.

Simple puzzle.

What kind of fucking simple puzzle was this? What kind of simple puzzle involved prime numbers?

"Hey, Vaughn?"

Vaughn raised his eyes.

"What's up?"

"Check this out."

Darnell made no move to get up, so Vaughn walked over to him.

His partner was on TikTok.

"Aren't you a little old for TikTok?"

"Never too old for TikTok. Anyway, I started searching for puzzle shows and prime numbers and this came up. It's going viral."

He pressed play.

It was a video from a classroom of sorts, the kind that was shaped like a caldera, the main lectern and display board down below, the seats rising in a semi-circle above.

Darnell turned the volume up on his phone.

The professor, a woman, three-quarter turned to the

camera, was saying, "Let's say that the probability of a first-year student of having an STI is 5 percent."

She wrote on the lectern, her words magically appearing on the board behind her.

"Now, let's say you were a bit . . . concerned after a particularly eventful weekend. You decide to get tested. The test isn't perfect—they rarely are. If you have an STI, it's pretty accurate—95 percent of the time, it will come back positive. But if you don't actually have an STI, the false positive rate is 10 percent."

The class chuckled.

"I don't get it," Vaughn admitted. "What's the link?"

"They're calling her the Bae-sian Prof."

"The what?"

"Bae-sian Prof."

"No, I heard you—what does it mean?"

Darnell pulled up the comments. There were hundreds of them.

"Looks like she was teaching Bayesian statistics. And, before you ask, I have no idea what that is. But *'bae'* means, like, girlfriend or something in millennial speak."

Vaughn frowned.

"Cute. What does this have to do with the barn? The gas?"

"Dunno. Searched for math, prime numbers, game show, New Jersey, and this popped up." Darnell shrugged. "Maybe she knows what the hell those boxes are all about."

"Got a name?"

Darnell scrolled.

"Dr. Ivy Reeves—math prof at Princeton." Princeton . . . this was getting more interesting. The idea of visiting someone at the university who might have a clue what the numbers meant had already crossed Vaughn's mind. But with everything going on—Dr. McGill and the gas canisters, searching Aaron Treadman's apartment, and Dr. Button at the morgue—it had slipped from his thoughts. "Wanna go have a chat with Dr. Reeves?"

"Why not? We can drop the laptop off with Bowes on the way." Vaughn set his full mug down. "And we can also pick up some real coffee."

"What do you mean? What's wrong with my coffee?"

"Tastes about as good as your pajamas look."

This, Darnell chuckled at.

CHAPTER 25

Ivy was flustered when she entered her office, more so when she saw that Tristan was seated behind his desk. She wanted to be alone.

"Dr. Reeves? You alright?"

"Yeah."

Her head hurt. Felt two sizes too big.

"Zeke's an asshole," Tristan said. "He's unpredictable."

Ivy nodded.

"You talk to Dr. Moorehead about him?"

"Yeah."

"And?"

Ivy shrugged. She still didn't feel like talking.

"Shit. He's an asshole, too. I can go to Moorehead, if you want. Tell him that—"

"No, that's okay."

Ivy didn't want to think about Zeke anymore. Zeke or Blake or Rebecca. What she wanted to do was lie down and take a nap, wake up tomorrow for a fresh start.

Damn you, Abs.

"I know this isn't a great time, Dr. Reeves, but there's—there's something you gotta see."

"What is it?"

"You're not going to like it."

No shit.

"Show me."

Tristan got up from his desk and passed his phone to her. Ivy made a face.

"TikTok?"

"Click play."

With every second that passed, Ivy felt the hangover knot in her stomach tighten.

"You have to be kidding me," she whispered. "Bae-sian Prof? Who the hell posted this?"

Ivy kept her eyes trained on the phone as heat rose in her cheeks.

"No idea. It's a new account, no other posts."

"How many people have seen it?"

Ivy wasn't a TikToker. Didn't know how to interpret the heart, the weird badge, or the curved arrow symbols. The extent of her social media knowledge started and stopped with an old Instagram account that she only rarely logged into. When Tristan didn't answer, Ivy raised her gaze. The TA's lips had curved downward.

"It's blowing up."

"What does that mean? A hundred people?"

Tristan's Adam's apple bobbed.

"More."

"Like how many—"

"150k."

Ivy's eyes bulged.

"*One hundred and fifty thousand?*"

"Yeah," Tristan said dryly.

"How the fu—we need to take this down."

"I've already reported it."

"Who recorded it?"

"Like I said, it's a new account—"

"I know, but the students didn't have their phones!"

Zeke—it had to be Zeke. He was pissed at her for reporting him for cheating, thought he could post a video of her to . . . what? Embarrass Ivy? Was he planning on posting lewd comments and, when the video took off, he just let it run? Well, if that was his goal, it had worked. Or perhaps Zeke knew that a professor posting a video of one of their lectures without departmental consent went against university policy. Sure, Ivy hadn't been the one who had posted it, but the department would still hate it. As for taking his phone, a guy like him probably had every iPhone iteration since inception. Likely had three or four burners in his possession at any given moment.

"I dunno if you can take it down, but if enough people report it . . ."

This nightmare was getting worse.

Ivy handed Tristan his phone back and took out her own. Navigated to the app store and downloaded TikTok. Took a minute or so to create an account. She used a made-up name—Euclid314—and skipped all the annoying questions.

She searched for "Bae-sian Prof" and the video of her immediately popped up. Tristan had been wrong. The video, posted by User999123, had 172,000 views and growing. The knot in her stomach was like an iron fist now. An iron fist wrapped in barbed wire.

This is the last thing I need.

As a liberal institution, Princeton was fully and completely progressive, but it was still a traditional establishment—the math department in particular. And then there was the code of conduct she'd signed when she'd won the Clay Fellowship. Had she broken the rules? Was using an STI analogy off-limits?

"How do you report it?"

"Click the share button, then report."

Ivy did. A dozen or so different reasons came up. Everything from suicide and self-harm to shocking and graphic content. No reason fit perfectly, so she just selected one at random. A check mark appeared thanking her for the report and telling her that a moderation team would review the video.

"That's it?"

Ivy closed the app, opened it again. Searched for "Bae-sian Prof." 180,000 views now.

"Yep."

"It's still there," she said desperately.

"Yeah, they'll have to review it. If enough people report it, then—"

A knock on the door startled them both.

Oh, fuck. Dr. Moorehead. He saw the video.

But it wasn't Dr. Moorehead. Through the frosted glass, she saw the outlines of two figures, both about the same height, one considerably thicker around the middle. Neither were bald.

"Open it," Ivy instructed.

Tristan opened the door and the thinner man who was standing slightly in front of the other spoke first.

"I'm Detective Ryan, and this is Detective Sacker with the PPD. We're looking for Dr. Ivy Reeves."

Ivy dropped her phone.

"Is it my dad? Please tell me my dad's okay."

CHAPTER 26

SURE, VAUGHN HAD seen the video of the Bae-sian Prof. But in it, she was half turned. Hard to see much of her face. In real life, Dr. Ivy Reeves was young. *Really* young. Pretty, too, despite not wearing a lick of makeup.

Vaughn thought that this might be a work thing, playing down her good looks to appear more professional. He suspected that if she put a little effort in, Dr. Reeves would be stunning.

"Your . . . dad?" Darnell said, squeezing into the small office behind Vaughn.

"Yes. Is he okay?"

"What's your dad's name?"

Confusion washed over Dr. Reeves's features.

"Gene—I mean, Eugene Reeves."

"No, this isn't about your father," Darnell said flatly.

Relief replaced confusion, but Dr. Reeves remained on edge.

It wasn't uncommon for civilians to become nervous—even good, law-abiding citizens—in the presence of cops.

Vaughn had a friend in college, a woman, who had family

who lived in Canada. She'd drive up to visit them for every major holiday. After a late-night study session, she'd offered to give Vaughn a ride home. He'd noticed a set of glasses on the dash and picked them up.

"I didn't know you wore contacts." A flirtatious opening. He liked her.

"I don't."

Vaughn waved at the glasses.

"Oh, those? I wear those for when I cross the border."

"But you don't need them?" They weren't the sexy secretary type. They were old, thick frames. A decade or two out of style.

"Naw. They just make me look less suspicious."

"You some sort of international drug smuggler?"

She'd laughed.

"Dr. Reeves, can we speak with you for a moment?" Vaughn said, clearing his mind of the reverie.

"Sure."

Darnell put a hand on his hip and narrowed his eyes at the man with the long hair who had opened the door for them.

"Right—*uh*, I was just leaving. I have class." He was nervous, too. Sweeping his hair behind his ears, he said to Dr. Reeves, "I'll catch up later. Excuse me."

Darnell moved just a little, forcing the man to turn sideways to get by him and out the door.

"Your father—he in some kind of trouble?" Darnell asked.

"N-no. It's just . . . I'm sorry, what is this about?"

The woman was clearly flustered. Her brow was sweating even though the AC unit inside the office was pumping out cool air.

"We saw your TikTok video," Darnell said.

This was usually how these things went. Darnell did the talking, Vaughn observed. But they generally reserved this approach for suspects.

And Dr. Reeves wasn't a suspect.

"Jesus, that was fast. I only just reported it. Is it gone?" She reached for her phone. "Was it taken down?"

Vaughn noticed that her hand was shaking.

"You didn't post it?" Darnell asked.

"No, of course not. I don't normally . . ." She sighed, checked her phone, darkened the screen. "I reported it—I want it taken down. I thought you were here because of the video."

"We are . . . sort of." Darnell took out his phone. "You want it taken down?"

"Yes." Exasperated.

"I can report it for you."

"Thank you. And because you're a cop—"

"—detective," Darnell corrected.

"Sorry, detective. That should get it taken down, right?"

"*Ehhh*, it's my personal account."

"I just want it gone."

Dr. Reeves's blue eyes flicked in Vaughn's direction.

"Sorry, I don't have TikTok."

She nodded. Looked to be in physical pain.

"I don't even know how someone recorded it. I always confiscate the students' phones before class." She cocked her head. "Oh, shit, wait a second. I was late, I . . ." Dr. Reeves stopped herself when she realized she was rambling. "I'm sorry, Detectives. It's been a day. But if this isn't about my dad or the video, then why are you here?"

CHAPTER 27

Ivy's mind was swimming again. TikTok, Bae-sian Prof, Zeke, her father, detectives.

Fucking Abs. Why did I listen to you and go out to the bar? I hate you, bitch.

"Can I sit?" she asked.

"Of course."

The thinner of the two cops was young, white, and about her age. The other Black detective was hefty. Like her, he too was sweating.

"You're not in any sort of trouble," the Black detective said.

Ivy tried to lower herself gracefully in her chair, but her legs failed to behave.

She didn't like the sound of that.

In her experience, "You're not in any sort of trouble" usually meant the opposite.

"I'm sorry, I forgot your names."

The young cop pointed at himself then his partner.

"Vaughn and Darnell. We're detectives with the Princeton

Police Department. Dr. Reeves, if this is a bad time, we can come back."

"No . . . it's fine. And call me Ivy. Dr. Reeves was my dad. *Is* . . . Dr. Reeves *is* my dad," she corrected herself.

"Sure, Ivy. We're here because we have a bit of a math problem we need help with."

This, Ivy had not been expecting.

"Okay . . ."

Vaughn looked uncomfortable. It was cute. The detective had medium length brown hair, parted to one side. A square jaw, a five o'clock shadow. Not 6'5", hazel eyes, not blue, and definitely no trust fund.

Ivy silently cursed Abby again, this time for getting that stupid song stuck in her head. She didn't even think that Abby was responsible—it was probably one of her students—but it just felt right to blame her friend for pretty much everything right now.

"It's sensitive, and we're not really sure if it is actually a math problem. It's just . . . there are these numbers, right? Prime numbers, and—"

Darnell grimaced as his partner stumbled over his words.

"What we're trying to say is that you can't mention anything we show you. And, I'll be honest, some of the images are pretty graphic."

What is happening in my life?

"You have no obligation to help. And if you want us to come back . . . ?" Vaughn let his sentence trail off.

"It's fine. I'm just not sure what you mean by a 'math problem.'"

Vaughn smirked.

"We're not either—that's part of the problem."

Another sidelong glance from his partner.

"We were at a crime scene and there were these prime numbers scattered all over the floor. We think it might be a math puzzle," Darnell said. "But we're way out of our league. Vaughn?"

The younger detective—twenty-five? Twenty-eight?—got out his phone. Swiped his finger, cocked his head. Pinched the screen. Squinted.

Ivy knew what he was doing. He was trying to hide some of the more 'graphic' images. She waited patiently. After a good thirty seconds, he seemed satisfied and held a photo out to her.

Ivy had no idea what she was looking at.

Smashed wood. A crumpled piece of paper with the number thirteen on it. A dirt floor.

"May I?"

"Sure."

Vaughn passed her the phone, and she accidentally touched the screen. The image reset to normal size and Ivy grimaced.

"Oh, shit—did it?"

Vaughn reached for the phone. Ivy kept it.

"It's okay."

The scene was disturbing. More wood—broken boxes or tables, maybe?—other sheets of paper with numbers on them. Ivy saw all this, but couldn't take her gaze off the man lying in the dirt. His eyes were open and cloudy.

Ivy had only ever seen one dead person before, and that situation had been entirely different. Intense, dangerous. No time to think or process. Just act.

"We found boxes with numbers engraved on the top and different ones inside. All prime numbers . . . you okay?"

Ivy shuddered, recalling the fire. The heat. The carnage.

The first two fingers and thumb on her right hand suddenly felt hot. Always did when she thought about the fire. All of her other wounds—scorched nose and throat from smoke inhalation, minor burns on her face and arms—had completely healed. But not her fingers.

"Is he . . . is he dead?"

Vaughn reached for the phone again, but for some reason, Ivy continued to hold it tightly, wouldn't let him have it.

"Yes. I'm sorry, I didn't mean to shock you."

He had to basically pry the phone from her hand.

"Yeah, sorry about that," Darnell said. "Maybe we'll just describe the scenario to you?"

"Okay."

Ivy had no idea why they hadn't just done that in the first place. To impress on her how important this was? Was the presence of two detectives in her office not enough?

"Right, so we found these boxes. Some were smashed. Vaughn how many boxes in total?" The younger cop was staring at her. "Vaughn?"

"We think ten," he said after a beat.

"So ten boxes. Each had a number on top, a prime number, and a different one inside. The victims—*uh*, the *players*—each had a number on their chest. That's pretty much all we know," Darnell said.

Victims. As in, plural? More than one?

This day could not possibly get any worse.

"I'm sorry, I don't—"

"Actually, we know a bit more. There were only ten numbers," Vaughn said, finding his tongue. "We found ten numbers, all prime numbers, repeated twice. One on the outside of the box, one inside. In some of the boxes, anyway—most were smashed."

"Three," Darnell corrected.

"Huh?"

"*Three* sets of numbers. One on their chests, one on the top of the boxes, one inside."

"Right. Three. Could they be, like—"

"Wait," Ivy interrupted. "There were *ten* victims?"

Darnell and Vaughn exchanged a look.

"Ten like . . . *that*?"

CHAPTER 28

THIS WAS FALLING apart. And quickly.

The poor woman, stressed about her father (for some reason) and the TikTok video, was now trying to deal with wrapping her mind around the idea of ten dead bodies.

Vaughn had seen it in Ivy's face.

Aaron Treadman was likely her first.

The first corpse that Vaughn had seen had been his grandmother's—Betty Ryan. His parents had talked about an open casket, but he, being only seven at the time, had no idea what that meant.

It had been a rude awakening, seeing the woman who lying in a coffin so still—impossibly still.

Ivy Reeves was no seven-year-old, but that didn't make it much easier. Darnell . . . God damn it, it had been his idea to come here.

"Dr. Reeves—I mean, Ivy—we shouldn't have bothered you."

"Ten boxes, you said?"

Ivy was deep in thought and her brow knitted.

Darnell: "Yeah."

Vaughn just wanted to leave the woman alone, but Darnell was blocking him in.

"Numbers on their chests, numbers on the boxes, different numbers in the boxes?" Ivy said. Her voice was different somehow. Far-off.

"Well, it's the same ten numbers repeated. *Uh*, two, three, seven . . . thirteen."

"Two, three, five, seven, eleven, thirteen, seventeen, nineteen, twenty-three, and twenty-nine."

"How'd you know?" Darnell asked.

"Those are the first ten prime numbers."

"Ah."

"The boxes . . . ?" Darnell pressed. "Any idea what this all means?"

Ivy didn't answer at first. Her brow still stitched, she ran a hand through her hair. It got stuck halfway and she teased her fingers free.

"Ten numbers, ten boxes, ten . . ." Ivy trailed off before saying the word "victims."

"Yes," Darnell confirmed. He kept shooting these looks at Vaughn, which he found particularly annoying.

"Have either of you ever heard of the 100 prisoners problem?"

Now it was Vaughn's turn to stare at Darnell. The big man shrugged.

"Can't say that I have," Vaughn admitted.

Ivy's forehead softened, and the '11' fold between her eyes disappeared completely. When she spoke again, she seemed more or less steady.

It was as if her brain switching into math mode had made her forget all about Aaron Treadman.

"It's a classic probability theory in the form of a game. One hundred prisoners are placed in a room and are given the rules: each one is assigned a unique number from one to one hundred, consecutive. They are all to enter an adjacent room alone, one at a time. They can discuss strategy beforehand, but once they are in the room, they can no longer communicate with the other players. The room has one hundred boxes in it, all labeled consecutively, again, from one to one hundred. They can open up to fifty boxes, and that's it. The numbers inside the boxes have been randomized. Their goal is to find their number—the one assigned to them—in one of those fifty boxes they open. If they do, they have effectively 'won.' The boxes are closed again, and the next person enters the room. Same rules apply. If all one hundred find their number, they're released from prison. If even one of them fails, they all lose."

"They die?" Vaughn blurted.

"Yes. These are prisoners, remember? Anyway, it's just a hypothetical game. Win the game, you live. Lose, you die."

"I mean, depending on the sentence, it seems like a good deal. Fifty-fifty, right?" Darnell said, playing along.

"Not exactly," Ivy continued. Vaughn recognized her now as the same woman in the video. Confident and sure of herself, despite the uncomfortable analogy she'd used on TikTok. "For the first person to enter the room, the odds are, like you said, fifty-fifty. But for every one of the one hundred prisoners to find their number? Opening only half the boxes? The formula is one in two to the exponent one hundred."

One of Vaughn's eyebrows lifted. He felt impossibly stupid at this moment.

"It's . . . not fifty-fifty?"

Darnell *sounded* impossibly stupid at this moment.

"No. It's more like less than one in a decillion."

What the fuck is a decillion?

Vaughn had just recalled *decuple*, as in decuple homicide. He wasn't in the mood to learn another number, and decillion sounded somehow even more ominous than decuple.

"A *what*?" Darnell asked.

If Darnell Sacker had a superpower, it was this: the ability to not give a shit how he looked in front of others. He just wanted to understand, to find the bad guy. He would ask question after question until he exhausted a suspect.

He wouldn't break down, wouldn't crack.

Never.

Vaughn had seen Darnell run a sixteen-hour interrogation by himself without so much as a break for a drink of water. Went against every rule the PPD had, but their suspect had eventually confessed.

"It's effectively zero," Ivy said. "The probability of all one hundred prisoners finding their number is zero."

"Well, I take back my previous answer. I'll take my chances behind bars."

Darnell's secondary power was humor. And his damn hunches—Vaughn couldn't forget those, either.

"But there weren't one hundred boxes or one hundred prisoners. There were only ten," Vaughn said, trying to get them back on track. "And they weren't prisoners."

Until they were.

The digital locks on the doors in the barn flashed in his mind.

"The odds improve with fewer participants." Vaughn noted that Ivy wasn't viewing them as victims anymore. Ivy had turned this into a true math problem, her way of dissociating herself from the image she'd seen on his phone. "But the probability of success is still only 0.1 percent with ten prisoners."

"What's with the—"

Vaughn wanted to say prime numbers, but Ivy wasn't done yet.

"But that's only if each contestant opens random boxes. If all of the prisoners utilized a permutation approach, they can vastly improve their odds of success."

"Permutation approach?" Darnell asked.

"Yeah, it's simple, really. Say you're prisoner number three. The first box you should open is the third one. Find your number by sheer chance? Great. You're done. If you don't—instead, you find number seven inside, for instance—then you go to the seventh box. Open that box. Repeat." Ivy drew a small circle in the air with her finger. "You form these permutations or loops. Using this strategy can vastly improve your odds. In the ten prisoner scenario, the odds of being successful goes from 0.1 percent to about 36 percent."

"36 percent?" Darnell was legitimately surprised, but him pretending to understand was a farce.

Ivy nodded.

"Yep. About a third of the time, you can beat the game."

Darnell whistled, laying it on thick.

"But the numbers aren't one to ten," Vaughn remarked. "They're prime numbers."

"Doesn't matter what the numbers are. Could be random, could be prime—as long as they're all the same, you can create loops. I'm guessing that's why the numbers were on the outside of the box, so that the contestants could follow the permutation approach."

Vaughn thought about Aaron Treadman lying on the gurney at the morgue, Dr. Button hovering over him.

Aaron Treadman had a high school education. He'd been a security guard at Princeton, but was unemployed at the time of his death.

Vaughn put the odds of Aaron knowing the "permutation approach" for solving the 100 prisoners problem at pretty close to zero.

One in a . . . *decillion*, maybe.

Hey, maybe he wasn't beyond learning new things.

Darnell shrugged.

"I don't . . . really get it, but okay."

Ivy blushed.

"Sorry, I nerd out sometimes. Math—"

"No, it's okay," Vaughn cut in. "But why prime numbers? Why not just use one to ten? Would make things easier, wouldn't it? Like to organize the game?"

Now Ivy shrugged.

"I have no idea. But, yeah, it would make things much easier from a design perspective."

"Hmm." Vaughn took all this in, realized that both Darnell and Ivy were waiting for him to say something. "Well, Ivy, thank you for your help. Again, I'm sorry about the photo."

"No problem."

With a curt nod, Darnell and Vaughn left the professor's office.

"You understand any of that?" Darnell said out of the corner of his mouth as they walked the hall.

"Not a fucking word."

CHAPTER 29

Ivy was still reeling from the photo.

She was also mortified that the cute cop had seen her video.

And the 100 prisoners problem? What the hell was that all about?

Her mind went there, thought about permutations. Looping, odds. This was her happy place. Math had always been her refuge, where she felt comfortable. Math was specific, math was undeniable, math was truth.

People, on the other hand, were unpredictable. Even people like her father.

Ivy's first introduction to math, even before fractals, had been through chess. On her third birthday, Ivy's mother had bought her a checkers board. At this point in her young life, she'd rarely seen her parents fight. That didn't happen until later, when her father was spending every waking hour on his work.

But they'd fought then.

Gene had been angry, saying that checkers was linear tic-tac-toe. Said it was for simpletons. He'd taken the board from Ivy, thrown it out. Ivy had cried.

Later that day, Gene had returned with a chess board. Said that chess was a real game, a smart game, a thinking person's game.

"There are more possible chess games than there are atoms in the universe, Ivy."

That was her father—that was Eugene Reeves. And that was Ivy.

Over the years, they'd played hundreds of games, with Eugene always coming out on top—he never let her win.

Wetness suddenly leaked into the corner of Ivy's mouth, and she absently licked at it. She hadn't even realized that she'd been crying.

Her phone buzzed, and she glanced at the call display. Sniffed, wiped more tears before answering.

"Hey, Abs."

"If it isn't the Bae-sian Prof!"

Ivy choked.

"What? You saw that?"

"How could I not? You're famous, bitch!"

"What the hell, Abs! I want it taken down!"

"Why? It's blowing up! You need to monetize that shit. 'Member the Hawk Tuah girl? She made hats and shirts . . . hell she even had a meme coin. Made millions."

Ivy closed her eyes and rubbed her temples.

"I just want it gone."

"I didn't think you had it in you," Abby continued, either not hearing Ivy or not caring. "The Bae-sian Prof." She laughed. "Although, after last night, I guess you've changed your prudish ways. What was that, anyway? I know you cheated at that coin flipping game."

Eyes still closed, Ivy said, "It's called Penney's game, and it isn't cheating. You just—"

"Yeah, yeah, yeah. Anyway, it was fun, wasn't it? That Blake guy . . . he was hot."

No, it wasn't fun. It was a disaster. I'm still hung over, and if I hadn't been, I would have never made the stupid STI example in stats class.

"Abs, I just want it taken down," she said for the hundredth time. "Can you report it—*please*?"

"Report it? You need to start a TikTok account and repost it. Get some of that influencer *guap*."

"Abs? Please?"

Abby groaned.

"You're no fun. But if you really want me to report it, I will." Ivy waited. "Okay, done. But I doubt it will do much. Unless—"

"Can you hack it?"

"Hack it?"

"Yeah, hack it to get it taken down."

"Ivy, TikTok isn't like Princeton's—"

"Fine, whatever."

Silence.

"What are you doing tonight? Wanna go out again?" Abby asked.

"No chance."

Abby chuckled.

"Yeah, probably for the best. My head is pounding. This morning, I had this client come in for Botox, just their forehead and crow's feet, and I almost injected her with lip filler."

Another laugh.

"I gotta go, Abs. Talk soon."

"Be good, Bae-sian Bitch."

Ivy hung up before she had to hear Abby's high-pitched titter again. Abby would laugh, though. Would probably be laughing all day.

Ivy, on the other hand, had work to do. She opened her computer, loaded a spreadsheet. Dr. Moorehead wanted her to upload an abstract for the ACM conference. That was impossible. She was so far behind. Dr. Moorehead also wanted her to continue her father's work. That, too, was impossible.

Ivy spent ten minutes just scrolling through data before giving up. It wasn't happening. Every time she blinked, she saw the dead body.

The numbers.

Yeah, Abby Granger definitely led the simpler life.

CHAPTER 30

"Wow, were you smitten or what?"

Vaughn started the car.

"What are you talking about?"

"You were fucking googly-eyed!"

"I was not."

Darnell placed a hand on his heart.

"I'm so sorry, I shouldn't have shown you the picture. Oh, Dr. Reeves, milady, please accept my apology."

His impression of Vaughn was terrible.

"Whatever. Let's just focus."

"Focus on what? I didn't understand anything the Bae-sian Prof said, either. Fucking math riddles."

"We've narrowed our suspect pool a little. Whoever sent that email knows math."

Darnell rolled his eyes.

"Great, so we're looking for a psycho math genius."

Beneath his partner's joking words were undertones of disbelief.

Vaughn understood.

The media often portrayed serial killers as these super

intelligent individuals—and the public ate that shit up, for reasons Vaughn didn't understand.

It simply wasn't true. Some were of average intelligence. Some were below. Occasionally above.

The only true fact that could be said about all serial killers Vaughn had ever come across or studied was that they were narcissists.

Each and every one of them.

Vaughn's dash radio came to life—it was Delaney.

Darnell grunted disapprovingly.

"Hey, Delaney, what's up?"

"I found Aaron's car. Two of the others', too."

The man sounded tired.

"Where?"

"Pizza place in Fredon Township. 'Bout a mile and a half from the barn."

"On our way."

PPD Officer Frank Delaney was standing with his hands on his hips when Vaughn and Darnell arrived.

The pizza joint, CiCi's Pizza, was located off Route 94 South. Large lot, old building. Red roof, wheelchair ramp out front.

Delaney looked spent. His hair, which Darnell had remarked on numerous occasions that the man fashioned to look exactly like Vaughn's, was a mess.

If the cop hadn't been so tired, Vaughn might have guessed that this was another deliberate, accurate attempt at copying him.

"You okay?"

Delaney nodded.

"Yeah. Just . . . you know how it is. Telling someone that their husband is dead is the fucking worst."

Oh, Vaughn knew, alright. And it was the one job that he was glad Darnell had passed off to Delaney.

"What happened?"

Delaney shrugged, let out a long breath.

"Just what she said on the phone. Basically, her husband went out for some game show thing and never came home. It was him—victim number three. Showed a photo and she confirmed it. Then she just . . . broke."

Delaney had a far-off look in his eyes, and Vaughn gave him a moment.

Darnell did not.

"What did she know about the game?"

"Nothing. I mean, she was completely destroyed. Said something about not having any money, about how they'd been forced to cancel Harrison's life insurance policy just a few weeks back. That's name, by the way. Harrison. This was supposed to be their chance, you know? And they had this kid . . . a fucking baby. Just kept wailing."

The man shuddered.

"She didn't know anything about the game?"

"No."

"You said she mentioned the game when she reported her missing husband on the 911 call."

"Yeah, I heard the call; that's what she said."

"Did you even ask her about it?"

"Darnell . . ." Vaughn warned.

"Of course I asked her," Delaney shot back. "She said she

didn't know. Only that Harrison said he was going to a game show, said that it was a secret and he couldn't say more."

"You sure you asked her?"

"Jesus fucking Christ, man! I asked her! She *didn't* know."

Darnell grimaced.

"The fuck were you guys doing? I've been running around all over the place trying to—"

"Hey, we're the detectives here. Not you. You do as we fucking say, alright? Got a problem with that, talk to the captain."

Darnell stepped forward aggressively and Vaughn slid between them.

"Calm down—just calm the fuck down, both of you."

And leave the captain out of this.

The fact that the grumpy old man hadn't butted in already was a miracle. Vaughn wanted to keep it this way for as long as possible.

Delaney backed off while Darnell remained rooted in place.

"Darnell, do me a solid?" Vaughn said.

"What?"

Darnell didn't take his eyes off Delaney.

"Head into CiCi's and ask the owner if they recognize Aaron or any of the other victims?"

I'm too old to be a babysitter. And he's *supposed to be the senior detective.*

When Darnell didn't move, Vaughn prodded again.

"Darnell?"

The man finally stopped glaring at Delaney.

"Yeah, whatever."

He stomped off.

"Sorry about that. Show me Aaron's car."

CHAPTER 31

"HE'S HOLDING YOU back, you know."

Delaney indicated a maroon Chevy parked in the back of the lot beside two other vehicles.

"What do you mean?"

"Darnell—everyone knows he's a fucking drunk. Captain likes to keep you partnered up because you keep him in check. Captain also knows he can't cut him after what happened. You'd be sergeant by now if you requested a new partner. Nobody would blame you, either. You've done your time."

"Let me worry about Darnell. Just stay out of his way."

"I'm trying. I try my best to just keep clear of that trainwreck."

He wasn't. Delaney had a way of just showing up at crime scenes that Vaughn and Darnell were working. PPD had fifty officers, but only six detectives. Delaney appeared at nearly every single case that Vaughn took on. He'd once asked a couple of the other detectives if Delaney showed up at their scenes, too—there was no question the man was dedicated and had detective aspirations—but they'd told him no.

Darnell had laughed when Vaughn had mentioned this, called Delaney a dick rider.

Well, dick rider or not, he was a hard worker. And that's what they needed right now. Someone to actually do something.

"You sure this is his car?"

"Yeah. Pulled Aaron's tag number from the DMV. It's his car."

Delaney had parked his PPD squad car right beside the Chevy and the two other civilian vehicles.

"You have a shim in your trunk?"

"Yep."

Vaughn peered through the Chevy's windows while Delaney went to go get it. Like the man's apartment, Aaron kept his car clean and neat.

He stepped aside to allow Delaney access to the window. The man slid the flat metal shim between the window and the frame, jiggled it a little, and then pushed. The door lock disengaged.

Vaughn was impressed. He hated the damn thing—always took him six or seven tries to get it to work. This was also the reason why he kept a crowbar in the trunk. The brute force method had always been Vaughn's favorite.

He let Delaney search the vehicle. The cop opened the center console first and hit gold: Aaron's cell phone.

This, Vaughn took. It was an older model iPhone. There was still some battery juice, and when he pressed the side button, the screen lit up.

New Jersey Devils logo as the background.

Unfortunately, unlike the laptop, the man's phone was

password protected. It was only four digits, and Vaughn tried a few basic combinations. When none of these worked, he gave up and slipped the phone into an evidence bag, and then put it in the pocket of his sport coat.

"Found the registration," Delaney said, removing a leather folder from the glove box. "Just like I said—"

"Way to crack the code, genius."

Darnell had returned. The time away from Delaney had done nothing to quell his anger, but the officer managed to bite his tongue.

"What about these other two cars?" A black Hyundai sedan and an old Ford Taurus. "You run their plates?"

"Didn't get a chance," Delaney said as he exited Aaron's car.

"What do you mean you didn't get a chance? You were standing with your dick in your hand when we got here!"

"Darnell!" Not a warning now, but a sharp retort from Vaughn.

Darnell scowled and shook his head dramatically. Rolled his eyes.

"Owner said he recognized Aaron. Said he came in with two other guys, grabbed a couple of slices, then walked off. Left their cars." Darnell pointed at the Hyundai and the Ford. "*Those* cars. Showed them photos of the other victims, but he couldn't be sure if it was any of them."

"I'll pop these cars open, as well. See if we can ID more victims."

"While you're at it, search other places around here. Talk to the owners. If any cars have been there since last night, pop 'em."

Delaney looked at Vaughn.

C'mon, the look said. *Give me a break. I'm running on fumes here.*

Vaughn might admonish his partner, try his best to keep him under wraps, but he wouldn't directly go against his superior's orders.

"Let us know if you find anything." Then, to Darnell, "Found Aaron's cell phone. Let's get it back to the precinct."

The PPD didn't have an official tech department—it wasn't big enough, neither in size nor in budget. What detectives and cops alike who worked in Princeton called the tech department was actually just two young cops, Bowes and Caine, who, despite constantly denying it, had to have been hackers in past lives. If Bowes and Caine couldn't get into something, then it was rare that anyone could.

In the past, when Bowes and Caine were unable to gain access to an electronic device, Vaughn had sent evidence to the New Jersey State Police Digital Technology Investigations Unit.

They too had been unsuccessful.

It was Bowes who Vaughn found in the hacker duo's shared office today. He was a lot like Dr. McGill at the Princeton CBE, only twenty years younger and forty pounds heavier.

Same hair and glasses, same energy drink addiction.

Thoughts of Dr. McGill reminded Vaughn to follow up with the other employees who had access to the tanks. He was convinced that the person who had taken the hydrogen sulfide had used Aaron Treadman's card. It could have been Aaron himself—unlikely, considering the possibility of being recognized—or he had either sold his card, or it had been stolen.

And whoever possessed the card had to be their unsub.

"Have something for you," Vaughn said, producing Aaron's cell phone still in the evidence bag.

Bowes took it, turned it over, inspected the back.

"iPhone 13 Pro. Midnight. 512Gb."

"Need to see if you can get in. Has a four digit password."

Bowes set the phone down.

"I can get in, but it has that annoying cool down thing. It'll take some time."

"How much time?"

"I mean . . ." Bowes pressed the side button and the phone illuminated. "Could be a couple of days. I'll start with some Devils players' numbers. Looks like he's a fan."

"What if we need it sooner?"

Bowes eyed Vaughn.

"What exactly do you need off of it?"

Vaughn considered the question. They didn't need location data—Aaron had left it behind before heading to the barn. Unlikely that he met up with their unsub beforehand.

"Texts and call logs," he decided.

Bowes did a little finger gun salute.

"That's easier. I can use Cellebrite and pull texts and calls in less than a day."

"Awesome. Thanks—appreciate it. Did you manage to work on that computer we dropped off earlier?"

Even from behind the thick lenses of his glasses, Vaughn could see that Bowes's eyes were bloodshot. His blood was ninety percent caffeine. No thin coffee for him.

"Yeah." Bowes grabbed a Ghost energy drink and sipped. Sucked his cheeks in. Vaughn had tried one of the man's drinks once. It had been so sour that all the muscles in his neck had contracted. "Good news and bad news."

"Bad first."

"Right—just like the router and remote gas release valve, I couldn't trace the email. No way. Just a dead end. The cell number, too."

"Well, shit . . . what's the *good* news?" Vaughn said.

Bowes finished his drink. "Looks like the computer itself was wiped about six months ago. Found an old user in the system metadata. Before Aaron Treadman, this computer was owned by an Ivy Reeves."

CHAPTER 32

"Guess you didn't think you'd see your girlfriend again so soon, huh?"

They were walking down the hallway of Fine Hall again, just a few hours after they'd left.

"How do you manage your time with both a boyfriend *and* a girlfriend? You ever get them mixed up?"

Darnell was talking about Delaney, of course.

"You gotta lay off the guy."

"To hell I will. Delaney—"

They turned a corner, and Ivy Reeves nearly ran right into them.

"Sorry," she said. Then she recognized who they were.

"Detectives Ryan and—"

"Sacker, yeah."

"Vaughn and Darnell, right?"

Vaughn smiled. "That's right."

"What can I do for you guys?"

"You wouldn't happen to have had a laptop stolen from you a while back?" Sometimes Darnell liked to get right to it. No playing the dumb guy this time.

Ivy frowned.

"Yeah," she said hesitantly. "About six months ago. I was working in the Lewis Annex and went to use the bathroom. Came back and it was gone. Had everything on the cloud though, so I didn't lose my data. Did you find it?"

Darnell acted as if he hadn't heard her question.

"Did you report it stolen?"

"Yes. There was this security guard wandering around at the time. Only other person in the library after hours—my card still works when it's closed. I told all this to campus security."

"The guard, do you know his name?"

Ivy thought about this.

"Adam . . . I think? They never found the laptop, but I heard they fired the guy. Never saw him again, anyway. Never left my computer on a desk unattended, either."

"Dr. Reeves—"

"Please, just Ivy."

"I'm going to stick with Dr. Reeves," Darnell said, and Vaughn frowned. "Dr. Reeves, we found your laptop. It was indeed in the possession of the security guard—whose name is Aaron, by the way, not Adam."

"No shit. Can I have it back? I already have another one, but—"

"It's part of an active investigation. When we're done, we'll have someone in the PPD return it to you."

"An active investigation? Into what? The theft?"

Ivy was confused, as was Vaughn.

Why the hell is Darnell treating her like a suspect again?

"No." Darnell adjusted his belt. Hiked up his pants.

"Dr. Reeves, do you think you'd recognize Aaron the security guard if you saw him again?"

Ivy scratched her chin.

"It was six months ago . . . but probably."

"Huh."

Vaughn took over. Darnell's direct approach had twisted into a charade.

And he didn't care for it.

"Ivy, that photo I showed you earlier, the guy with the thirteen on his chest? That was Aaron the security guard."

As he spoke, Vaughn scanned Ivy's face. Searched for any signs of deception. Shifty eyes. Toes pointed away from them. Animated hand gestures. Suspect or not, it was difficult to turn off detective mode. He saw none.

"Are you kidding?"

"No, we're not," Darnell said. "Did you recognize him?"

"No. I don't get it. The security guard . . . he stole my laptop? The *dead* guy in the picture you showed me?"

Again, Darnell ignored the woman's questions.

"You just said you'd recognize him if you saw him again."

"I said I'd *probably* recognize him," Ivy corrected. Her cheeks had started to turn scarlet. "I guess I didn't. He was . . . his eyes and—"

"It's okay." Vaughn tried to calm Ivy's growing agitation. "Here, take my card. If you don't hear from someone in the PPD in the next few days, give me a call. I'll see if I can get your laptop back to you."

"Thanks."

They left with Ivy even more confused than the last time they'd visited.

"Seriously?" Darnell altered his voice. "Take my card, I'll get your laptop back to you."

"You were treating her like a suspect."

"Isn't she?"

"How so?"

Darnell ticked items off his fingers as he spoke.

"The gas is taken from her university. Her laptop is stolen by the same guy whose card was probably used to steal said gas. Security guard then ends up dead. She pretends she doesn't recognize him. And that math shit? She definitely knows that math shit."

"I don't think she 'pretended' not to know him. She was shaken by that photo."

"Good actress."

Vaughn clenched his jaw. He didn't like the path they were headed down, but he knew that if he didn't at least entertain his partner, he'd never hear the end of it.

"Fine, I'll bite. What's her motive?"

"No clue. But we don't need a motive."

They didn't. It was a common misconception that a motive was necessary for a conviction. It helped the DA form a narrative that the jury could follow, but killers didn't always need a rhyme or reason. Vaughn had learned early in his career that applying rational logic to irrational actions was pointless.

"Look, Vaughn, I know how you feel about my hunches, but I got a big one right now. Dr. Reeves is holding something back." Vaughn fought back a sigh, but it slipped out of the corner of his mouth. "Remember Armand Reese? The Princeton Pervert?"

"Yeah." It wasn't something you forgot.

Vaughn expected Darnell to continue, but he didn't. Clearly, the man thought he'd said enough. Vaughn was tempted to repeat something that Darnell liked to say—*even a blind squirrel finds a nut every once in a while*—but held back.

"Anyway, you wanna go for dinner?" Darnell asked.

Vaughn checked his watch.

"Sure, why not. Maybe we should invite Delaney."

"Fuck off."

CHAPTER 33

Despite accepting the invitation, Vaughn didn't really feel like going to dinner with his partner. Not after Darnell had been an asshole pretty much all day. But the more time they spent together, the less time his partner had to get shitfaced.

And Darnell behaved during the meal, a middle of the road steak and burger joint. Two beers each.

That being said, Darnell was typically good company. Liked to crack jokes, primarily at Delaney's expense. Mostly good-natured ribbing.

Puppy dog, dick rider, simp. Beta.

Not today.

Today, Darnell read the room—Vaughn wouldn't put up with any more of that shit.

Twice, Vaughn considered bringing up AA again. Psychotherapy.

Darnell had passed his evals following his reinstatement, but there was clearly something wrong with him. And it was getting worse.

The insults were one thing, but seeing Darnell this

morning in bed, half-naked, sweaty, with his gun lying beside him, holding hands with a bottle of Jack?

That was something else.

After—he said after this case.

Vaughn would hold Darnell to his word.

Dinner was bland, both steaks slightly overcooked. The beer was good, though.

When he dropped Darnell off, Vaughn told the man to be ready at eight the next morning. A surrogate for *don't drink too much.*

Darnell promised he'd be up.

Vaughn popped open another beer when he got home and sat in front of the TV. He was a hockey guy, but the Devils game was already over. They lost 3-2 to the Senators. There was another game on, a Western Conference matchup, but Vaughn wasn't interested.

Wasn't really tired, either.

He decided to call Bowes. It was late, but there was no way someone could sleep after consuming upwards of a gram of caffeine throughout the day.

Bowes answered on the first ring.

"Yello?"

"Bowes? You still up?"

"Yep—still at the station."

"Really?"

"Yeah—just finishing up. Pulled that data you wanted off the phone. Was gonna wait until morning but . . . I'm guessing that's why you called?"

"Yes. Sorry for calling so late."

"No prob. Like I said, I'm still at the station."

"What've you got?"

"Still going through the texts. Looks like our man Aaron was trying to score some testosterone from some guy named Ronnie. Anyway, he did make a call to that number in the ad. Two of them. First time around, nobody picked up. The second call lasted two minutes and forty-three seconds."

"When was that?"

"Three nights ago. Then last night, two texts came in from the same number. Both at 10:45 p.m. Here, let me read the first to you: *Welcome, contestant. Congratulations on being accepted to participate in our new puzzle game show. This event will be a team event. If all members complete the puzzle, each will be awarded 1 Bitcoin. Please read the following instructions carefully. Failure to comply with any of the rules will result in immediate disqualification.*

"That was the first text. The second: *Drive to CiCi's Pizza in Fredon Township. Park there or anywhere else in the vicinity. DO NOT drive to the game address (to follow). Do not mention the address to anyone. Do not speak to anyone about the game show. NO CELL PHONES ALLOWED. NO IDENTIFICATION ALLOWED. Leave your wallets at home or in your car. You must arrive before midnight. Remember, failure to comply will result in IMMEDIATE DISQUALIFICATION. Good luck!*"

Bowes read off the address, which was the barn where they'd found the bodies, as Vaughn mulled this information over.

The ME, Dr. Button, said that Aaron and the other victims died around 1:30 in the morning, plus or minus half an hour. The texts had come in at 10:45 p.m., and Aaron had to drive from his home in Trenton to CiCi's in Fredon Township. At that hour, there would be no traffic—takes about ten minutes. He grabs a slice. Maybe speaks to the other contestants for a little while. Probably nervous—the NO IDENTIFICATION ALLOWED was an odd request. But he's not alone now. Aaron and the other men are also excited, bragging about what they're going to do with the nearly eighty grand they're about to win. Then they walk from CiCi's to the barn. How far did Delaney say that was? A mile and a half? That takes, what? Thirty minutes?

11:30ish arrival.

Then the rules of the 100 prisoners problem are explained over the speaker.

If Ivy was right about the set-up, then Aaron was the victim who failed, who didn't find his number. If the rooms were assigned from left to right, which made the most sense, then that meant seven people had already found their numbers in the boxes.

Vaughn wondered what the odds of that were. Maybe not one in a decillion, but pretty damn low.

He sipped his beer.

Everything in the barn was automated, from the door locks to the gas release valve.

"Detective Ryan? You still there?"

"Yeah, sorry. Been a long one."

"Don't I know it. So, the phone that made the 911 call to report the location of the gassing is the same phone—same IMEI number—as the one that sent the texts and received the initial calls from Aaron Treadman."

Their assumptions had been correct. The anonymous call had been made by their unsub.

"Any way to tell who else called that phone? Received texts from it?"

"Not without the actual device."

Vaughn had thought as much, but figured it pertinent to ask. That phone was probably at the bottom of the Delaware River by now.

"You tracking it?"

"Yep—if it's used again, I'll get an immediate notification."

Unlikely.

"Great. You manage to get any location data from when the texts were sent or when it answered the call from Aaron?"

Vaughn's phone beeped and he pulled it away from his ear. It was Delaney calling.

"Yes to the call from Aaron's phone. It pinged the same towers as the 911 call."

That was three days prior to the gassing. Their unsub was probably out at the barn putting up drywall.

Did he know the area well? Is that why he chose that location? Or was it just easy because it was abandoned and secluded?

Vaughn had driven around the location, although he wasn't sure what he'd been looking for.

Building supplies?

It was farmland. Every farmer worth his salt had equipment to do home or barn repairs.

"The texts didn't ping a tower," Bowes continued. "Probably sent through WiFi. Haven't been able to trace them and doubt I ever will; same circle jerk runaround VPNs like the speaker and door locks."

Another beep.

Delaney was still trying to reach him.

"I'm getting another call. Thanks, Bowes. Let me know if that phone is used again." Vaughn clicked over. "Delaney? What's—"

"Detective Ryan, we got another call! I was looking for the victims' cars at gas stations when dispatch reached out. I passed someone on the road, but had to get to the site—"

Delaney was excited, out of breath. Vaughn was having a hard time following.

"What the hell are you talking about?"

"Another 911 call! Same as the last! Gas leak. One dead."

Vaughn was on his feet in an instant. He grabbed his gun belt and coat and flew out the front door.

"Where, Delaney? *Where*?"

CHAPTER 34

Ivy put her phone on silent and crawled into bed, not expecting sleep to come—every time she closed her eyes, she saw Aaron the security guard's dead face—but the man's blank expression was the last thing she remembered before conking out.

She woke before dawn.

Her phone.

Beep, beep. Beep. The only number that would come through no matter what.

She answered groggily, then dressed. Rushed out of her house.

Ivy found Sarah Kachinski waiting outside Delta Assisted Living—DAL, for short—less than fifteen minutes after she'd called.

The matronly, overweight woman was wearing some sort of blue smock that made her look like a giant blueberry. Her face was pinched.

"Ivy, I don't know where he went. I checked the field, the Queen . . . whatever field, but I couldn't find him. Sorry for calling you so late, but I'm worried."

Sarah cared.

Maybe a bit too much. It would have been easier for Ivy to deal with someone more militant and straightforward.

When was he last seen? What time? How was his general demeanor?

The rapid-fire questions that flashed in her mind reminded her of Detective Sacker and his partner.

It was difficult to focus working on such little actual, restorative sleep.

"No—thank you, I appreciate it." Ivy's eyes drifted in the direction of the Queen Anne's lace to the northwest. The DAL building was mostly dark, but the bright lights over the front entrance made everything else pitch-black by comparison.

She couldn't even make out the flowers.

"I've managed to keep this quiet, but if management . . ."

"I know, I know. When's the last time you saw him?"

"He was in his room for lights out, but I went to check on him at around midnight because of what happened yesterday, and he wasn't there."

Sarah's voice dripped with desperation.

"Do you have a flashlight?" Ivy silently cursed herself for not bringing her own.

The nurse offered her a tired smile. Produced two thick black Maglites from an unseen pocket and handed one to her.

"I'm going to go look for him. Sarah, if I can't find him in half an hour, I want you to go to management. Tell them he's missing. Alert the troops or whatever—full-scale search."

Now she was thinking like a cop, and sounding like one, too.

Sarah's round face tensed as much as the thick layers of

fat would allow. Ivy knew what was coming even before the woman opened her mouth.

"Management..." Sarah let out a heavy sigh. "Management's upset. Frustrated. I think it's an insurance thing, you know? The place is already over capacity. Money is tight. I heard them grumbling about enforcing the rules."

Ivy had heard all this before. Disregarded it again.

"I just want to get him back safe."

Sarah nodded.

"Okay, but I'm coming with you."

Ivy wasn't going to let the big woman slow her down, but two sets of eyes were better than one.

"If management asks why you didn't inform them earlier, tell them I told you not to. Got it?"

"'Kay."

Ivy switched on the Maglite.

Goddamn, it was bright.

Sarah shielded her eyes, and Ivy swung the beam away from the woman and the building.

"Let's go."

Ivy bounded off toward the field. Sarah might have said she searched the area, but Ivy wanted to see for herself.

Everything in the flashlight's direct path glowed an artificial, ghostly white, while everything else remained black.

Ivy found herself in a sea of flowers.

"Dad?" she said loudly, falling just short of shouting. "Dad? You in here?"

She found the path from yesterday, half-jogged until she reached the end. The area was still depressed from where she'd found the man sitting, twirling the flower between his mangled fingers.

He wasn't there now.

"Dad?" A little louder this time. "*Dad?*"

Ivy continued to scan the surrounding area, gradually raising the flashlight beam. Only saw those damn fractal flowers.

"Dad!"

"Ivy?"

Sarah Kachinski, being a much bigger and slower woman, was only arriving now. Her thick chest was heaving.

"What?"

"There's something . . ." Sarah sucked in a deep breath, placed her hands on her thighs. "There's something going on over there."

Sarah pulled one hand off her leg, pointed.

Ivy saw it immediately: blue and red flashing lights in the distance.

"No," she moaned and broke into a run.

Sprinting. Flashlight beam bouncing up and down.

The police lights were about a quarter mile away, reflecting off some sort of structure. A small barn, maybe, judging by the peaked roof.

Not one car, but two—two cop cars.

Please . . . please . . . please . . .

She was a quarter of the way there. Half.

Breathing hard. Legs and arms pumping. Flashlight swinging.

Ivy almost lost her footing in a boulder-sized divot.

Grunted.

Winced.

Was forced to slow.

The beam of light steadied, and that's when she saw him.

A man, standing unmoving in the middle of an open field, his back to her, seemingly transfixed by the police cherries.

Ivy skidded to a halt.

"Dad?"

CHAPTER 35

Fucking Darnell.

Vaughn called his partner three times as he sped across the city toward the address that Delaney had given him, the address he'd passed along from the 911 call.

Gas leak. One dead.

No answer.

Vaughn saw the flashing lights. Pressed the gas a little harder.

He screeched to a stop within just inches of one of two PPD squad cars.

A uniform was standing near the doors of a barn, green this time, and smaller than the last. He was wearing a gas mask.

"Delaney?" Vaughn asked as he jumped out of his car.

It wasn't Delaney. This cop was about six inches shorter.

"Where's Delaney?"

The cop pointed to the east.

"He went that way on foot." The mask muffled the man's voice, making it difficult to understand.

Vaughn looked toward the barn.

"How many inside?"

"Just one. DOA."

"Stay here."

Vaughn broke into a jog, pulling out his flashlight as he went.

He didn't have to go far. Three minutes later, he saw Delaney, easily recognizable by his uniform. Two others stood in front of the cop. With their flashlights aimed at the ground, all Vaughn could tell was that one of them was tall, the other short.

Vaughn unclipped the strap on his gun holster. Didn't draw. Continued forward, but at a slower pace now.

"I said put your hands in the air!" Delaney shouted.

"He doesn't understand!" A woman's voice.

Familiar, but Vaughn couldn't place it. The blood roaring in his ears warped the sound.

A fourth person arrived. Squat, round. Clearly struggling to breathe.

Unlike Vaughn, Delaney had his weapon out. He aimed it at this new person.

"Hands up! *Hands up!*"

The fat woman screeched and did as Delaney asked, cowering at the same time.

"All of you, *hands up!*"

"He doesn't understand what you're saying!" the first woman countered. "Please, he doesn't understand!"

"I don't give a fuck!" Delaney roared. "If you don't—"

Vaughn announced his presence.

"Delaney! Detective Ryan!"

Delaney turned, leading with his gun. For a split second, Vaughn thought the cop was going to shoot him.

"Jesus Christ! Put your gun down, Delaney! It's Detective Ryan!"

Delaney held Vaughn in his crosshairs.

Vaughn made himself small.

"Vaughn?"

"Yes! God damn it, stop pointing your gun at me!"

Delaney finally listened, turning back to the trio of people standing in the open field.

Both the newcomer and the woman Vaughn had heard speaking earlier had their hands high in the air.

The tall man did not.

"I saw this guy running from the scene," Delaney said over his shoulder.

"He wasn't running! He was lost!"

Vaughn made his way next to Delaney and raised his flashlight. The woman turned her eyes away, brought one of her hands in front of her face.

"Keep your hands up!" Delaney ordered.

"Ivy?"

It was Ivy—Ivy Reeves.

What the fuck?

"Delaney, holster your weapon."

"But—"

"Do it now!"

Delaney begrudgingly jammed his gun into his belt.

"I saw—"

"I've got this."

"What?"

"I said *I've got this*. Back away."

"But—"

"Back off, Delaney. Don't make me say it again." Vaughn glared at the cop.

"Okay, okay, shit. I'm backing off."

Delaney put his own hands up now, not quite as high as the others, and took three large steps backward.

"Good. Stay calm." To Ivy, "What the hell is going on?"

He lowered his flashlight, and she squinted one eye.

"Detective Ryan?"

"Yes. What are you doing here?"

"My—my dad. Shit." Ivy was having a hard time catching her breath, but Vaughn suspected that this was for a different reason than the woman in what he now saw was a blue muumuu.

"It's okay, take your time."

As she collected herself, Vaughn observed the other two. One was a fat woman in her forties, the other a man in his sixties. Tall, thin. There was something on his face and head. A skin-colored mask of some sort.

It looked . . . well, frightening.

"My father, he's sick. He doesn't understand." Such pain in Ivy's voice. "He wanders off. This is Sarah. She's his nurse at the home."

Ivy took a deep, shuddering breath.

"I'm Dr. Reeves's resident care aide," the big woman squeaked.

Vaughn recalled what Ivy had said when they'd first approached her in her office back at Princeton.

"Is it my dad? Please tell me my dad's okay."

"Where's the home?"

"Back there." Ivy pointed in the opposite direction that Vaughn had come from.

Vaughn felt a headache begin to form behind his eyes.

"Is he okay?" He indicated Ivy's father.

Ivy moved to her dad, gently placed a hand on his back.

"Dad? You going to be okay?"

No response. Not even a blink.

"I think he's fine," Ivy said. "Sarah?"

The nurse or resident care aide, or whatever the hell she was called, twisted her hands.

"Can I—"

"Yes, put your arms down."

"Thank you."

She moved slowly, never taking her gaze off Delaney, who was still standing behind Vaughn. Reached for the man's wrist, pressed two fingers against the thin skin just below his palm. Her lips moved slightly as she counted.

"Pulse is good," she told Ivy. Then she rambled, "I'm sorry about this, Officer. Really sorry. Dr. Reeves gets confused and wanders off sometimes. Especially around this time of year. Around the time of the accident."

"He was running—"

"Quiet, Delaney!" Vaughn hissed. "What's your name?" he asked the woman.

"Sarah."

"Sarah, I want you to take him back to the home, okay?"

A nod sent a ripple cascading through the woman's multiple chins.

Expecting a protest from Delaney, Vaughn held a finger up and out to his side as a warning.

"Thank you."

"It's okay, Dad," Ivy whispered. Then she turned to Sarah. "I thought you didn't tell management?" Accusing.

"I didn't! I didn't!" the woman protested.

Vaughn clued into what was going on.

"Ivy, the cops aren't here because of your father."

Ivy's eyes shot in his direction.

"They're not?"

"No. They're here because there's been another gassing."

CHAPTER 36

"GASSING?" IVY WAS still reeling from a cop threatening to shoot them.

Vaughn squirmed—he clearly hadn't meant to say so much.

"Yeah. The body you saw . . ." he trailed off.

Ivy had heard enough.

Gassing, as ambiguous as the term was, explained the white paste she'd seen on Aaron Treadman's face.

She shuddered.

"And there's been another one? *Here*?"

"Yes. I just got the call. That's why I came."

"Ryan, why'd you let the other two go?" Delany demanded.

Vaughn whipped around. Glared at the cop.

"What the hell were you thinking, Delaney? Drawing on three unarmed civilians?"

"I saw a man running! How was I supposed to know—"

"It wasn't my father," Ivy interrupted, trying to restore calm. "He doesn't run. And he doesn't understand."

"I'm sorry—who the hell are you?"

Ivy noticed Vaughn tense a little, even moved in front of her.

"This is Dr. Ivy Reeves. She's helping us with the case."

Delaney looked confused.

"This case?"

"The other case," Vaughn snapped.

Now Delaney was taken aback.

"Really?"

"Really."

"Well, I didn't know." Delaney did his best to backpedal. "You didn't say anything, and I saw—"

"Someone running, yeah, I got that. Tell me what happened."

"Like I said on the phone, I was close when the 911 call came in and rushed to the address. Passed someone on the way. Officer Horowitz arrived around the same time as me. We used a crowbar to open the door and found the body. Already dead. I came back out, started searching for the person I saw. Noticed someone running." Delaney pointed at Ivy. "That's when I found your father."

When Vaughn laid eyes on her, Ivy shook her head.

"It wasn't him," Vaughn said. "Whoever you saw might still be out here. Get on the radio, set up a search. *Now.*"

During this conversation, Sarah and Ivy's father had started back toward the DAL. Ivy could just make out their silhouettes.

As Delaney said something into his radio, Vaughn moved closer to her.

"You going to be okay?"

"Yeah," she lied. Everything about this ordeal had fried

her nerves. Hell, everything about the last two days had put her on edge.

"You should probably go with them," he suggested.

Ivy considered this.

With all the yelling and police lights, it would be a miracle if others at the DAL failed to notice. If she moved quickly—difficult, but not impossible—Sarah might be able to pass off her father's absence as being related to the commotion.

The man was confused, heard shouting and saw the lights. Went out to investigate, like a moth to a lightbulb. But if Ivy showed up, that would raise questions. Questions she couldn't and wouldn't be able to answer. Not in this frazzled state, anyway.

"It's better if I don't," Ivy said in a tone that she hoped expressed her unwillingness to explain.

Vaughn got it.

"I have to process the crime scene. I can take you home afterward, but it might take a while."

"I'm parked back at the home."

Vaughn looked over her shoulder. Squinted.

"Search party ordered," Delaney said. "We'll have this entire place lit up in under an hour."

"Good. Delaney, you think you can walk Ivy back to her car? She shouldn't be alone if there's someone still out there."

Delaney seemed less than enthused about this prospect. Ivy didn't know much about PPD hierarchy, but figured that detective was above officer. Doubted someone in plainclothes—the same clothes she'd seen Vaughn in earlier in the day, minus the jacket—took orders from a man in uniform.

Made sense.

"Where's your car?" Delaney said. He sounded almost petulant.

"At the home. But wait. Is this another prisoners problem?"

"A what?" Delaney asked.

"It's the name of the game at the other crime scene," Vaughn clarified. "We think that the numbers and boxes were all part of a complex math game."

Delaney made a face. Ivy might have, too. She wouldn't have classified the 100 prisoners problem as a "math game." Still, Vaughn was trying his best.

"Oh. Well, no, this is different than the other. To be honest, I don't know what the hell was going on in there, didn't spend too long inside the barn. As soon as I confirmed the vic was DOA, I rushed back out."

"You see anything in the barn?"

"Sure. A couple of buttons—green, red—some fucking display screens. I don't know. Just checked the guy's pulse and then headed out."

"Buttons?" Vaughn queried.

"Yeah—buttons. There were two rooms, each had a red and a green button on a table."

This triggered something in Ivy.

"And the screens, did they show red and green dots?" she asked.

Delaney looked at her, eyebrows rising up his forehead.

"Yeah," he said hesitantly.

"You recognize it?" Vaughn said to Ivy.

"I might. Not sure."

Vaughn scratched his head, appeared torn.

"If she helped with the other scene, it might be worth

having her look at this one, too." Ivy got the impression this was more about Delaney keeping in the loop than believing that she could help. "It smelled like eggs. Vic looked the same, too. Eyes cloudy, foam—"

"Got it," Vaughn said quickly, clearly to protect her. "I don't know if that's a good idea."

"It's fine. If I can help . . ."

"Seeing a photo is different than seeing the real thing." Vaughn chewed his lower lip. "But you might be right. Delaney, you have something in your car you can put over the body?"

"I've got a tarp."

"Okay, snap some photos and cover it."

"Gotcha."

Delaney scampered off. Vaughn waited a moment before indicating for Ivy to join him up the small grassy embankment toward the barn. She started to feel pressure in her chest when she saw a cop wearing a gas mask. Vaughn quickly introduced her. He referred to Ivy as Dr. Reeves, a consultant on the case.

"You have any more of those?" Vaughn said, indicating Officer Horowitz's mask.

"Delaney said it's okay now, used this handheld thingy to check the air. It's just in case."

"You have any more?" Vaughn repeated.

"In the car."

"Grab them."

Delaney exited the barn around the same time that Horowitz returned with masks.

"Let me help you with that." Vaughn took one of the

masks and slipped it over Ivy's head. Tightened the straps. "Should stop fogging in a few seconds."

Vaughn put his own mask on and said, "Ready?"

Ivy felt her pulse pounding in her throat.

No, not really.

"Yeah," she lied. "Ready."

CHAPTER 37

VAUGHN WASN'T KEEN on the idea of bringing Ivy into the crime scene. Liked the idea of sending her home alone less.

He entered first. Scoped it out before indicating for Ivy to follow.

His first impression was that the interior of the barn was eerily similar to the first. Same unpainted walls. Same vent, same speaker. Cheap doors, expensive locks. Hint of rotten egg smell, muted by the mask, but still detectable.

This is where the similarities ended, however.

No boxes, broken or otherwise. No numbers.

As Delaney had told them outside, the first room they entered contained a generic table. A chair, too. Tipped over, lying in the dirt.

A tarp masked the outline of a body half under the desk.

Sitting atop the desk were two raised buttons roughly the size of drink coasters: one green, one red. Opposite the desk, hanging from the wall, a digital display, like a stock ticker, three feet long, maybe ten inches high. It showed green and red dots in a line. Ten of them. No apparent pattern.

To Vaughn, anyway.

"What the hell is this?" he said quietly. His words rebounded off the mask, echoed.

The door they entered, the one that Delaney had said they'd used a crowbar to open, was on one side. There was an identical door on the other.

Like the first, the frame had also been splintered near the lock on this one.

"Delaney, you—" Vaughn was turning as he spoke, but stopped when he saw Ivy. Her eyes were locked on the tarp-covered body on the ground. "Ivy?"

She stood in place, unmoving.

"Ivy." He placed a hand on her shoulder and she jumped. "Don't look down."

A slow nod.

She obliged, raising her head, and Vaughn addressed Delaney again.

"This door," he said, pointing at the one to their right. "You crack it open?"

"Horowitz did. Same kind of digital locks as the first scene."

Vaughn glanced at Ivy again, checked to see if she was okay.

Her attention was firmly locked on the digital display hanging from the wall.

She nodded to herself.

Vaughn stepped around the body, pushed the door to the adjoining room open with the back of his hand.

An identical room. desk, chair. Buttons, display.

Just no body.

There was a different pattern of red and green dots on this digital screen.

Vaughn scratched his head, and his eyes drifted to a third door. The frame was intact. Vaughn tried the knob, was surprised to find it unlocked.

It opened to the outside.

"Delaney?"

"Oh," the man said. "That's weird. I didn't check that one. Thought it was locked like the other two."

This was strange. Vaughn inspected the knob, the keypad. Digital. WiFi symbol on the black, matte finish.

He located a camera mounted in the corner of the room.

"You think someone got out?" Delaney asked.

It sure looked that way to Vaughn. The door might have been unlocked remotely by whoever was watching the live feed. Alternatively, the passcode could have been given over the speaker.

One person exits, the other stays behind, locked in, and is gassed. It certainly did seem like some sort of game. Red light, green light.

Wasn't that a Squid Game, too?

Vaughn considered another option: the person in this room had been their unsub, posing as a contestant. He was mulling this possibility over when Ivy, who had been silent until this point, suddenly spoke up.

"You said you saw someone running from the scene?" she asked in a small voice.

"Yeah, when I first drove up. Thought it was your father, but—"

"It wasn't."

"I guess not. I'm thinking it might be the guy who set this thing up, whatever the fuck it is."

"It wasn't him either."

Vaughn admired the woman's confidence. She was rattled from seeing the body, covered or not, probably thinking about the photo he'd stupidly shown her of Aaron Treadman. But even so, when Ivy spoke, there was no hesitation to her words. No suggestion of doubt. No maybe, perhaps, could be.

Before visiting Ivy the first time, Darnell had done a quick background check on the woman. Dr. Ivy Reeves had just turned twenty-six years old. She was the youngest tenured mathematics professor in Princeton University's nearly three hundred-year history. Won a bunch of awards that sounded prestigious, although Vaughn had never heard of them before.

And now this stuff about her father, which had clearly her rattled.

Out of her element, wearing a mask, seeing a dead body for the first time. And yet she was still confident.

"Who was it then?" Delaney asked.

Ivy looked directly at Vaughn when she answered.

"The person you saw wasn't my father, and it wasn't the person behind this. It was the person who *won*."

CHAPTER 38

"Won? What do you mean *won*?" Vaughn asked.

Ivy indicated the green and red buttons on the desk.

"I recognize this setup. It's a game theory experiment called the prisoner's dilemma. And whoever was in this room won the game. That's why the door was unlocked—they were permitted to leave."

She almost said, *while the other was killed.*

That damn mental image of Aaron Treadman again.

"The prisoner's dilemma?" Vaughn repeated. "I thought the other one was the prisoner's dilemma. This looks hella different."

Ivy shook her head.

"That was the 100 prisoners problem. This is the prisoner's *dilemma*. Like I said, it's a very different experiment. The game is broken into rounds." She pointed at the display board now. "Looks like they played ten rounds. Each player can select either green or red for each round. They won't know what their opponent chose for that round until their decision is locked in. Points are attributed . . ." Ivy trailed off. She'd lost Vaughn. It was the stupid mask muffling her words.

"It would help if I had a piece of paper," she said.

Vaughn looked to Delaney, who patted his pockets.

"In the car," he said, moving to leave.

"Let's head outside," Vaughn suggested.

Ivy didn't need to be asked twice. The night air was cool. Felt good on her skin. They walked toward Delaney's car. As the cop rooted through his glove box, Vaughn took off his mask, inhaled. Helped Ivy with hers.

That was better.

Ivy scrunched her nose, stretched her face.

"I had paper in here somewhere," Delaney muttered.

"Don't worry about it," Vaughn said. "Any word from the troops on the ground?"

Delaney pulled out of his car. He squeezed the radio on his shoulder, leaned down, and said a few words. Waited. Someone replied.

"They're still getting set up. Coupla boots on the ground but nothing yet."

"What about the ME?"

"I got here just before you—haven't called him. Where is your partner, anyway?" Delaney asked.

"Getting some rest."

Delaney had since removed his mask, too, and Ivy saw distaste cross the man's features.

She pictured Darnell, his tone and mannerisms, the way he'd spoken to her—abrupt, curt—when she'd been cornered in the hall. Detective Sacker's approach couldn't be more different than Vaughn's. Was it a good cop, bad cop thing? Could be. But Ivy had thought that this approach was reserved for suspects. That's the way it was in all those cop dramas.

"I'll give the ME a call." Vaughn did, speaking concisely. The phone call lasted only a few seconds. "Dr. Button was already made aware of the situation."

"That was me," Horowitz informed them. He was still wearing his mask.

"Good. He'll be here within the hour. Delaney, how do you feel about holding down the fort? Waiting for Dr. Button? Taking photos—those 3D ones again?"

"I can do that once Landon arrives."

"Give me a call if the ME notices anything different. Fingerprint the vic, secure the gas canister. If your men find anybody, call me."

Ivy was impressed. She liked how Vaughn took control. Was grateful that his partner had decided to sit this one out.

"Got it."

Delaney moved to his trunk and leaned inside while Vaughn turned to her.

"Want to go somewhere quiet where you can tell me about this prisoner's dilemma? Fair warning, though, you're going to have to go slow. *Real* slow."

The quiet place that Vaughn chose was a hole-in-the-wall called Wailen's on the east side of Jersey. A handful of men sat at the bar—a giant, single chunk of wood—but Vaughn led them to a private booth at the back. The way he moved suggested that this wasn't his first time here.

A waiter approached. Old, gruff.

"Detective Ryan, how you doin' tonight?"

Yep—he'd been here before.

"Been better."

"I hear you. What'll it be?"

"Pint for me. Guinness." Vaughn looked at Ivy. "You?"

Ivy thought about it. She didn't really feel like drinking. The effects of her late night out with Abby had faded, but she'd only slept a few hours before Sarah Kachinski called. Water would be ideal, but she crumbled under the pressure.

"I'll have a lager."

"Sure."

"Hey, Mike? Can we get a couple of pieces of paper and a pen when you have a chance?"

"No problem. I'll be right back."

He left.

"So, I'm a special consultant now?" Ivy said with a smirk. Something to ease the tension. Take her mind off that tarp. Because beneath that tarp was a man. A man with . . .

Stop it.

"If you want to be. To be honest, we're going to need you. Prisoners problem, dilemma, it's all Greek to me."

"Well, there's some Greek to it, that's for sure," Ivy said with a chuckle.

Vaughn didn't get the joke.

The waiter returned with their drinks and the paper. Vaughn took a long sip, three swallows worth. When he placed the beer glass down, Ivy saw him tilt his head and look at the word "Guinness" printed on the side.

"Not bad—split the G," he said.

Ivy took a small sip of her own beer. Stared at Vaughn. "Now *you're* speaking Greek."

"More like Irish. First sip, you want to drink all the way

to the middle of the G in Guinness." Vaughn turned the glass around and showed her. The dark brown liquid came to just above the straight part of the letter G. "I went to Ireland a couple of years back. They all do it there."

"Interesting."

"Not really. So you wanna teach me about the prisoner's dilemma?"

She grabbed the paper and pen. Ivy didn't know much about "splitting the G," but she knew math.

"Absolutely."

CHAPTER 39

Vaughn found Ivy's way of speaking, what he was mentally starting to refer to as her *professor mode*, captivating.

And attractive. *Very* attractive.

Fuck you, Darnell, for putting these thoughts in my head.

"The game itself is simple. Two players, two buttons each: red and green. You can't see what your opponent has chosen until both have selected a color. The point system varies, but the most accepted one is as follows." Ivy scribbled on the paper, but Vaughn's eyes were locked on her face. She pushed her tongue lightly into the inside of her cheek as she worked the pen. "If both players select green, they both get three points. If one chooses red and the other green, red gets five points, green zero. If they both choose red, they both get one point."

Ivy spun the paper around, and Vaughn was forced to look at it.

Player 1: G, R, R, G, G, G, R, G, R, G.

Player 2: R, R, G, G, G, R, G, R, G, R.

Player 1: 17

Player 2: 23

"So player two wins? Just like at the scene?"

Ivy frowned.

"These *are* the colors from the board."

"Really? You remembered them all?"

"I have a thing for numbers. They just kinda stick."

Vaughn made a face. He was about to comment that these were colors, not numbers, undoubtedly making a fool of himself, but Ivy saved him the embarrassment.

"I just converted G to 0 and R to 1—simple binary. Easier for me to remember that way."

"Ah."

Still impressive. Vaughn had stared at the digital boards for as long as Ivy had and would have been hard-pressed to remember a single three-color sequence correctly.

Their minds were wired differently, it seemed.

He focused on victims and victimology, Ivy on math and numbers.

"I still don't understand these math games. Random . . ." He stopped himself again, recalling Ivy's lecture on the 100 prisoners problem. "Wait, you're about to tell me that this game isn't random, either?"

Ivy laughed. She had a pretty laugh. High-pitched, but also somehow soft. Not shrill.

"There is a strategy to it. A mathematician named Robert Axelrod held a tournament, a computer tournament, in the 1980s. He wanted to know the optimal strategy to win the game. People from all over the world submitted their strategies in the form of simple computer programs. Then he pitted them against each other and tallied their total scores. One strategy came out on top: the tit-for-tat strategy. Essentially, you start out green and only switch to red when, in the previous round, the opponent chose red. If they chose green again, then the tit-for-tat strategist picks green."

Vaughn drank more of his beer.

"I get it."

I think.

"Axelrod ran the tournament several more times, with different strategies that mathematicians submitted, and barring a few exceptions, tit-for-tat came out on top. So, intrigued by this, he dug a little deeper. Realized that this strategy could be described simply as starting out 'nice' but becoming 'mean' if the opponent is 'mean.' The key is, though, to be 'forgiving.' If the opponent goes back to being 'nice,' then you go 'nice,' too. I'm not positive, but I'm pretty sure that more papers have been published about the prisoner's dilemma than any other math problem in history."

"Really?" They'd both finished their beers and ordered another round. Ivy went for Guinness this time. "All this for a simple math game?"

"That's the thing. Axelrod realized that it was more than just a game. It was an allegory for life. Biology follows this pattern; ecosystems, too. A species needs a level of cooperation with other species for the betterment of both. And within species, packs, families, everything—this tit-for-tat strategy wins out. You can't be a complete pushover. If someone does something bad to you, then you need to hit back. But you also need to be forgiving. The 'tit-for-tat' or 'nice guy' strategy has been applied to everything from war, business, and trade to cybersecurity."

"Interesting." Vaughn wasn't just paying lip service. He had no idea about the widespread application of such a simple game. To him, math was reserved for calculating sales taxes and interest rates. "I just don't understand why someone is using these games to kill people."

Ivy's face dropped.

"That I can't help you with," she said solemnly. She took several large gulps of her Guinness. "What *I* don't understand is why someone would go to an abandoned barn in the middle of nowhere to play."

"That's the easy part. We found an ad on Aaron Treadman's computer, in his email. It advertised a game show for a streaming service, offered a payout of 1 Bitcoin to the winner."

"So it's about the money?"

"It's always about the money."

Their eyes met again, and Vaughn immediately dropped his gaze. He noticed Ivy's glass.

"Look at that. You split the G."

"Of course. The volume of the glass is sixteen ounces. The glass itself is tulip-shaped, and the middle of the G is roughly 3.75 inches from the rim. Applying a volume-height curve, that makes the volume of beer to be removed roughly seven ounces. A typical mouthful of beer is three ounces, so I calculated the number of mouthfuls to be two plus an additional third."

Vaughn craned his neck forward. His eyes widened.

"You . . . you calculated all that in . . . seconds? The . . . volume . . . the—"

Ivy broke into laughter. "No, I just guessed."

Vaughn laughed, too.

After they were finished, he drove her back to the assisted living home to retrieve her car. He no longer saw flashing police cherries in the distance. Instead, the entire field had been lit up with massive floodlights. It looked like an evening baseball field, ready for the opening pitch.

"Thank you for your help tonight, Ivy."

He saw lines around her eyes and reached out with his thumb. She pulled back at first, then let him touch her. He gently rubbed her skin.

"Just marks from the mask."

Ivy leaned forward. Vaughn did the same.

Their lips almost met.

"Thank you," Ivy said, stepping back.

Vaughn nodded.

As much as he'd enjoyed and needed the reprieve, it was time to get back to work.

CHAPTER 40

VAUGHN WAS THOROUGHLY spent. After dropping Ivy off, he'd gone back to the crime scene. Relieved Delaney.

Dr. Button was still there, and CSU tech Landon was with him. Vaughn helped finish processing the scene. The ME wasn't yet prepared to confirm that the victim's cause of death was H2S poisoning, but that was just the man's profession peeking through. They all knew this was the case.

They'd found an identical canister of gas. Remote switch. Router. Speaker. The victim was a man in his mid-thirties.

Vaughn didn't get home until close to three in the morning. Dr. Button was destined to have a longer night still.

The fuzzy feelings that had come over him following his drinks with Ivy faded.

They were long gone the next morning when he arrived at Darnell's house forty-five minutes later than he told his partner to be ready, and the man still wasn't answering his phone.

He knocked heavily on the door, shouted Darnell's name. Didn't bother checking to see if it was locked.

Vaughn wasn't in the mood to rouse his partner, nor clean up the man's shit. This shtick was getting old.

He knocked again.

"Darnell! Time to go!"

He heard movement from inside.

Satisfied that he'd done his part, Vaughn got back in the car and waited. Gave Darnell fifteen minutes—if he didn't come out by then, he'd go into the precinct by himself.

Darnell emerged at the thirteen minute mark.

The man groaned as he got in the car.

"No coffee this morning?"

Vaughn said nothing as he pulled onto the road.

"You look like shit, by the way."

That did it.

Vaughn was fed up.

Maybe it was what Delaney had said about Darnell holding him back. Maybe it was the cumulative effects of dealing with the man's shit for months now.

"*I* look like shit? *Me*? You smell like a distillery."

Darnell sniffed his armpits.

"Ran out of deodorant."

Typically, these types of jokes would tickle Vaughn.

Not today.

"Where the fuck were you last night?"

"At home. My blind date stood me up."

"Darnell, there was another murder."

This finally slapped the smile of his partner's face.

"*What?*"

As he drove, Vaughn briefly outlined what had happened, leaving Ivy out of his account.

"Jesus Christ, man, why didn't you come get me?"

"I'm not your babysitter."

"Fuck. I'm your goddamn superior, Ryan. Don't you forget that."

Vaughn's eyes flashed to his partner. He was about to say something, something he couldn't take back. And Darnell seemed to be daring him to do it. His eyes were bloodshot. The pupils pinpricks.

But there was a deep sadness in them too, hidden beneath a thin veneer of anger.

Vaughn looked away.

"Let's just find this fucking guy."

Delaney wasn't in the bullpen. Vaughn and Darnell had missed the morning briefing, which wasn't terribly uncommon while working a case. The whiteboard on the back wall was filled with manic scribblings.

Vaughn recognized Captain Daniels's terrible writing.

This was a little odd. Captain Daniels rarely attended these meetings, leaving Lieutenant Carlo to run the briefings.

Vaughn found Bowes tucked into the corner of the room, a half dozen cell phones in front of him, a laptop open. The man had headphones on and didn't notice either Vaughn or Darnell.

"Bowes? You seen Delaney?" Vaughn asked.

The man was bobbing his head to a song that Vaughn recognized when he got closer.

"Save Me," by Jelly Roll.

Vaughn reached out and pulled one of the headphone cups off his ear.

"Oh—hey. Captain was in this morning." He hadn't heard Vaughn's question. "Looked pissed."

"Why?"

Bowes shrugged.

It was barely nine, and there were already two energy drinks—Ghost and C4 this time, both open—on his desk.

"Dunno. I was just going through the phones that Delaney brought in. And—"

"Phones?" Darnell asked.

"Yeah. He found two more, one in each of the cars at the pizza joint. Belong to, *uh*," Bowes's eyes flicked to his screen, "Thomas Altman and Geoff Lane."

The names meant nothing to Vaughn, but he assumed that they were two of the first ten victims. Likely the two that Aaron had shared his final slice of pizza with.

"And?" Darnell said.

"And they all got the same text messages, the ones with the rules."

Made sense; their cars were parked at CiCi's Pizza.

"Where is Delaney, anyway?"

"Haven't seen him. But I don't think he clocked out last night."

"Really? I sent him home after—"

The bullpen door opened.

"Sacker, Ryan, my office."

It was Captain Daniels, and Bowes was right. He did look pissed. The PPD Captain was in his sixties, but on any given day, he could have passed as eighty or fifty. Hard eyes, thick gray, almost white hair. Built like a slab of granite. Today, he was eighty.

"Bowes, you working the gas case with them?"

"He's helping with the tech," Vaughn offered.

"You too, then. In my office, *now*."

CHAPTER 41

"WHAT THE FUCK were you thinking?" Captain Daniels bellowed.

Vaughn didn't know what the man was talking about. He knew, however, that Daniels would expound. And the man did—after a pregnant pause.

"Bringing a civilian into a crime scene? A fucking *gas* scene?"

Vaughn felt Darnell's eyes on him.

He didn't look at his partner, but he knew what the man was thinking.

How did Daniels know? Delaney? It had to be Delaney. That's why the prick wasn't in the bullpen waiting for you, like he usually is.

Puppy dog dick-riding simp.

Captain Daniels had a hands-off approach. Let the detectives, and to a lesser degree the officers, go about their business without interfering.

But the one thing the captain hated was being left out of the loop.

Daniels waved a hand indicating that it was Vaughn's turn to speak.

"Dr. Ivy Reeves is from Princeton—a math professor. She helped us understand the first scene."

Daniels's icy eyes narrowed.

"*How?*"

"Our unsub is using some weird math games to kill his victims. They seem random, but Dr. Reeves says that there's a way to increase their odds of winning. In the most recent crime scene, she's fairly certain that one of the participants made it out."

"You need her help?"

Vaughn nodded.

"Yes. I think—"

"Wait—Dr. Reeves? Did you say Dr. *Reeves*?"

"Yes. A prof—"

"Dr. Reeves?" Daniels repeated a third time.

"Yes, Dr. Ivy Reeves." Vaughn couldn't mask his annoyance.

"Dr. Ivy . . ." Daniels shook his head. He was pissed before but now the captain bordered on furious. "I want you to listen to me: under no circumstances is Dr. Reeves to be involved in the case."

Why? was on the tip of Vaughn's tongue.

Never got the chance to say it.

Daniels got worked up about a lot of things. Had a resting blood pressure of 200 over 100. But this was extreme even for him.

"Do you understand me?"

"Yes, sir."

Even though the captain's anger had peaked at the mention of Ivy, his reaction didn't make sense to Vaughn. The man's fury had to be the result of the press getting wind of this.

The only thing that pissed Daniels off more than being left out of the loop was the press getting on his ass about something.

Vaughn was surprised it had taken this long. Delaney had spoken to the caller about her missing husband. When she didn't hear anything about her husband's murder on the news, she probably went looking.

Looking and asking questions.

"I mean it. Bowes?"

The caffeine-laced officer's legs were bouncing up and down. Vaughn wanted to reach out and grab his knee, make him stop.

"Everything was operated remotely. Whoever's behind this knew what they were doing. Covered their tracks."

Vaughn didn't think that Captain Daniels's frown could get any deeper.

It did.

"What about this guy who managed to get away?"

"Delaney dispatched a team to look for him. Haven't seen him yet this morning," Vaughn said.

"We're making progress," Darnell blurted.

Vaughn cringed, glanced at his partner.

Why the fuck would you say that?

But he knew why. Senior detective and all that. Trying to save face, trying to make it seem like he hadn't passed out and missed last night's ordeal.

Daniels cocked his head, ran a hand through his thick white hair.

"Progress?"

"I mean—"

"Eleven dead? Two crime scenes? Two more missing canisters of gas?" *Fucking Delaney.* "You call that progress?"

Vaughn saw Darnell open his mouth to say something, but he smartly remained silent.

"Didn't think so. And where the fuck were you last night?"

Darnell scowled and Bowes shifted uncomfortably. It was a rhetorical question. Everyone in the room where Darnell was. If not *where*, for sure *what* he was doing.

"You guys have forty-eight hours. Forty-eight hours and then I'm—Detective Ryan, would you answer your fucking phone?"

"What?"

"Your phone," Bowes said under his breath.

Vaughn looked down. At some point, he must have switched his phone to silent—probably before he'd gone to bed—and turned off the vibrate function, too. The flashlight, however, was lighting up his slacks. He took it out.

"It's Delaney."

"Answer it."

Vaughn did.

"Delan—"

"I caught him! I fucking caught him, Vaughn!"

"What? Who?"

"The unsub! Our guy!"

Darnell was on his feet now. Vaughn wasn't sure if it was because he could overhear Delaney shouting or if he was only reacting to Vaughn's change in posture.

"What are you talking about, Delaney?"

"He was in a field near the Cedar Ridge Preserve. Vaughn, you ain't gonna believe this, but the fucker got lost. He was like a zombie, talking some bullshit about Bitcoin . . . he was delirious."

Delaney was clearly amped up, excited about the idea of catching this collar. Vaughn was of a different mind, considering what Ivy had said, how the man who had been permitted to leave the barn was likely the winner of the game, not the orchestrator.

"Where are you?"

"I have him in the back of my car. I'm heading to the station now."

"Don't talk to him, Delaney. Wait for us to meet you outside."

"I'm going to fucking kill Delaney," Darnell said.

"Keep your shit together."

"He ratted us out. He told all that bullshit to Daniels, couldn't keep his goddamn mouth shut. And what the fuck is this about you bringing Ivy to the second crime scene? I may have been hungover, but I'm pretty sure that you never mentioned that little detail in the car this morning."

Delaney's squad car raced into the lot. Stopped directly in front of them before Vaughn could defend himself, explain. Delaney jumped out. He was wired, clearly hadn't slept all night.

"I got him!"

"Calm down," Vaughn said.

"Sorry, it's—"

"I get it—just calm down. We don't know that this is our guy."

Delaney's eyes bulged.

"He is! The man was—"

"He could just be the winner," Vaughn said flatly. "We

don't know that he had anything to do with this other than trying to make a quick buck."

Delaney's eyes sucked back into his head. He hadn't considered this possibility, and the idea of not being the man who had brought this nightmare to a close took some of the wind out of his sails. He paused just long enough for Darnell to jump in.

"Did he say anything to you in the car?"

Delaney shook his head, and they all moved closer to the vehicle, peered into the backseat.

"No. He . . . he fell asleep."

And the man was still sleeping, his cheek pressed up against the glass. There was a thin trail of spit on the window. It was difficult to get a full picture of the man with his face compressed the way it was, but Vaughn got a general idea. Wiry, with dark circles around his eyes. Shaggy blond hair.

"You have a name?"

"When I found him in the field," Delaney said, speaking at a rapid clip, "he said he was Joshua Perry. Gave his DOB, too. Punched it in on the ride over. No priors in the system. Could be a made-up name, though. We need to get him printed."

"Thanks, tips," Darnell growled.

"I'll wake him up; Delaney, you bring him in," Vaughn said.

"Fuck that, *I'll* bring him in," Darnell said.

"You weren't even there last night. This is *my* collar."

"We don't even know if this *is* a collar, Delaney. This is—"

Vaughn didn't get a chance to finish. Darnell reached out and grabbed Delaney by the throat, surprising all of them.

Delaney's eyelids peeled back, and Vaughn clawed at his partner's arm.

"You trying to steal this from me too, you fucking worm? Like you tried to steal my job?"

"Darnell!" Vaughn shouted. He tried to pull his partner's hand off, to no avail. "Darnell!"

The man bared his teeth.

"Little fucking—"

Vaughn used his free hand to rabbit punch Darnell in the armpit. Not hard, but with enough force to make Darnell grunt and curl his body protectively on that side. He finally let go and Delaney coughed as he massaged his throat. Vaughn immediately got between them.

"What the fuck is wrong with you?" Vaughn snarled.

The anger leaked from Darnell's face.

"Back up," Vaughn ordered.

When Darnell continued to just stand there, Vaughn gave him a little push. His partner took two steps back.

"Don't you move."

Vaughn whipped around. Delaney had recovered and looked more shocked than injured.

"You good?"

"Y-yeah."

"Bring him in. Print him and throw him in a room. Don't talk to him. And don't say a word to Darnell. Got it?"

Delaney nodded, and Vaughn held the stare for a moment longer. Then he rapped two knuckles against the window, startling the man in the backseat.

"*You,*" he hissed. "Wake the fuck up."

CHAPTER 42

Any notion Ivy might have had of her colleagues and the students *not* seeing the TikTok of the Bae-sian Prof were dashed the moment she parked outside Fine Hall. Three separate groups of people—one of which she recognized as faculty—started shooting glances her way and chatting amongst themselves.

High school shit. Whispering into their hands.

Ivy refused to let this get her down. She felt oddly refreshed. If anything, the terrifying events of the night prior should have only added to her anxiety. Maybe it was the two beers that she'd had with Vaughn that had calmed her. Maybe she was just getting used to being around death.

Can it happen that quickly? Can one become jaded to murder after witnessing just two crime scenes?

A ridiculous thought, but regardless, she'd slept well.

She'd also predicted that something like this might happen—the gossip about the TikTok video—so Ivy had decided to arrive just before class started to avoid any awkward encounters.

Tristan was holding the door open for her.

"Got the phones today?" she said.

Tristan raised a bag.

"Yep."

"Good."

Ivy entered the class. Saw the students' smirks. Ignored them. She didn't notice Zeke—his usual seat was empty—and this lifted her mood even more.

"Alright class, before we start . . ." Murmurs, a smattering of chuckles. "Yeah, exactly. Let's get this out of the way. Go on, laugh. I'll wait."

Some did, most remained silent.

"Good. It looks like everyone has seen the TikTok video. Not much to say about it—I just hope that you learned something yesterday. And sorry to disappoint, but today we go back to our regular scheduled programming."

This was met by a chorus of boos, and Ivy couldn't help but grin. Just a little.

"Now that we got that out of the way, today's lesson is on Monte Carlo simulations. And before you ask, no, I won't be talking about casinos or gambling. Monte Carlo simulation is used to predict outcomes from uncertain events."

The lecture went well. The students were looser than usual. More engaged, even though Ivy stayed far from any taboo subject matter. She wrapped up the lesson, saved her digital scribblings as the students collected their phones from Tristan.

"Dr. Reeves?"

Ivy raised her head from the lectern.

"Rebecca, how can I help you?"

"I—"

"Dr. Reeves? I have to get to my own class."

Ivy turned to Tristan.

"Sure, go ahead. I'll meet you in my office later." Ivy waited for Tristan to pack up his computer and leave before addressing Rebecca again. "You wanted—Rebecca? What's wrong?" The woman was crying. "Rebecca?"

Ivy reached out and gently stroked the back of her arm.

"I'm sorry." She sniffed, wiped her face. "It's just . . . it's Zeke."

Ivy tensed, let her hand fall.

"What about him?"

"I know he's—well, his dad is like this big shot. But it's just—"

"Rebecca, what did he do?"

Ivy's eyes narrowed as she pictured Zeke at the bar, yelling in her face.

Do you know who my father is?

"He said that if I told anyone, he'd get his dad to talk to the department. Get my scholarship revoked. I can't—I can't lose my scholarship."

Rebecca's gaze was locked on the floor. Tears streamed from her green eyes.

"That's not going to happen. If he did something to you, you need to tell me."

"But—"

"No, stop that." The words came out a little more sternly than Ivy had intended. "You need to tell me what he did. I'll go to bat for you with Dr. Moorehead. You're a smart kid, a pleasure to have in class. Zeke is . . ." Ivy trailed off.

Rebecca wiped her face again. Now, she looked skyward. Exhaled loudly.

"I was leaving yesterday afternoon, and he came up to me.

Got in my face. Y-yelled at me, said I told on him for cheating. B-but I didn't say anything. I just want to do my work."

Ivy nodded, waited for the fear-stricken girl to continue.

"Then he . . . he *grabbed* me."

Ivy was taken aback.

"He grabbed you? Where?"

Rebecca was wearing a rust-colored sweater, loose, and she began teasing up her right sleeve.

"I told him to let go, then that's when he said that stuff about his dad. Said that if I *ever* said anything about him cheating again, he'd ruin me. His . . . his eyes. I was so scared."

Rebecca's sleeve was up now past her bicep, and Ivy inhaled sharply. There were deep red marks on her pale skin, four of them. Circular. Half crescents outlined in purple.

"Jesus. He did that to you?"

Rebecca nodded.

"He grabbed me," she repeated. "Squeezed *hard*."

"Hold on—keep your sleeve like that."

Ivy snapped a photo with her phone. Asked Rebecca to supinate her hand. There was a mark on the inside from Zeke's thumb. She took another photo.

"You can put it down now."

Rebecca did.

"I didn't even want to come in today, I was so scared. Waited in the hall for everyone to pass. Only entered when I didn't see Zeke. I'm scared, Dr. Reeves. Scared that if he knows I talked to you, he's going to do something. Something worse."

Ivy had felt the same fear when Zeke came up to her at the bar. She suspected that he was capable of violence then but didn't want to believe it. The bruises on Rebecca's arm left no doubt.

"You did the right thing coming to me. I'm going to speak with Dr. Moorehead, okay? You should go to the police. Tell them what he did to you."

Rebecca's eyes widened.

"No—I can't. I do that, and he's going to know. He'll *know*."

"You have to."

"I can't! I thought—I thought you'd understand."

This made no sense to Ivy, but she understood the woman's intense reaction. Knew what it was like to be completely overwhelmed by fear. It had happened to her at the fire.

She'd barely made it out alive.

"Rebecca, I want you to listen to me."

"My scholarship, I—"

"Rebecca! Listen to me. I want you to go home, okay?"

"I have class, I need—"

"*Go home*. Take the rest of the day off. If any of your other professors give you any trouble, tell them to call me. In fact, you have your cell?"

Rebecca must have gotten it from Tristan already because she took it out.

"Good. Put my number in." Rebecca did. "If you see Zeke again, anywhere, even if he doesn't say anything to you, I want you to call me, okay?"

"Okay."

"Good. Did you drive here?"

Nod.

"I'm going to walk you to your car."

Rebecca must have arrived early, sat in her car debating whether or not to go to class, because her old Hyundai was parked in one of the closest spaces to the front of the building.

"Ice those bruises. I'm going get this sorted for you. Zeke won't hurt you again."

Ivy waited for Rebecca to drive off before storming back inside.

Fuck you, Zeke. You and your father.

CHAPTER 43

It took half an hour to get the man in the backseat of Delaney's car through processing. He again provided his name and DOB—Joshua Perry—but his prints weren't in the system.

Vaughn let Delaney take care of this part, making Perry the cop's collar, if he was actually responsible for the murders. Vaughn remained unconvinced. Either way, this was fine by him. Delaney deserved whatever credit was to be had. He'd been working his ass off.

But it was still their case.

During this entire process, Darnell hung back, saying nothing.

They put Joshua in Interview Room 2, let him sweat a little.

"I'll talk to him with Darnell." No argument from Delaney—he'd already gotten what he wanted. "In the meantime, let's assume he is Joshua Perry. Delaney, look into his past. I want you to focus on his education. He said he got lost, right?"

"Yeah."

"No phone on him?"

"No phone or wallet."

"Okay, so I'll ask him where he parked. If he gives up the location, head out there, see if you can find it. If you do and his phone is in his car, give it to Bowes."

Delaney nodded.

"Darnell, I'll do the talking, got it?"

Darnell grunted an affirmative.

"Okay, we're going in. Delaney, make sure the camera's recording."

Vaughn Mirandized Perry the second he walked into the room. Asked the man three times if he understood. He said he did.

"Good. We're going to start with the easy stuff. What's your name?"

"Josh Perry. I told the—"

"What were you doing by the Cedar Ridge Preserve?"

"I was lost," he said desperately. "It was dark, and I got lost."

"What were you doing out there?"

"I just . . . I'm so tired, man."

"What were you doing out there?" Vaughn asked again.

"I was playing this game. This . . . button game. And then the voice on the speaker says that I won, that I could go free. So I left. Got outta there."

"Josh, you ever heard of the prisoner's dilemma?"

"The *what*?"

"How about the tit-for-tat strategy?"

Perry scrunched his nose.

"I mean, I heard of tit-for-tat, but I don't know what it means. Like give and take?"

If this was an act, it was a fucking good one.

"Tell me about the game."

"It was this thing with red and green buttons—"

"Start earlier. How did you hear about it?"

"Oh. I, *uh*, I got this flyer thing under my wiper when I was parked at a gas station. It—"

"Where?"

"*Uh*, the one on Belt Line Road. QuikTrip?"

Vaughn waited a beat, made sure that Delaney on the other side of the one-way glass overheard.

"What'd it say?"

"It was an ad for a TV show. Wanted players for a puzzle game to win some crypto—"

"You still have the ad?"

"Yeah, in my car."

"Okay, so you got the ad, then what?"

"I called the number, but there was no answer. To be honest, I kinda forgot about it—thought it was a scam. Then I got a text the next day from the same number with a list of instructions."

"Which were?"

"Like, go to this parking lot, leave your phone and wallet in the car. Don't tell nobody, that kind of stuff."

Darnell cleared his throat—a signal. Vaughn was tired of talking, tired in general, so he allowed his partner to say a few words. Sometimes—almost all the time—sitting and listening was the best approach. Not here, not now. As per his own admission, Perry, like Vaughn, was exhausted. They needed to keep peppering him, keep the man off balance.

"You didn't think that was a little weird?"

"Of course, but I need the cash. Lost my job and I need the money, man."

Vaughn nodded, trying to look understanding and sympathetic.

"Okay, so you get the instructions and then what? You drive to the parking lot?"

"Yep."

"Which one?"

Joshua scratched his head. He had stubby fingernails that weren't quite grimy but definitely weren't clean.

"Stillwater Cafe."

"Then?"

"I got the address for the game. Put it in my GPS, did my best to memorize it. Read that screen like fifty times. Wasn't far. Less than a mile. But I suck at directions. Like, real bad. I got lost. The text said that I had to arrive by midnight, so I had lots of time—at least I thought I did. But I just couldn't find the damn place. Musta walked in circles for twenty minutes. Don't have no watch, so I didn't know the time. Got to the barn on time—well, I musta got there on time, 'cause I didn't get kicked out."

"You just walked in? Then what?" Vaughn now.

"A voice from a speaker told me to shut the door—I did. Then he told me to sit at the desk. I was tired and sweating . . . just sat, then I got instructions. Didn't have no time to think."

"So you play the game?"

"Yeah. Then the voice said I won, just like that. After ten rounds. Told me to go, said I'd get paid. The door clicked open and I left. Started to walk back to my car. At least, I tried to. Like I said, I got lost. Walked around for hours . . . all friggin' night. Then that cop . . . man, he was angry. Told me to get on the ground. Pulled his gun on me 'n everything."

Not surprising. Delaney had done the same thing with Ivy, her father, and the nurse.

"Josh, from my side of the table, all of this, everything you're saying, sounds incredibly unbelievable."

Josh wiggled his nose as if it itched.

"Honestly? I know. Too good to be true, right? Especially with my luck. But I thought what the fu—sorry, what the heck? Worth a shot. And it kinda looked legit. There was a camera, and the voice was, like, computerized or something? Am I . . . am I gonna get that Bitcoin?"

"No idea. Josh, did you see anyone else there? Anyone other than the cop who found you in the field?"

"Naw. Not a single person. Just that voice over the speaker."

CHAPTER 44

"Dr. Reeves, Dr. Moorehead is in his office with a student right now. You can't—"

To hell, I can't.

Ivy yanked the door open.

"Dr. Moorehead, we need to—"

Ivy's mouth snapped shut. The student was none other than Zeke Godfrey. He looked demure. Head down, hands folded in his lap.

"What the hell is he doing here?"

"Dr. Reeves, sit down."

"Dr. Moorehead, Zeke—"

"Sit down."

Ivy grabbed the chair next to Zeke, pulled it across the office, and sat.

"Dr. Reeves, there have been some serious allegations made against you. It has come to—"

"Me? *Me?* This is—" Ivy was aghast.

"You'll get your chance to speak."

Dr. Moorehead dared her to interrupt. When Ivy didn't,

he continued, "The allegations involve you at a bar, intoxicated, approaching a student."

Ivy couldn't believe what she was hearing. Had to literally bite her tongue to stop from speaking out.

"At said bar, it's alleged that you made inappropriate comments. These come on the back of previous innuendos made during class time, in reference to STIs." Dr. Moorehead leaned forward. "Now, I've seen the little TikTok video that you posted, Dr. Reeves. Posting lectures on any social media without prior approval by the department is in direct violation of your contract."

Dr. Moorehead, his lips a thin line, stopped speaking.

Ivy waited.

"Now, you may go ahead."

Calm, Ivy. Calm.

"First of all, I never approached anybody at the bar. *I* was approached. Zeke was aggressive and threatening. I was not. As for the comment in the class, it was made by a student—not by me. And the video? I did not post the video. I have no idea who did." Ivy leaned back hard in her chair. "This is insane."

It was. Ivy couldn't believe that she was being forced to defend herself.

"Insane or not, these are serious allegations."

"I agree. Couple this with the cheating and we have more than enough to expel Zeke."

"*Both* of your allegations are serious. The way I see it, we have a he said, she said situation."

Ivy almost blurted, *Bullshit.*

She was a goddamn professor, Zeke an entitled asshole student.

"I have witnesses."

"As does Zeke."

Of course he does. His fellow douchebags from the bar. She had Abby and—*blegh*—Blake, but they'd all been drinking. Abby had an ace up her sleeve, however.

"One more thing," she said, daring to look at Zeke. He still had his chin pressed to his chest, but now, he was nervously alternating interlacing his fingers and spreading them out. Jesus, he was a good actor. Pretending to be nervous, ashamed, even. Goddamn psychopath was what he was.

"Yes?"

Ivy got her phone out.

"A student came up to me after class this morning. This woman said that Zeke not only threatened her, but also assaulted her. I have photos."

Zeke's head shot up.

"No way, I didn't—"

"Mr. Godfrey, please remain silent. Dr. Reeves, show me the photos."

Ivy pulled them up and started toward Dr. Moorehead's desk, phone in hand.

"This is a lie!" Zeke's placid demeanor vanished completely.

"Mr. God—"

"It's a *fucking* lie!"

Zeke leapt to his feet.

"Rebecca's lying! I didn't touch her!"

Ivy suppressed a smile. She hadn't mentioned Rebecca by name. This was an admission of guilt if she'd ever heard one.

"Sit down!" Dr. Moorehead yelled.

Zeke had no intention of sitting down.

"Samantha, call security!"

Zeke snarled. This was the angry student that Ivy knew from the bar, finally showing his true colors. And this time, Dr. Moorehead was here to witness it.

"Give me the phone!"

Someone took the phone, but it wasn't Zeke. Dr. Moorehead snatched it from Ivy's hand and moved around the front of his desk, putting himself between Zeke and Ivy. Zeke didn't back down. Reached for the phone again.

"Mr. Godfrey!"

Ivy cowered, thinking that Zeke was actually going to hit the department head.

"Give me the phone!" Zeke screamed. He grabbed Moorehead's wrist. "Give me—"

The door flew open and two Princeton security guards stormed in. One of them wrapped an arm around Zeke's waist and pulled him back.

"Do you know what my father will do to you?! Do you have any idea—"

"Get him out of here!" Dr. Moorehead shouted.

It took both of the guards to remove Zeke from the office.

"Escort him off campus! If he even steps back on Princeton property, arrest him!"

"My dad—"

"Quiet, kid," one of the guards warned. They dragged Zeke down the hall, past a terrified-looking secretary.

"Dr. Moorehead, are you okay? I heard shouting, so I called security even before you—"

"I'm fine." He rubbed his wrist where Zeke had grabbed him. "Thank you, Samantha."

"Are you sure—"

"I'm fine. Put in a report with security. I'm serious; if Zeke Godfrey is seen on campus by anyone, call Princeton PD."

"Okay."

Samantha, still reeling, went back to her desk and picked up the phone.

"I told you he was unhinged." Ivy was sweating. "You should call the cops now. He grabbed you and he—"

"Zeke is just angry. And I'll be fine."

Ivy felt her upper lip curl.

"He's a psycho. You need to call the cops."

"Let me deal with Mr. Godfrey."

"Stop calling him Mr. Godfrey! His name is Zeke. I told you about the cheating and you did nothing. Now he's assaulted a student and you!"

"Dr. Reeves—"

Ivy knew that she should stop now. Couldn't do it.

"It's because his father donates money to the school, isn't it? If it were any other student who did *any* of this shit, you'd get his ass hauled out of here in cuffs. Get him thrown in a cell, right?"

"Dr. Reeves, that's enough. You're suspended pending a full investigation."

She'd gone too far. Still couldn't reel herself in, though.

"No hesitation acting now, *huh*?"

Dr. Moorehead stared her down.

"You going to leave on your own, Dr. Reeves? Or am I going to have to call security for you, too?"

Ivy ground her teeth.

"No, I'll leave. But first, I want my goddamn phone back."

CHAPTER 45

VAUGHN WAS SURPRISED to find Delaney still on the other side of the glass in the adjacent room.

"What are you doing here? Didn't you hear where Perry parked his car? The gas station?"

Vaughn expected Darnell to say something too, something more aggressive.

He didn't.

"I heard—I told Horowitz and some of the other guys to check it out."

And I told you *to do it.*

As much as he wanted to, Vaughn couldn't admonish him. If Delaney wanted to, he could go to Captain Daniels, tell him what Darnell had done. And that'd be it for Darnell.

This is all I got, man.

It was no secret that with Darnell coming in hungover, probably still drunk, and Vaughn always having to cover for him, most people thought the PPD would be better off with him gone.

They felt for him, sure, for what happened to his family, but everyone had their limits.

"Fine. You're here. You watched. What did you think?"

"I think he's a lying piece of shit."

Predictable. If Joshua Perry was their man and Delaney brought him in, he'd get that promotion to detective he was vying for.

Even if Darnell kept his post.

"I don't," Vaughn countered.

"You don't think he's lying?" Delaney sounded shocked.

"No," Vaughn said. "I don't."

"C'mon—this is all an act. He did it. He killed all those people."

"Darnell?"

"I don't know."

Great, thanks for your help. Got another one of those hunches, Darnell?

"Did you look into Josh's background? Education?"

"Yeah—GED. No college. Worked in construction last year."

"I don't think someone with no college education set up the 100 prisoners problem and the prisoner's dilemma," Vaughn said, shaking his head. "I mean, the construction worker thing would come into play building those rooms, but Darnell said that pretty much anybody can do that."

"*If* it's actually Josh Perry in that room," Delaney countered. "It could be anyone. Prints didn't ping in the system. Josh has no record."

"Did you reach out to his ex-employer?"

"No, not yet. But I'm telling you, this is our—"

Vaughn's phone rang and he held up a finger as he answered.

"Horowitz? You find his car?"

"Yes, sir. Perry had his keys on him—Delaney gave them to me. Found his wallet and phone inside."

"Name on the license?"

"Joshua Perry. Sure as hell looks like the guy that Delaney brought in."

Vaughn eyed Delaney.

"Send me photos of everything you got. Did you find an ad in there? A piece of paper?"

"I can look."

"Do it. You have someone there with you?"

"Stanley came with me."

"Good—you drive Josh's car back here, have Stanley take your car."

"Got it."

Vaughn hung up. Delaney was staring at him expectantly, but Vaughn let him squirm.

A few seconds later, Horowitz's photos came through. A couple of the exterior of a wallet, one of a black iPhone. The last was a photo of Joshua Perry's driver's license.

Vaughn frowned, turned his screen around and thrust it in Delaney's direction.

"It's Joshua Perry alright. And he's not our guy."

Even Delaney couldn't deny the resemblance.

He shrugged.

"Could still be our guy."

Vaughn didn't blame the officer for sticking to his guns. He was young and eager, and if Perry had been behind this, it would have been an incredible boon for his career.

He let it go.

"*Hmm.* Darnell and I are going upstairs. Don't talk to Perry. If he gets squirrelly or asks for a lawyer, let me know. And when Horowitz arrives, come get us."

Captain Daniels had given them a forty-eight-hour window to catch this guy. Forty-eight hours . . .

Vaughn wasn't sure they had that long before the man set up another one of his games. Usually there was an escalation with these types of crimes, these types of violent criminals.

Slow start, hesitant.

Serial killers' first murders were sloppy. They panicked, afraid of being caught, and when they weren't, they gradually became bolder.

The cool off period shortened.

This unsub had no cool off period.

Ten dead yesterday, one today.

And the planning . . . the flyers had to go out. The interiors of the barns had to be constructed. No, they weren't cooling off. They were getting hotter.

Josh Perry had said it, and all evidence indicated that at least Aaron Treadman felt the same: the ad was sketchy, but the allure of money—crypto or not—was too hard to ignore.

Something occurred to Vaughn then.

The game show. This entire time, Vaughn had been thinking of the game show as a ruse.

What if it wasn't?

It wasn't airing on a 'major streaming platform,' but what if it was airing somewhere else? What if someone was broadcasting the contestants' deaths? Possible.

Vaughn swirled his mouse, woke up his computer.

Snuff films were as old as time. It sickened him to think that people got off on watching other people die, but there was nothing he could do about it.

"Maybe this guy is—"

"Why didn't you tell me that the math chick was there?" Darnell interrupted.

"What?"

"The math chick and her father. Why didn't you tell me that they were there?"

"I don't know, man."

He knew—Vaughn didn't want Darnell to propose Ivy as a suspect again.

"Don't you think it's a little odd?"

"What?"

"Dr. Reeves's laptop was in Aaron's possession, she shows up at one of the crime scenes. She definitely knows the games. Nobody would bat an eye if she was seen wandering around the chem building, either."

Darnell had said all this before, and his hunch was beginning to bore Vaughn.

Don't bite, don't bite.

He bit.

"Why would she help us? Tell us about the games?"

"It wouldn't be the first time that an unsub inserted themselves into an investigation—you know that."

Vaughn did. Didn't believe it in this case, though. He took a different approach.

"A female serial killer? Unlikely."

"Agree in principle. But we're not talking about a mass shooting or stabbing. This is hands-off. You know the profile."

Female serial killers were rare—maybe ten percent. And when they killed, it was usually at a distance. Poisoning. Drowning. More 'quiet' methods.

Darnell saw the look on Vaughn's face and clawed back a little.

"Look, I'm not saying she's behind this, I'm just saying that she knows something. Something she's not telling us. And I want you to make sure you're not so blinded by your feelings for Dr. Ivy Reeves that you miss it."

Vaughn had been loading up a TOR browser during his conversation with his partner, but now he glanced at Darnell.

"I'm not."

At least, he didn't think he was.

CHAPTER 46

VAUGHN DIDN'T FIND anything relevant on the dark web. Two snuff films, at least one of which was likely a fake, but no game shows. But this wasn't his domain. Vaughn had just reached out to Bowes to ask him to do a deeper dive when Horowitz called.

"I'm here with Perry's car."

"Good. I'll meet you downstairs."

Horowitz must have also called Delaney because he was already outside.

"Found that ad you were looking for," Horowitz said.

He passed Vaughn a piece of paper. With gloved hands, he unfolded it.

The ad was pretty much the way that Perry described it. Simple, to the point.

Vaughn still couldn't believe that someone—twelve some-ones—had fallen for the scam. The ad mentioned a streaming service, but didn't include a name. No logos, nothing that made it appear even remotely legitimate. But money was a powerful motivator.

The most powerful motivator.

The number at the bottom was different from the one that had made the 911 call. Their unsub was using burner phones. Vaughn didn't think that tracing the number would lead anywhere, but he relayed the phone number to Bowes via text just in case.

"Hey, can I see that?"

Vaughn gave the ad to Darnell.

Next up, Perry's wallet.

The photo of the man on the New Jersey license was definitely the same person holed up in the interview room. Perry's face was a little fuller, and the man's eyes were less racooned in the picture, but it was him.

Finally, the phone. It was locked.

"Anything else in the car?"

Horowitz shook his head.

"Nothing related to either of the cases. No building materials, no receipts from hardware stores."

"Alright, let's go see if Perry will let us into the phone."

The man didn't hesitate in giving up the six digit pin.

"Did . . . did something happen to the other guy?" Perry asked hesitantly. He'd been so dazed earlier that he was only now piecing things together.

The fact that Delaney had accused him of murder. That all of this definitely wasn't just about a game show.

"Yeah, he's dead," Delaney said flatly.

"He's *dead?*"

"Delaney . . ."

"Dead?" Perry repeated.

They left Perry there, went back to the adjacent room. With Darnell and Delaney peering over his shoulder, Vaughn unlocked the phone. Navigated to the man's text messages. Again, they were just like Perry said. Same wording as the texts they'd found in Aaron's phone.

"Fuck," Vaughn muttered.

He hadn't thought that Perry was their guy, but things would be so much easier if he was.

"Cut him loose," Vaughn instructed, no longer even entertaining the idea that he was their unsub.

"But—"

"Cut him loose, Delaney. If you want, have one of your guys tail him for a bit."

Delaney straightened.

"I'll follow him."

Vaughn pictured Delaney in the field again, gun drawn. The last thing they wanted was for Delaney to do something stupid.

Stupider.

"No. Have Horowitz do it."

"But—"

"I said no, Delaney. I want you to head out to the gas station where the ad was placed under Josh's wiper—QuikTrip on Belt Line Road. See if they have security footage."

Delaney looked as if he was going to continue the argument, but let it go. Left in a huff.

Vaughn slowly headed upstairs to his and Darnell's shared office.

He hated murder boards. Thought they were mainly a waste of time, just something to do when a case stalls. And that's exactly why he decided to set one up now.

Darnell helped, but was mostly preoccupied with his phone.

Vaughn started with the ad that had been left on Josh Perry's windshield. A copy, because for some reason, Darnell insisted on keeping the original. Moved outward from there, printing out all the text messages as well as the transcripts from the two 911 calls. These calls themselves were a bit of an oddity. Whoever was behind these killings wanted the cops to know about them.

Why?

In Vaughn's experience, most unsubs did things like this for one purpose: notoriety. He made a mental note to follow up with Bowes later regarding his search of the dark web.

Delaney, for all his faults, had put in the most hours on this case. Had done some good work, too. Identified all but one of the first ten victims, had even let their significant others know when there was a significant other to notify, which was only in three of the cases.

If their unsub had a type, it was this: male, between twenty-five and fifty years old. Low socioeconomic status. Desperate enough to accept a budget ad and play a sketchy game in hopes of winning crypto. The issue with this 'type' is that it applied to nearly half of the American population.

"Darnell, you think that these victims are all chosen at random?"

Darnell's face was still buried in his phone.

"Probably. My guess is that he just put these ads in areas where he thinks desperate people hang out."

The QuikTrip on Belt Line Road fit the bill.

"Or sends them emails."

This was an assumption, but a fair one. They were still working on search warrants for the laptops of the other victims. Vaughn wasn't hopeful that this would get them anywhere. Their unsub had already proven himself perfectly capable of hiding his digital fingerprints.

Vaughn continued putting photos on the board. Added images of Dr. McGill, and the three other members in the department who had access to the gas. None of those leads had panned out. He hesitated, but then added Ivy's image, noting that her laptop had been in Treadman's possession.

Vaughn took a step back, cocked his head.

"There's one more name you might want to add," Darnell said.

"Yeah? Who's that?"

"Eugene Reeves—Ivy's father."

CHAPTER 47

Ivy was fuming. Fucking Zeke.

Fucking Dr. Moorehead, fucking donations, fucking Princeton.

Fucking *gas*.

On the short drive home, Abby called. Ivy didn't feel like answering, but she needed to vent.

"That's bullshit," Abby said after Ivy had explained the situation. "I don't understand how someone posting a video of you on TikTok is your fault."

"It's this stupid code of conduct. But you're missing the point, Abs—this Zeke kid, he's dangerous. You should have seen the look in his eyes when the security guards pulled him out of my boss's office. He was insane."

"You want me to come over? I'm at work now, but—"

"No, I'll be okay. The security guards took Zeke away."

"But if he's pissed, he might—"

"It's okay, Abs. I'll be fine. Just needed someone to talk to."

"Forget it, I'm coming over."

"Abs—"

"I'm coming, Ivy. Nothing you can say about it. Just need to wrap up a few patients first."

"I'm not—"

"I'm coming."

Ivy sighed. Abby was as stubborn as she was loyal. Besides, Abby had already hung up.

Ivy pulled into her driveway and went inside, making sure to lock the door behind her.

She didn't know what to do. Work, probably. Get going on that abstract for the conference. But that wasn't happening.

Ivy kept picturing Zeke's face. The anger in it.

The fury.

Jesus, the kid was off his rocker.

Ivy tossed her keys on the table by the door a little too aggressively, and they smacked into the only framed picture on it. It teetered, but Ivy grabbed it before it fell.

It was a photo of her family—of Ivy, her father, and her mother, taken just a few weeks before her father's accident, outside Fine Hall. The day that Ivy completed her PhD dissertation.

They all looked so happy, their smiles genuine.

Ivy stroked the side of her father's unblemished face. There was such intelligence behind those hazel eyes.

Such brilliance.

And that fucking fire . . . it took it all away.

Ivy's gaze drifted to her mother's face next. Everyone always commented on how much they looked alike. Ivy knew that this wasn't necessarily complimentary. Women didn't often like being compared to someone twenty-five years their elder. But in this case, Ivy didn't mind.

Wendy Reeves was a beautiful woman. Understated, with hair that was the same color but less curly than Ivy's own. Same heart-shaped face. Same small, slightly upturned nose.

A tear dropped on the glass and Ivy wiped it away with her thumb.

Why'd you leave, Mom? We could have gone through this together.

Ivy's thoughts turned to the night of the fire. Remembered calling her mother because her father had dialed Ivy instead of Wendy.

How things might have been different if her father had called his wife that night. Ivy had wanted to tell her mother everything. Tried to, several times. But Wendy had been so devastated by what had happened that she was intractable.

They'd both stayed by her father in the hospital, answered all the grumpy police captain's questions. Held hands.

Promised that this wouldn't break them.

For an entire week, Ivy and her mother went home only to shower and change. The rest of the time, they were at Gene's side.

Being a daughter of a professor—of mathematics, no less—and following in her father's footsteps, Ivy wasn't religious. But Ivy had prayed then. Prayed that none of this had ever happened.

God, wind back the clock. Please.

If Ivy was anything, she was a realist, the praying notwithstanding. She knew that Gene wasn't the *best* father—his work always came first. And toward the end, it had completely consumed him. Working through the night. Forgetting to shower, to eat. And when Gene had woken up from his coma, which the doctors had warned them would probably never happen, her mother knew what had really occurred. By then, it was too late for Ivy to explain. Wendy was a broken woman, and the next day, she was just gone.

No note, no email, not even a text.

She grabbed a small suitcase, packed up a few belongings, and just vanished.

Ivy stayed behind. Dealt with the—

There was a knock on the door and Ivy startled, nearly dropped the photo. Her fingers and thumb burned. She placed it down before unlocking the door.

"Abs, I think—"

Ivy had just started to turn the knob when the door was flung inward, pushing her back.

"Abs?"

A hand reached out and gripped her by the throat.

CHAPTER 48

"MATH GENIUS DEAD in Mysterious Fire," Darnell read off his phone. "Dr. Steve Neely, professor of mathematics and statistics at Princeton University, co-winner of the Fields Medal, and a strong candidate for the Nobel Prize in mathematics, was found dead in the early hours of the morning. The medical examiner reports that Dr. Neely died from asphyxiation following a fire in his rural New Jersey home. Princeton Police are investigating. Dr. Neely's partner, also a professor at Princeton, Dr. Eugene Reeves, suffered major injuries in the fire and his condition is listed as critical. He is currently in the ICU at Penn Medicine Princeton Medical Center. More details to follow."

Vaughn pictured Ivy's father and that horrible face mask. The way he just stared blankly, even when Delaney had a gun trained on him, ordering him to put up his hands.

The lack of any semblance of a response or understanding.

"Do you have access to the police report?"

Darnell nodded, swiped his screen, then continued to read.

"On June 5, 2022, at approximately 01:34 a.m., PPD responded to a residential fire at 63 Windemere Road. Two bodies were recovered from the scene. One was DOA, the other unconscious. The body inside the building was later identified as Dr. Steve Neely. Official cause of death was asphyxiation. There was evidence of blunt force trauma to the skull consistent with a fall from loss of consciousness. Impossible to determine if there was the presence of defensive wounds due to extreme burns on over 90 percent of the victim's body."

Darnell cleared his throat.

"Dr. Eugene Reeves was discovered by his daughter, who received a phone call from her father and was first on the scene—Ivy Reeves was also the one who placed the 911 call alerting PPD of the fire. Ivy dragged her father's unconscious body from the house. He had severe burns on his face. Ivy had minor burns and was treated at the scene. Dr. Reeves was unconscious and taken to PMC. He was admitted to the ICU at 2:46 a.m. A joint investigation between the fire marshal and the PPD revealed that the fire was electrical in nature. No evidence of an accelerant was present. PPD subsequently exercised a warrant on both parties' cell phones and computers. No computers were found at the scene or in either party's place of work. An escalating series of text messages between the two mathematicians was discovered (see accompanying notes). These appeared to be work-related—Dr. Neely and Dr. Reeves were colleagues at Princeton. The final message was written by Dr. Reeves and had a read receipt: *Don't you dare fucking do anything. This is my work.*"

Darnell scrolled a little. Paused. His thick brow lowered.

"Ah, here we go: 'Due to the lack of material witnesses and the origin of the fire being consistent with a faulty circuit breaker, the case is officially marked as suspicious. Dr. Reeves awoke from a coma seven days after being admitted to the hospital, an outcome that the doctors initially claimed was unlikely. Interview attempts with Dr. Reeves proved unsuccessful; degradation of the Broca's area of the brain from oxygen deprivation was observed, which appears to have affected the victim's ability to communicate verbally or in writing. Interviews with the man's wife and daughter did not reveal anything pertinent to the investigation. They claimed to be unaware of any strife between the two men.'" Darnell raised his eyes. "Now, you wanna put Eugene Reeves on the board?"

Vaughn frowned.

"He's nonverbal. Can't write."

"Still ambulatory, though—according to you," Darnell countered.

"I saw him in the field. The man is practically a vegetable."

"Maybe that's what Dr. Reeves is hiding. Maybe she's covering for her dad, maybe he's behind this."

"Yeah right." Vaughn paused. "Wait—You serious?"

"I'm serious.

"C'mon, Darnell. That's ridiculous. Delaney had a gun on him, told him to put his hands up. He just stood there."

"An unarmed old white dude in a field? With two witnesses? Not much risk of being shot."

"Delaney was screaming at him, at all of them. Darnell—Hey, where are you going?"

Darnell flashed his phone.

"To visit the detective who investigated the fire. 'Practically a vegetable' isn't good enough for me, Vaughn. Not by a long shot." It looked as if Darnell was about to wink, but smartly decided not to. "And I've got a hunch."

CHAPTER 49

Retired Detective Doug Howe sat in a wicker chair on his front porch, smoking a cigarette. He was fat with unruly gray hair. A wide nose, heavily lined face. Pockmarked skin, a telltale sign of long-term alcohol abuse. The man was a weathered detective if Vaughn had ever seen one. Beside the ashtray overflowing with cigarettes was a half-empty bottle of vodka.

The man said nothing as they approached, just butted out his smoke and sipped from a glass of clear liquid and ice. Howe's flowing movements suggested that this wasn't his first drink of the day. As did his flushed complexion.

"Doug? Doug Howe?" Vaughn said as he and Darnell approached.

"What do you want, officers?"

Doug's voice matched his appearance: gruff.

"Detectives—Ryan and Sacker."

Doug had no reaction to this. He lit another smoke, took another sip.

"If you want to talk about Neely and Reeves, I can get you a glass. You're going to need one." Doug tilted his drink in their direction.

"No thanks."

Vaughn was surprised with how fast Darnell responded. Probably didn't want to let this sit, give Howe an opportunity to convince him. Wouldn't have taken much.

"Suit yourself."

"How did you know we were here about the fire?" Vaughn asked as Howe refilled his glass with a healthy pour.

"It's coming up on the third anniversary." Howe shrugged. "And it's always on my mind. You know how they say that when you retire, there's that one case that just messes with you? That you can't get out of your head?"

Vaughn nodded just to humor the man. It wasn't the claim he disagreed with, it was the use of the word 'one.' Vaughn wasn't close to retiring, not by a long shot, but already several cases nagged him daily.

"That was my case. And before you ask, yes, I think that Eugene Reeves started the fire."

Vaughn didn't think that this was anywhere close to what Darnell was going to ask, but it didn't seem to faze his partner.

"What makes you say that?" Darnell said.

Another shrug.

"Experience."

"I read the report—we both did," Vaughn said. He knew that not everything made it into these reports. Still . . . "Fire was consistent with a faulty circuit—"

"Due to the lack of material witnesses and the origin of the fire being consistent with a faulty circuit breaker, the case is officially marked as suspicious," Howe said, citing the words from the report verbatim. "The captain made me write that. I know Dr. Reeves started the fire, just couldn't prove it. I read the text messages. The two professors were in a fight, something to do with their work. And don't ask me what the hell they were working on. Spent weeks trying to understand it, but didn't come close to figuring it out." Howe took a heavy pull on his drink. Licked his lips. "The two are fighting and Reeves heads over to Neely's house. Reeves starts the fire, plunks Neely on the head. Don't know for sure with what, but if I had to guess, it was this giant paperweight shaped like a chess piece. ME said that it wasn't 'inconsistent' with a fall from lack of consciousness."

Vaughn thought about Dr. Button, how he spoke exactly like that. Not inconsistent. Likely. Probably. Nothing definitive. MEs always created a loophole for themselves to avoid contradicting an expert witness in court.

"But you still signed off on it." Vaughn was trying not to come off as defensive, but was doing a piss-poor job.

"No choice. No witnesses, no hard evidence. I tried to keep the case open, but the university got involved."

"The university?" Vaughn was taken aback.

"You surprised? Princeton's operating budget is almost three billion dollars annually. So, yeah, when two of their biggest stars get into a fight and one of them dies in a fire? The other in a coma? They want that mess cleaned up real quick. No loose ends. They pressured the captain, and he made me close the case."

"Who was the captain back then?"

"Daniels."

Vaughn glanced over at his partner.

That explained why Daniels had been so adamant about not wanting Ivy involved. Her father a walking vegetable, his partner dead, and the daughter a special consultant on a case involving a series of mass murders? That was the epitome of 'messy.' Daniels didn't like being left out of the loop, the press, and definitely didn't like 'messy.'

"The real question is, why the hell are you guys here asking about the professors? I know Daniels is still in charge, and he sure as shit ain't letting you reopen the case."

Vaughn hesitated, not sure how much he wanted to share with the retired detective. Darnell had no such qualms.

"There's been a series of murders—all part of these weird math games."

"Hmm." Doug took a drag of his cigarette . "And you think that Dr. Reeves might have something to do with them?"

"Or his daughter," Darnell said sharply.

Howe's eyebrows rose.

"Ivy?"

"You remember her?" Vaughn asked a little too quickly.

"Of course. Interviewed her a couple of times about the fire—she was first on the scene. Dr. Reeves called her from inside the house. Call lasted almost a minute, but when I asked her, she said that she couldn't remember exactly what her father said. A lot of yelling, panic. Always felt that something was a little off about her."

"You think she was lying?"

"I don't know."

"Let's back up a second. If your theory is correct," Vaughn said, "what happened to Dr. Reeves? He brains his partner and then doesn't leave the burning house? Why didn't he just run out?"

"Don't know that either. Maybe he wanted to make sure

the fire destroyed the evidence, which it did. Maybe he just tripped and fell. He was a math professor, after all. A real *mathlete.*"

"How did Ivy seem?"

Vaughn wished Darnell would stop asking about her. It felt . . . dirty, somehow.

"How did she seem? Devastated. She and her mother stayed by her father's side the entire time he was in the hospital. Stayed even after he woke up and her mother left."

Now it was Vaughn's turn to lift his brow. This was the first mention of Ivy's mother.

"Her mother?"

"Yep—Wendy Reeves. Couldn't handle the idea of looking after her vegetable of a husband for the rest of her—or his—life. Don't blame her."

"How long—"

Darnell interrupted Vaughn.

"*Is* he a vegetable?"

For a long time, Howe said nothing. He just smoked and drank.

And then, "You know what? That's something I've asked myself a thousand times. I honestly have no idea."

CHAPTER 50

Ivy batted at the arm that gripped her throat, scratched at it. She was struggling to breathe, her airway slowly being closed off.

Shoved backward, Ivy barely managed to stay on her feet. Then her ass hit something—a table?—and she fell, her head bouncing off the hard tile.

The man went with her, knocking what little air she had left out of her lungs.

The fall, however, forced her attacker to release his hold on her throat.

Ivy blinked, tried to clear her darkening vision. Her head swelled. She barely had enough presence of mind to kick with her legs.

Hit something.

Heard a grunt.

Ivy scooted backward. Finally got a clear look at her attacker.

It was Zeke, and the man was brandishing an eight-inch blade.

A blade that was covered in blood.

My blood?

Ivy did a quick mental inventory of her body. Her head ached and her throat was raw. But she didn't feel any stab wounds.

"Don't move," Zeke warned. "Don't you fucking move."

Ivy wasn't sure she could, even if she thought Zeke was bluffing.

She knew he wasn't.

"Please . . ."

Zeke looked like he was in physical pain, the way he was snarling, but Ivy didn't think that her weak kick could have done that much damage.

The blue polo he'd been wearing earlier in Dr. Moorehead's office, and was still wearing now, was heavy and dark with blood.

"Zeke, think about what you're doing."

Ivy coughed. It felt as if she'd swallowed a cactus.

Zeke came forward, leading with the knife.

Ivy screamed and closed her eyes. When she didn't feel the cold metal slip into her chest or stomach, she slowly opened them again.

Zeke seemed confused, as if he wasn't sure how he'd gotten here. The man was staring at the knife. Turning it over in his hand. Eyes locked on the blood; it had a jelly-like consistency as it clotted on the metal.

"My dad . . . you don't understand . . ."

Ivy wasn't sure what to do, what to say.

"Why didn't you just let it go?" Zeke sobbed now. "Why couldn't you just let it the *fuck* go?"

"I will." Speaking made Ivy's throat hurt. Nodding made

her head throb even more. "I'll forget all about the cheating, and I'll even tell Rebecca—"

"It's all your fault! All your *fucking* fault! My dad is going to kill me!" Zeke roared.

He lunged again with his knife, but this time, Ivy didn't close her eyes or scream.

Wouldn't give him the satisfaction of enjoying her fear.

Zeke stopped himself. Pulled the knife back a second time.

"I didn't . . . oh, God . . . I didn't mean to hurt anyone . . . I just . . . I wanted to talk . . ."

Ivy coughed again. Spat something thick on the floor beside her.

"Who? Zeke, who did you hurt?"

"Hurt?" His eyes watered. "I . . . I killed . . . oh, *fuck* . . ." Zeke brought the blade to within inches of her face. Tears wet his cheeks as he bared his teeth. "You made me do this, Ivy. *You* made me do this."

CHAPTER 51

"You wanna add Eugene Reeves to the murder board now, Vaughn?"

Vaughn did not and said as much.

"You can't think this is all a coincidence. The fact that he—"

"Look, I agreed to go speak to him. Let's start with that."

"You heard Detective Howe. He thinks that Dr. Reeves is faking his injuries."

That wasn't even close to what the retired detective had actually said, but Vaughn let it lie.

They parked in the assisted living facility lot. It looked much different up close during the day; less ominous.

Vaughn made his way to the front desk, which was unoccupied. There was one of those old-fashioned bells sitting atop it and he reached out to make it chime.

Before he did, however, a woman turned the corner.

It was the same woman that had been in the field with Ivy last night. She was wearing a similar smock, but it was white with small pink flowers instead of blue.

Her head was down.

"Sarah, right?"

She stopped and Vaughn tried to smile. Wasn't sure he succeeded.

"Ms. Kachinski," she corrected. It was clear that in the intervening hours since their last meeting, she'd gone over things in her head.

And she wasn't happy about what had transpired.

Fucking Delaney.

"Sorry—Ms. Kachinski. I'm Detective Vaughn Ryan and this is Detective Darnell Sacker."

"I remember you," Sarah said, meaning Vaughn.

Vaughn was on the fence about apologizing for what had gone down in the field, but before he could say anything, Darnell spoke up.

"Ms. Kachinski, can we ask you a few questions?"

She put her hands on her hips. Didn't say yes, but didn't say no, either.

"Just a couple of questions about Dr. Reeves—Eugene Reeves."

"What about him?"

"Can you tell us where he was two nights ago?"

"He was—" Her brow furrowed. "Two nights ago?"

"Yes."

"He was in the field."

"The same field as last night?" Vaughn said.

"No, not that one. There's a field of Queen Anne's lace behind the home. Dr. Reeves wanders there sometimes."

"And he was there two nights ago?" Vaughn asked, deliberately avoiding looking at Darnell.

"Yes."

"Unattended?"

Vaughn didn't appreciate Darnell's word choice. It made the esteemed doctor sound like a child. A once brilliant math professor being led around by the hand or worse, by one of those humiliating body harnesses attached to a leash.

"Like I said, around this time of year, Dr. Reeves wanders a lot."

"Because of the fire?"

Ms. Kachinski nodded.

"We would like to speak to Dr. Reeves," Darnell said.

The request seemed to annoy the aide.

"Dr. Reeves does not speak. Hasn't said a single word in three years."

Annoyed or not, she seemed broken up about this.

"We're aware," Darnell said. "How bad is he?"

"What do you mean?"

"Can he . . . I dunno, look after himself?" Darnell was at least trying to be considerate.

"Sure. He can feed himself, go to the bathroom on his own. Sometimes needs help with his food, depending on what it is. Cutting smaller pieces, that sort of thing. But he can't speak and he can't write."

"We'd still like to try."

Ms. Kachinski reluctantly agreed. Dr. Reeves, despite his injuries, was still a grown man, after all. The rules regarding interviewing an adult of diminished capacity were sketchy. Because you couldn't Mirandize a man who didn't understand, it was unlikely that anything Dr. Reeves told them here today would be admissible.

But if he gave them something that could set them on the right path, that was a different story.

He won't. He can't speak. Doesn't understand.

"You're wasting your time," Sarah muttered under her breath.

She navigated the hallways, stopped in front of a door before opening it for them.

They found Dr. Reeves sitting on a chair in the center of the small, boxy apartment, his back to them. He didn't react to his door being opened. The man's mangled right hand—comprised of fingers that were unnaturally short and lacked fingernails—was gripping a chess piece. A rook.

He moved it straight across a small, thin chessboard resting on a table. Placed it on the other side. It was the only piece on the board.

Dr. Reeves starts the fire, plunks Neely on the head. Don't know for sure with what, but if I had to guess, it was this giant paperweight shaped like a chess piece.

"Dr. Reeves?" Darnell said.

No response.

They walked around to Dr. Reeves's front.

Darnell stopped abruptly when they got a clear view of his face. Vaughn had already seen the strange peach mask that Dr. Reeves wore, but it was only marginally less unsettling now.

It smoothed all his features, like the thick nylon stockings that bank robbers always wore in the movies. Only in this case, his nose jutted from a hole, and there were additional openings for his eyes and lips.

The man's eyes appeared more or less normal, and even

his nose, pink and smooth, seemed only slightly unusual. In fairness, his nose looked better than retired Detective Howe's. But the color of Dr. Reeves's lips was wrong, and they lacked defined borders.

"I—I—" Darnell was too flustered to form sentences.

As petty as it was, Vaughn relished seeing his partner, who always had an insult or quip at the ready, at a loss for words. He let the awkwardness settle for a moment before taking over.

Vaughn also mentally rescinded roughly half of his scathing remarks about Delaney from last night. Coming across Dr. Reeves in this mask in the middle of a field, after just seeing another person dead to gas, must have been a shocking sight.

"Dr. Reeves, my name is Detective Vaughn Ryan, and this is Detective Darnell Sacker. Mind if we ask you a few questions?"

No response.

"Can you tell us what you were doing in the field last night?" Vaughn asked.

Nothing.

"Dr. Reeves, are you familiar with the 100 prisoners problem or the prisoner's dilemma?" Vaughn asked, thinking that appealing to the mathematical part of the man's brain might trigger something. If anything clicked with him, it would be this.

Still nothing.

"Dr. Reeves—"

"Tell us about your daughter, Dr. Reeves. Tell us about Ivy."

Darnell had found his tongue. Vaughn wasn't positive, but

he thought Dr. Reeves cocked his head, just a little. Then he grabbed the rook and squeezed it in his mangled hand.

"Dr. Reeves? Tell us about Ivy."

No movement this time.

"Dr. Reeves—"

"Darnell, let's go," Vaughn said. Darnell didn't move. "Darnell?"

"I told you he doesn't speak. If you think that he is somehow responsible for whatever happened last night—"

"Ms. Kachinski, do you guys have a printer here?" Darnell interrupted.

Sarah was taken aback.

"Of course—in the main office."

"Think I could use it real quick?"

"For what?" Kachinski was suspicious now.

"Need to print something out for my taxes."

"Seriously?"

"Seriously. The printer at the PD is busted."

Darnell was lying, but Vaughn had no idea where his partner was going with this.

"S-sure. I guess?"

They left Dr. Reeves standing where he was, hovering over the small chess board, and Ms. Kachinski led them down the hall. They passed several other patients, one in a wheelchair, but none wearing a mask.

"He always wear that mask?" Vaughn asked.

"Not always. But his face . . . some of the other guests find his appearance disturbing."

"That bad, huh?"

Ms. Kachinski nodded.

"The printer's in here."

Darnell thanked the nurse and ducked into a small office.

When they were alone, Kachinski said, unprompted, "Ivy's a good woman. She stayed by her father's side. It would have been so easy for her to just bury herself in her work. Drop him off here and never come back. But she didn't. The man's insurance pays the bills, so . . ." Ms. Kachisnki paused, considering what she'd said earlier. "Even Gene's wife left."

This was the second mention of Wendy Reeves in as many hours.

"You ever meet her?"

The nurse shook her head.

"No. But Ivy visits at least once a week. Plays chess with her dad."

Vaughn cocked his head.

"He plays chess?"

"No. He just sits there while Ivy moves the pieces around. Talks math with him."

Darnell exited the office, a piece of paper in one hand.

"Got it," he said. Vaughn tried to look at what the man had printed, but couldn't make it out. "Thanks again." Darnell produced a card. "Can you do us a favor? If Dr. Reeves leaves again, can you give us a call?"

Ms. Kachinski made the card disappear.

"Thank you."

Another business card. So far, their investigation amounted to little more to handing out damn cards.

CHAPTER 52

"What's with the printer thing?" Vaughn asked.

Darnell grabbed the printout, which Vaughn now saw seemed to be random words. The ol' *lorem ipsum* Latin placeholder text repeated over and over. Then Darnell produced the ad that had been in Josh Perry's possession. Darnell held them side by side.

"Bowes told me a couple of months back that printed pages are like fingerprints—they can be matched to the exact printer."

"C'mon, you can't honestly think that the man we saw back there had anything to do with these murders."

Darnell shrugged.

"I dunno . . . math games . . . being at the site? That creepy mask?"

Vaughn pressed his lips together.

"C'mon, Darnell."

"Maybe it's his daughter."

"For fuck's sake. She's *helping* us."

"She's inserting herself into the case. Guiding us where she wants us to go, where to look. Sure, she might be helping us, but maybe she's also helping *him*."

Again, Vaughn found himself entertaining his partner's ludicrous theories. Couldn't help it.

"We went to *her*, we asked *her* about the crime scenes, not the other way around."

Darnell refused to give it up.

"Yeah, sure, but *why*?"

"Why what?"

"Why did we go to her?"

"Because she knows math?"

Darnell shook his head.

"No, we went to her because when I started looking up prime numbers, she was the first name to pop up."

Now Vaughn understood. Didn't agree, though.

"You can't possibly think she posted that video herself so that we would notice her. Besides, even if there was no video, we would have probably eventually gone to the math department to help us out."

Darnell tilted his head dramatically.

Vaughn hated when his partner did this. Somehow tricked you into saying what he was thinking, then twisting it around.

"To the math department, yes, but probably not specifically to her. I know you've got a thing for her, Vaughn. Don't let that—"

"I don't have a thing for her."

"Yeah, right," he scoffed. "We should interview her. Find out if Ivy has an alibi for the past two nights."

The last thing Vaughn wanted was for Darnell to speak to Ivy.

"I'll tell you what: I'll drop you at the station to get Bowes to do his forensic printer shit. *I'll* speak with Ivy."

Darnell winked.

"Private time. I get it."

As Darnell was getting out of the car, Vaughn thought about changing his mind. If Delaney was still hanging around, things could get ugly.

"Darnell?"

The man turned.

"Yeah?"

Vaughn's partner was momentarily unguarded. Like in the car when Vaughn had torn a strip off him, he saw the real Darnell. The one who was hurting so badly that the only way he could get through the day was to drink, crack inappropriate jokes, and lash out. And drink some more.

"Earth to Vaughn?"

"Stay away from Delaney, okay?"

"Wouldn't go near that little shit with a ten-foot pole."

As long as you stay out of arm's reach, Vaughn thought as he drove off.

Being the middle of a weekday, Vaughn assumed that Ivy was at work. Decided to call ahead just to make sure. Vaughn was surprised when a man answered the number that he'd found in the campus directory for Ivy's office. He identified himself as her TA, Tristan Coates.

The response he got when asking for Ivy perplexed Vaughn even more.

"What do you mean she's on temporary leave?" Vaughn asked. "I just saw her yesterday."

"I'm just telling you what I was told by the department head. Dr. Reeves is on temporary leave until further notice."

His first thought was that after what had happened with her father and the gun-toting Delaney, Ivy had taken a personal day. But "temporary leave until further notice" sounded more disciplinary than voluntary.

"Listen, Tristan, any way you can give me Ivy's home address?"

"I'm not supposed to do that."

"I get it, but it'll save me time. She's a special consultant on a case we're working." Vaughn pictured Captain Daniels's red face as he said this. "If I have to call the math department and go through regular channels—"

"You said you were a detective?"

"Yeah, I saw you the other day in her office. I'm Detective Vaughn Ryan with the PPD." Vaughn gave his badge number too, hoping to reassure the man.

"Hold on a second."

The phone muted. Vaughn tapped his foot as he waited. Grew impatient.

Figuring that Ivy probably lived close to Fine Hall where she worked, he started driving in that direction.

Tristan came back on the line.

"Okay, your name and badge number check out."

He gave Vaughn Ivy's home address.

"Appreciate it."

Vaughn hung up and stepped on the gas a little.

Something felt off about this.

About all of this.

CHAPTER 53

"You don't have to do this, Zeke. *Please.*"

The kid had gone mad. Lost his fucking mind.

And he'd killed someone.

More than one person? The people in the barn?

Rebecca?

Ivy had heard stories about people in dire situations such as this. How victims had humanized themselves, even went as far as to sympathize with their captors.

Do anything and everything to avoid becoming a victim themselves.

Ivy considered what Vaughn had told her about the 100 prisoners problem and the prisoner's dilemma. How the detective had just assumed that these were random guessing games.

Thought of Penney's game for some reason, too. The coin flip sequence contest that she'd exploited to win countless times in a row.

And Blake.

Six-foot-five, blue eyes, trust fund.

If Blake was here now, he'd have no problem taking the knife away from this psycho.

"Those people? The ones who were gassed? If they'd been smarter, if they'd been smart like you and I, they would have made it. It's *their* fault they died."

It pained her to say this, but she was desperate.

Zeke's lips twisted.

"Gassed?"

"The prisoner's dilemma, the 100 prisoners problem. They could have gotten out. If only they'd—"

"What the hell are you talking about?"

"The—"

"You and your stupid fucking math. I didn't want to hurt her. I just wanted to talk. Tell her I was sorry, that I didn't mean to . . . oh, fuck . . . this is so fucked up. So fucked—"

"Zeke—"

The door that Zeke had barged through was still hanging open.

Now it flew inward, and as much as she tried to resist, Ivy couldn't help but scream again.

CHAPTER 54

VAUGHN WAS ABOUT to knock on the half-open door when he heard a man's voice from inside Ivy's home.

"You and your stupid fucking math. I didn't want to hurt her. I just wanted to talk. Tell her I was sorry, that I didn't mean to . . . oh, fuck . . . this is so fucked up. So fucked—"

Vaughn didn't hesitate. While reaching for his gun, he kicked the door. It smacked into a table and something fell.

Shattered.

Saw Ivy on the floor, on her back, a man in a blue shirt hovering over her. Vaughn charged, intent on driving his shoulder into the man's spine, open field tackle style.

At the last second, the man turned—just a kid, Vaughn's mind had enough time to register—and slashed at him with a knife. The blade cut into Vaughn's forearm, but he kept charging.

Instead of hitting the kid in the back, he struck him in the side, his shoulder connecting with the man's kidney. Vaughn heard him grunt, heard all the air *whoosh* out of his lungs.

They went to the ground together, the kid beneath Vaughn taking the brunt of the fall. The knife skittered across the floor.

"Ivy!" Vaughn yelled. He laced a forearm—bloody, he saw—across the kid's throat, pushed all his weight down. "Ivy, you okay?"

The kid bucked, and Vaughn moved his knee to his chest, keeping his forearm pressed to his windpipe.

"I'm okay. I'm fine."

"Stop fucking moving," Vaughn warned.

The kid on the ground was making a strange hissing noise and spit flew from his lips. Landed back on his red face.

He stopped wriggling.

Vaughn grabbed his handcuffs from the back of his belt. With his free hand, he gripped the kid's wrist and then lifted his knee. In a practiced move, he flipped him over, replaced his knee in the small of his back. When he pushed the man's arm up toward his shoulder blade, the kid cried out.

Vaughn applied the cuffs. One hand first, then the next.

"Stay on your stomach," Vaughn said. "You so much as move and I'm going to pin you down again."

The kid tried to say something, but only managed to cough instead. Vaughn lifted his knee, stayed low.

"Ivy?"

She came over to him.

"You okay?"

Ivy was rubbing her throat, which was raw and red. Vaughn couldn't see any other injuries.

"Yeah."

Her eyes were wide.

"You're . . . you've been cut."

"Huh?"

Vaughn followed her gaze to his left forearm. There was a

six-inch gash that ran from his elbow to just beyond the meaty part. Vaughn probed it gently. It wasn't deep. Blood leaked from the wound, but he didn't think it warranted stitches.

"Who the hell is this kid?"

"He's one of my students. Zeke Godfrey."

The surname tickled something in the back of Vaughn's mind.

He removed his phone, thought about calling Darnell. Decided to dial Delaney instead. Told the cop he needed backup and EMS. Gave Ivy's address and hung up quickly before the man could ask questions.

"What happened?" Vaughn asked Ivy.

"He broke in." She continued to massage her throat. "Grabbed me. Threatened to *kill* me."

Vaughn had been squatting over the kid, but now dropped his knee back down. Ground it into his spine.

"I said stop moving."

Zeke hadn't moved.

"And he's a student of yours?" Vaughn's mind went to the two crime scenes. "A math student?"

"Yes."

"Did he say anything about the—?"

"Lawy—"

"Shut up." Vaughn pressed harder.

"He said he didn't mean to hurt—" Ivy cleared her throat. Grimaced. "He blamed me."

"You like to kill people, kid? Play these fucking math games?"

"Lawy—lawyer."

"I'll get something for your arm."

Ivy darted from the front hall, returned a few seconds later with some alcohol pads and tissue. She quickly cleaned the wound. Now that he could see it better, Vaughn confirmed that it wouldn't require stitches.

"What else did he say? Did he admit to the other murders?"

Zeke twisted a little at this.

"Stop!"

"No . . . he said . . . he said . . . Vaughn, I don't think this about the gassing. I think—I think he killed Rebecca."

CHAPTER 55

Ivy was standing outside with Vaughn while Zeke sat on his heels, his wrists cuffed behind him, his chin down. Her heart was still racing, and no amount of deep breathing could coerce it into slowing down.

Zeke had only said one word since Vaughn had taken him down: "Lawyer."

"Who is he?" Vaughn asked as they waited for backup to arrive.

Ivy briefly told Vaughn about the cheating, about what Zeke had said at the bar. Him standing outside her building and the alleged confrontation between Rebecca and Zeke.

"Jesus, why didn't you tell me?"

Ivy opened her mouth, but no words came out.

Why *didn't* she tell him?

She'd had ample opportunity. And she'd helped him with his case.

Cases.

Tit-for-tat.

She inhaled sharply.

"I don't know."

A squad car pulled up and a cop Ivy recognized hopped out. The one from the field.

The one who had pointed a gun at them.

She moved a little closer to Vaughn.

"Who the fuck is this guy?" Delaney asked, hooking a chin toward Zeke. "Is he—"

"Don't know. Book him for B&E, ag assault on an LEO, weapons charges. Throw the fucking book at him. Haven't Mirandized him, but he's asked for a lawyer."

"Jesus."

"I need to head to a secondary location—take him in." Then to Ivy, "You stay here."

Ivy shook her head; she didn't want to be anywhere near this cop.

A knowing look passed over Vaughn's face.

"Never mind—I'm taking her with me. I'll bring her into the station after."

Delaney was about to question this, but a stern look from Vaughn shut him down. Seniority and all that.

"You know where this Rebecca lives?"

Vaughn started to walk toward his car, and Ivy went with him.

"I can find out."

She called Tristan.

"Tristan, I need—"

"Hey, did you hear from that cop? Detective Ryan? I gave him your address. Wasn't sure—"

"It's fine. I need your help."

"With what?"

"Log into the student database, find an address for Rebecca Quinn."

"Rebecca? Is she okay?"

"I don't know. Please, hurry."

Tristan gave her the address and Ivy relayed it to Vaughn.

"It's not far."

Rebecca was a scholarship kid and lived in a cheap apartment that was part of student housing. First floor, motel style.

Vaughn double-parked in front of her door.

"Stay here, okay?" Vaughn said, placing a hand on her arm.

Ivy nodded.

"I'll be right back."

Vaughn exited the car, drawing his weapon as he did.

Ivy watched for a moment, saw that like hers, Rebecca's front door hung open.

This is my fault. I should have pushed Dr. Moorehead harder. Forced him to call the cops. And if he refused to do it, I should have done it myself.

Without thinking, Ivy found herself getting out of the car just as Vaughn ducked inside Rebecca's apartment.

It's all my fault.

Ivy pushed open the door.

The air was heavy with the smell of blood.

Coppery, thick.

The apartment was small, maybe seven hundred square feet, with an open layout.

She found Vaughn in the kitchen, hunched over. A chair had been knocked to the ground and a rectangular kitchen table was askew.

Something in the back of Ivy's mind told her to get out. To not look.

To do anything *but* look.

She couldn't help herself.

Ivy took three steps to her left, and her line of sight cleared the laminate countertop. Vaughn was pressing the first two fingers of his hand to the side of Rebecca's neck.

There was blood everywhere—sticky puddles on the ground.

Rebecca's eyes were wide open.

When Vaughn exhaled and pulled his hand back, Ivy gasped.

CHAPTER 56

You should've waited in the car.

Vaughn wrapped his arm around Ivy and escorted her from the building. She was trembling. Whispering that this was all her fault.

"It's not—it's *not* your fault."

Ivy sobbed once. Rebecca Quinn was dead, knife wound to the throat, God only knew where else. Still holding Ivy, Vaughn called Darnell.

"What the hell is going on, Vaughn? I'm hearing from Delaney that—"

"I need CSU." Vaughn gave the address. "One dead."

"*Dead*? Another gassing?"

"No, knife wound."

Ivy whimpered.

"It's not your fault," he repeated. "Darnell, hurry the fuck up."

After he got off the phone, he called Delaney again.

"What's up? CSU just arrived."

"Stack murder one to those charges, Delaney. Throw Zeke Godfrey in a cell. I want to be the first to speak to him."

"Murder—"

"Just do it."

He hung up.

"I should have called you," Ivy whined. "I should have told you about Zeke, about—"

Vaughn removed his arm from Ivy's shoulder and spun her around. Looked directly into her watery eyes.

"Look at me."

She did.

"This is not your fault, okay? You didn't do this. You are not responsible for this. You went to your department head with your concerns, right?"

Ivy didn't answer.

"Ivy," Vaughn said, more sternly now. "This isn't your fault."

"But if I'd—"

"And if my grandma had wheels, she'd be a bicycle," Vaughn said, pulling out his best Darnell-ism.

Ivy made a face.

"Wh-what?"

"Come here."

He embraced her. Held her tightly to his chest until her breathing regulated. Only let go when Darnell arrived on scene.

"What the hell, Vaughn? What—" He noticed Ivy. "What is *she* doing here? The captain—"

"A student attacked her in her home. He told her that he'd hurt someone, and she suspected another student. Got the address. She's DOA inside. Apparent knife wound."

"Jesus. What about the suspect?"

"In custody."

Vaughn glanced down at his arm. Ivy had done a good job of cleaning him up. It was nothing more than a scratch.

"Who—"

"Delaney has him—in booking now."

"Delaney? You called *Delaney*?"

A CSU van pulled up and Landon got out.

"I'll brief Landon. Get him to coordinate with the tech at Ivy's place—the knife is still there. Probable murder weapon."

"This related to the other murders?"

Ivy shook her head.

"Not sure. Maybe. The suspect has already lawyered up."

"His father is Devon Godfrey," Ivy said in a small voice.

"Shit, *the* Devon Godfrey?" Darnell swore.

It clicked—why the surname had sounded familiar to Vaughn. Devon Godfrey was a power broker in Jersey. If he wasn't worth a billion yet, he was damn close. Vaughn was also aware that Devon had donated quite a bit of money to the PPD.

"Yeah, *that* Devon Godfrey," Ivy confirmed.

"Fuck. I'll call the captain," Darnell said. His eyes drifted to Ivy. "He's not going to be happy about this."

"No, he won't. We meet Delaney at the station, interview Ivy first. Then we call the captain."

"He's not going to be happy about that either," Darnell reiterated.

"I don't give a fuck. Ivy, I'll be right back."

Vaughn whistled, called Landon over. Met him halfway.

"We need masks for this one?"

"No. Knife wound. One victim—deceased. Weapon should be at the secondary location."

Landon nodded.

"Delaney called that in already. I have a team over there."

"Good. I need everything by the book with this one. Suspect's father is a heavy hitter."

"Understood."

Vaughn returned to Darnell and Ivy. The way they fell silent the moment he came near suggested that they must have been conversing. His efforts to calm Ivy down had been erased. She seemed more agitated than ever.

Fucking Darnell.

"This is all over the radio, Vaughn. If we want to get an interview in before the captain catches wind of it, we should move now. I can take—"

"No. I'll take Ivy. You take your own car."

"You think that's a good idea?"

"I don't care if it's a good idea. She's coming with me."

And I'm running the interview.

CHAPTER 57

"You want some more water?" Vaughn asked.

Ivy shook her head.

"You know you're being recorded, right?"

A nod.

"Okay, so we're just going to ask you a few questions about what happened. If you need a break or want to end the interview at any moment, that is your right. You are not a suspect, but you can seek legal counsel if you want."

"I understand. I'm good."

Ivy was a tough woman. Had to be, to have gone through what she had with her father. But she'd seen more death in the past two days than most cops did during their first few years on the job.

"Tell us a little about your student, about Zeke Godfrey."

"He's in my class. First year student. About two weeks ago, my TA and I suspected that he had cheated on a test. Brought it to the attention of my department head, Dr. Moorehead. Then just this week, my TA caught him again. His answers were identical to another student's: Rebecca Quinn. Again, I told my department head. He said he would investigate. I was also made aware of the fact that Zeke's father was a big donor." Ivy paused to sip her water. "I was at a bar with a friend when Zeke first approached me. He was angry, somehow found out about the accusations—angry and aggressive."

"Did he touch you?" Vaughn asked.

"No."

"Do you remember exactly what he said?"

"Not exactly, no. But he was so mad . . ."

"Any witnesses?" Darnell piped in.

"My friend Abby Granger and a guy named Blake, but I don't have his number—Abby does. Don't know his last name." She stopped then, glanced off to one side.

Darnell scribbled this down.

"What happened next?"

"Zeke didn't show up to class two days later. Rebecca did and told me that Zeke came up to her the day prior, threatened her. Grabbed her arm, demanded that she take back the cheating allegations. The thing is, Rebecca didn't say anything about the cheating. It was the TA who brought it to my attention. Wait—I have a photo." Ivy started to reach into her pocket for her phone.

"We can get that later," Darnell said sternly.

Vaughn frowned. Darnell refused to meet his eyes.

"Did you go back to your boss?" Darnell asked. "After you found out what the other student said Zeke did to her?"

"I did. But I was ambushed. Zeke was already there. He made up this story about me harassing him at the bar. Then, in class—well, you guys know about the video, the TikTok thing. In the video, one of the other students made a comment, something about Zeke and . . . gonorrhea, I think. He told the department head that *I* made the comment, which I did not. I countered with what Rebecca told me, and he went crazy. Dr. Moorehead had to call security. Moorehead said—" Ivy sighed, rubbed her eyes. "He said that if Zeke stepped back onto the campus, he was to be arrested. Then he suspended me for breach of contract. It's bullshit."

"Huh." Darnell playing the old, dumb cop now. The man had a million personas. "At any point did you think of calling the police? I mean, your student was assaulted, and you were harassed."

"Darnell!"

Ivy answered anyway.

"I—I wanted to. But I thought—"

"You thought what? You already told us that this student had threatened you and assaulted a fellow student. Did you not think that—"

"Darnell!"

Vaughn sidled closer to the man.

"What? She's a smart woman. She—"

"—is not a suspect. She hasn't been Mirandized. If you keep interrogating—"

"I'm not interrogating her."

Darnell fidgeted and his eyes darted.

Unbelievable.

"Take a walk."

Darnell completely ignored him.

"Where were you last night? Did you meet with your father before we found—"

"Darnell, take a walk. *Now.*"

Vaughn was at his wit's end. If Darnell didn't leave now, he would physically remove his partner.

A series of shouts from the hallway saved Vaughn from cutting whatever fine thread of friendship remained between the two of them.

"Where's Captain Daniels?"

"Damn it—that must be Zeke's father," Vaughn mumbled.

Both he and Darnell stood.

He was only partially correct; it wasn't just one person, but judging by the sheer number of footsteps, at least four.

"And his team of lawyers," Vaughn added. "Darnell, go check it out."

Darnell finally left the interview room.

"I'm sorry about that, Ivy. My partner is a little amped up."

"Is he drunk? He smells like alcohol."

"He's . . ." Vaughn gave up. "I think you should take off before things get dicey. Is there someone you can call? A friend to come get you?"

"Yeah, my friend Abby. She was supposed to be coming over. I thought it was her at the door when Zeke—"

"It's okay, take a breath." More shouting from outside the room. "Call your friend, okay? I'll check in later."

He squeezed her hand.

"Remember what I said?"

"That your grandmother was a bicycle?"

Vaughn smiled at this.

"It's not your fault, Ivy."

CHAPTER 58

"Abs?"

"Ivy, what the fuck? I went to your place and there were cops everywhere! They wouldn't tell me anything! Are you okay?"

"I'm fine. That student—" Ivy choked up. "Can you come get me? Please? My car is at my place."

"Of course. Where are you?"

"Princeton PD."

"I'm on my way."

Even though she was standing outside now, Ivy could still hear the yelling from within the building. Suspected that the main culprit was Devon Godfrey.

She couldn't get over what Vaughn's drunk partner had said.

Why *didn't* she call the cops?

Because of Dr. Moorehead. Because he'd told her that he'd take care of it. And now Rebecca Quinn was dead because of his inaction.

Ivy clenched her jaw so hard that it began to ache.

Abby arrived moments later and immediately jumped out of her car. Ran over and hugged Ivy, who leaned into it.

What a fucking day.

They stayed this way for several moments, only separating when someone bellowed behind them.

Devon again.

"Let's go."

They started to drive.

Abby didn't ask questions, knew Ivy needed time.

All that blood, all this death.

They arrived at her house.

The black CSU van was still there, as were several squad cars.

"I'm over there."

Abby parked beside her car. Thankfully, it was far enough away that the cops didn't notice them.

"You want to go to my place?" Abby offered.

"Yes—but there's something I need to do first."

"I hate when you say that. I don't want to leave you alone."

"I'll swing by after. I gotta go."

"I'm coming with you."

No fucking way.

"No," Ivy said forcefully.

Abby's manicured eyebrows rose up her pale forehead. "Ivy, I'm scared."

"Me, too."

Now it was Ivy who hugged her friend.

"Thank you, Abs. I'll come by as soon as I'm done."

Dr. Moorehead—if anyone other than Zeke was to blame, it was him. If the asshole had only called the cops like she'd told him to, Rebecca would still be alive.

Fuck him.

Ivy knew that doing anything now was a bad idea. She was paradoxically exhausted and energized at the same time. She should just go to Abby's house. Finally get some rest, let this simmer. Figure things out in the morning.

Bold decisions made during times of stress never ended well.

Instead, Ivy stormed into Dr. Moorehead's office, surprised when there was no secretary there to stop her.

More surprised to not find the bald man behind his desk.

Ivy felt her anger dissipate a little. She was about to leave when she spotted a crisp, clean envelope on the desk. Ivy strode forward.

Her name was scrawled across the front in big, bold, capital letters: "IVY."

An apology? A resignation?

Did Dr. Moorehead hear about what Zeke had done already?

Ivy didn't know. Thought it was best to just leave it.

But fuck Dr. Moorehead.

Ivy picked it up. It wasn't sealed, and she flipped the flap back. Teased out a folded piece of paper. Unfolded it.

At first, Ivy wasn't sure what she was looking at. A piece of paper with printed words on it. She'd been expecting an apology, but this wasn't that.

It was . . . a poem?

At the top, in bold, was the number, "**8001**."

Then,

Not quite perfect, but close to right,
Add the missing number, reveal the site.
You have 29 minutes—so don't be late,
Fail, and a life meets its final, sulfurous fate.

This was followed by two numbers: 40.3299 and -74.6510.

Ivy read the note three times.

It made less sense after each reading. But the poem and the numbers seemed somehow familiar to her.

Where have I seen this before? Ivy wasn't sure.

She nervously looked around the room.

Spotted a camera in the corner, up high. Similar, if not identical to the one she recalled seeing in the barn in which the prisoner's dilemma had been played.

Her heart rate spiked again, and she reread the note a fourth time.

One word stood out to her: "sulfurous."

As in, *hydrogen sulfide gas.*

She fumbled with her phone.

"Vaughn, I think we've got another one . . . I think there's going to be another attack." Her voice cracked. "I think there's going to be another murder."

CHAPTER 59

VAUGHN HAD A lot to say to Darnell, but now was not the time.

"I want my son released," Devon Godfrey demanded. He was like a puffed-up version of his kid. Blond hair, tall. A little soft, but still imposing.

Vaughn took one look at him and pictured the man on his back, lacing his forearm across his neck as he'd done with Zeke.

"Your son has been—"

"I don't care. He didn't do anything. I want him released."

"Mr. Godfrey—"

"Where's Captain Daniels?"

Devon was flanked by three men and one woman. Lawyers. Expensive, tailored suits. Luxury attaché cases and million-dollar haircuts.

"Mr. Godfrey, I'm Detective Ryan. Your son attacked me with a knife." Vaughn held his arm up and the big man squinted at it.

"Doesn't look like a knife wound. Looks like a scratch. You have a cat, Mr. Ryan?"

Mr. Ryan?

Vaughn didn't hate many people in this world, but he instantly hated this man.

Time to put him in his place.

"Zeke also murdered a fellow student. Twenty-one-year-old Rebecca Quinn." That shut him up. "Good—now that I've got your attention—"

"What the hell is going on?"

Captain Daniels had arrived.

And, as Darnell had predicted, the man didn't look happy. Would be even less so when he realized that one of the PPD's big donor's sons had been arrested for murder, along with a litany of other charges. What would he do when he found out that Ivy had been involved?

Vaughn's phone rang.

"Captain Daniels, I want my son released."

Devon was no longer interested in Mr. Ryan, and Vaughn used the distraction to slip away and answer his phone. There was no caller ID.

"Hello?"

"Vaughn, I think we've got another one . . . I think there's going to be another attack. I think there's going to be another murder."

It was Ivy, and she sounded desperate. Vaughn couldn't believe his ears.

"What? What are you talking about? What the hell is going on?"

Vaughn heard Ivy struggle to swallow.

"I found a note . . . I went back to my boss's office and found a note addressed to me."

"A note? What kind of note?"

"I don't know! A . . . math note? There's a mention of gas and . . . twenty-nine minutes or someone else is going to die!"

Vaughn's blood surged. His ears grew hot.

"Where are you?"

"I'm at Fine Hall. You need to hurry. Hurry, *please.*"

"Meet me outside."

Vaughn started to move when someone grabbed his arm.

It was Darnell.

"Where you going?"

"Ivy's in trouble. Stay here. Deal with Devon."

"I'm coming with—"

"Stay here, Darnell! And brush your fucking teeth before you speak to anyone else. Got it?"

CHAPTER 60

Not quite perfect . . .

Missing number . . .

Ivy was too tired to figure out the riddle.

The last two numbers, at least, were self-explanatory: they were GPS coordinates.

Outside Dr. Moorehead's office, she spotted one of her colleagues. One of the few other female professors in the math department.

"Hey, have you seen Dr. Moorehead?" Ivy was having a hard time speaking. Her throat was raw and bone-dry.

"He left about an hour ago."

"Know where he went?"

"No idea. Seemed to be in a hurry, though."

"Thanks."

She coughed a little. Frowned when she felt the burn.

"Hey, Dr. Reeves, you hear anything about a student?" The woman scratched her head nervously. Her eyes kept darting to the angry red marks on Ivy's throat.

"Student?"

"Yeah—a rumor's going around that a student stabbed someone. Can you believe that?"

"No, no I can't." Deep down, Ivy knew she was lying, but it didn't feel like one. Everything from the time that Zeke had gripped her throat to seeing Rebecca lying on her back, Vaughn's fingers pressed to her skin, seemed like a terrible nightmare.

One that couldn't possibly be real.

Ivy went outside. The PPD station was only a stone's throw from Fine Hall, and Vaughn arrived in six minutes. Twenty-nine minutes . . . twenty-one remaining. Why twenty-nine? And why did that seem familiar?

Vaughn started to get out of his car, his face pinched.

"No, stay in."

Ivy slid into the passenger seat.

"What the hell's going on?"

Ivy produced the note and passed it to him.

"Found this in Dr. Moorehead's office—the envelope had my name on it."

"What the fuck . . ." Vaughn muttered. He turned to her. "You sure this is—"

"Look here: 'sulfurous fate.' That's gotta be the gas, right? The hydrogen sulfide gas?"

"I guess. I still don't—" Vaughn stiffened. "You think it might be your boss? Dr. Moorehead? Could he be behind this?"

Ivy blinked.

"I don't . . . I don't know. But I don't want anyone else to die."

"Why the hell is this note addressed to you?"

"I don't know, Vaughn—maybe . . . maybe whoever is behind this figured out that I was helping you. These are GPS coordinates. I don't know what the rest means, but I think we should go there. *Now*. We have twenty-one minutes left." She checked her phone. Shook her head. "No—only twenty now."

Vaughn nodded, kicked the car into drive while Ivy punched the GPS coordinates into the app on her phone.

"It's the Basin—the Princeton Basin," she said.

"The Basin?"

"Yeah—go."

The coordinates didn't lead precisely to the Princeton Basin, but to a forested area just on the eastern side of the Delaware Canal. On the opposite bank, a residential subdivision, but this specific bordered on an area that was mostly trees and trails.

The perfect spot for another one of those retrofitted barns.

Perfect . . .

8001.

29 minutes.

Add the missing number, reveal the site.

"If it was Zeke who set this up, everything could still be on a timer. The gas could still go off," Vaughn mused out loud.

He was picking up speed as he spoke, but Ivy was barely registering his words.

Perfect . . . perfect . . . not quite perfect, but close to right.

8001.

Something clicked.

"But if it's your boss who—"

"Do you have a pen?"

"Yeah, sure."

Vaughn popped open the middle armrest, pulled out a pen.

Ivy saw a PPD pad of paper inside and took that, too. As she wrote, she heard Vaughn's phone ring. Saw him click decline the call out of the corner of her eye. The phone immediately chimed again, and he cursed under his breath before declining that call, too.

Focus, Ivy.

"What's going on?" Vaughn asked.

Ivy didn't answer.

Twenty-nine was a prime number. All of the numbers from the 100 prisoners problem were prime. Hell, come to think of it, Joshua Perry and his opponent's scores—twenty-three and seventeen—were prime numbers, as well.

But 8001 was not. Close, just like the poem said.

But the poem didn't ask for a prime number. It wanted a *perfect* number. A number that was equal to the sum of all its proper divisors. The closest perfect number to 8001 was 8128. The difference between 8001 and 8128 was 127. 127 was also a divisor of 8128.

Ivy quickly scribbled numbers on the page to check her math.

1 + 2 + 4 + 8 + 16 + 32 + 64 + 127 + 254 + 508 + 1016 + 2032 + 4064 = 8128.

127 was missing . . .

Ivy referred to the poem again.

Add the missing number, reveal the site.

Ivy added 127 to the tails of both GPS coordinates. 40.3299 became 40.3426. -74.6637 became -74.6510.

She shook her head.

"It's not the right address. It's not the Basin."

Ivy grabbed her phone, typed in the new coordinates. As she did, Vaughn's phone rang for what seemed like the hundredth time. He finally answered.

"Delaney! We've got another attack," he shouted. "We—"

"It's the Thomas Clarke House!" Ivy interrupted.

"What the fuck is that?" Vaughn said out of the corner of his mouth.

"It's in the Princeton Battlefield."

"Where—"

Ivy shoved her phone toward Vaughn. She could hear Delaney saying something, but couldn't make out the words. He squinted as he read her screen.

"You hear that, Delaney? Battlefield State Park. Get there, *now!*" Vaughn ended the call. To Ivy, he said, "I know it. Hold on." He wrenched the wheel, started back toward Fine Hall, raced up Alexander Street.

"Hurry," Ivy said.

They had thirteen minutes left.

Somewhere in the back of Ivy's head she thought, *Hey, that's a prime number, too.*

CHAPTER 61

Vaughn raced down Mercer Road, saw the sign for the Princeton Battlefield State Park, and yanked the wheel so hard that two of the car's tires lifted off the ground.

"Where to now?"

The dirt road curved a little before being flanked by sections of old wooden fences.

He was familiar with Battlefield State Park, but not the Clarke . . . whatever House. There was a fork up ahead. Left, a gravel road flanked by pines. Right, a little more open.

"Don't know . . . right, I think," Ivy said.

Vaughn went right.

It didn't matter.

The road was short and looped back, connecting with the left fork, but there was no Clarke House.

"Where is it?" Vaughn hammered the brakes and hopped out.

"There!"

Ivy was already out of the car, pointing at a white structure about two hundred feet in the distance, on the other side of an empty field.

Vaughn was tempted to tell her to stay in the vehicle, but he knew she wouldn't listen.

They broke into a run.

"How much time?" Vaughn yelled.

Ivy was fast, already about twenty feet in front of him.

"I don't know!"

Minutes—there had to be only single digit minutes left.

Ivy got to the front doors first, barely breathing hard. Vaughn joined her moments later and looked up, blinking rapidly to clear sweat from his eyes.

The Thomas Clarke House was old, constructed of sun-bleached horizontal slats. A small overhang roof on the left half offered shade to what appeared to be the main entrance.

Ivy was at the door, yanking on it.

"It's locked!"

It was the middle of the afternoon—why the fuck was it locked?

There was another door halfway down the building. Vaughn rushed to it but was met with the same result.

He pounded on the worn wood with his fist.

"Hey! Anyone in there! PPD, open up!"

He banged again.

Heard Ivy say something along the lines of, "It can't be here."

"*PPD!*"

He took a step back, went further left. There were two windows on the ground level. Vaughn cupped his hands and peered through the first. The lights were off, and it was dark inside.

"Hey! Anyone in there!"

Vaughn pulled away from the window.

"Ivy, you sure about—" He stopped. Ivy was no longer at the other door. "Ivy? *Ivy!*"

Where the hell did she go?

"*Ivy!*"

He heard a faint beeping. An alarm—Ivy had put a timer for twenty-nine minutes on her phone after finding the note. Vaughn followed the sound, calling Ivy's name as he headed around the side of the building. He saw some sort of shed or barn, older even than the main building, just a couple dozen paces away.

"Ivy!"

Enter another sound, louder than her phone alarm.

A high-pressure hiss.

"Over here!"

Vaughn dashed around the back of the barn, finally saw her. Ivy was wrenching on the barn door, but it was locked. Firmly, judging by the way that it didn't even rattle in its frame when Ivy heaved.

"It won't open!"

"Out of the way."

Ivy stepped back and Vaughn tried the door—no luck.

He kicked it next, but it barely budged.

Old-ass shed was fitted with a reinforced door and a lock worthy of a prison cell. He could kick the damn thing for hours but would only end up with a broken foot.

The hissing sound had grown so loud now that it was impossible to hear if there was anyone inside.

"Wait here," Vaughn told Ivy and then was off again, running back toward his car.

He popped the trunk, grabbed two masks that he'd asked Delaney to put in there for this very possibility, and a crowbar.

When he returned to the barn, Ivy was still at the door, grabbing, pulling, doing everything she could to try and break in.

"Put this on!" Vaughn ordered.

Ivy didn't hear him.

"Put this on!"

He thrust the mask at her, made sure she took it before he pulled his own mask over his head. As Ivy adjusted the straps for a snug fit, Vaughn wedged the crowbar between the door and the frame.

Leaned on it, grunting with the effort.

"C'mon . . ."

He pushed harder, sweat dripping from his forehead and dotting the plastic shield in front of his eyes. The frame finally splintered and popped. Vaughn dropped the crowbar and kicked the door. It flew inward. A wave of cool air struck him.

Cool air that reeked of rotten eggs.

"Stay outside!" he shouted over his shoulder as he entered the shed.

The sound was deafening, and Vaughn identified the source of the gas immediately. A crude hole had been made—broken?—in the wall. Same shitty dryer duct.

Same death trap.

Vaughn saw the man next.

He was bald, glasses askew on his face. Lying motionless on his back. Tape covered his mouth, and the way his arms were angled behind him suggested that they were bound.

A piece of paper was attached to his chest.

Vaughn started to gag, but wasn't sure if this was because of the horrible smell or the actual toxicity of the hydrogen sulfide.

Didn't care.

He grabbed one of the man's legs and pulled. Ivy grabbed the other—of course, she hadn't listened about remaining outside.

Together they dragged him onto the grass.

Ivy was saying something, repeating the same word over and over again, but with the gas still hissing and the blood pumping in his ears, Vaughn couldn't make it out.

He could, however, read the note on the man's chest.

Too late.

Judging by the man'sgrayed-over eyes, whoever had written the note was right.

They were too fucking late.

CHAPTER 62

"Ben! *Ben!*"

Ivy dropped down, placed her head to Dr. Moorehead's chest. The paper crinkled.

No heartbeat.

She ripped the tape from the man's mouth. A frothy substance spewed forth, and at first, she thought that he was actively vomiting.

Except Dr. Moorehead hadn't moved, hadn't even blinked. It was just some sort of bile foam that had been trapped by the tape.

"He's gone, Ivy."

Ivy started chest compressions while Vaughn went back to the shed or whatever the fuck it was and closed the door as best he could.

"C'mon, Ben—wake up!"

"He's gone."

Vaughn put a hand on her shoulder.

She shrugged him off and continued with the chest compressions.

Vaughn got on his phone, called it in.

When Ivy felt his hand on her shoulder again, she finally stopped and sat down. Started to take off her mask.

Vaughn stopped her.

"Best to keep it on."

"It's . . . it's Dr. Moorehead," she whimpered.

Vaughn nodded. He'd figured as much.

"If only I'd been faster. If only I'd figured the riddle out sooner."

Ivy ripped the paper from her boss's chest.

Cursed loudly.

Too late.

She crumpled the page, went to throw it, but Vaughn took it from her.

"I'm going to need that."

Ivy handed it over and tried to stand. Her legs were like rubber, and she gripped Vaughn's arm to hoist herself up. Braced herself against him to keep from falling down again.

"We need to turn off the gas." Her voice sounded strange, mostly because of the mask, partly because of the surreal nature of everything.

They moved together, found the tank down the side of the shed. Like the others, it was hooked up to some sort of dryer exhaust tube.

Same digital, remote release valve.

Using the bottom of his shirt to cover his hand, Vaughn fiddled with the knob. When this did nothing, he tore off the digital valve and then turned the knob beneath one way, then the other. A sharp, intense whine, then the gas stopped flowing.

Ivy returned to Dr. Moorehead, hoping that, by some miracle, he'd be up, coughing and vomiting.

Pissed off.

Adding being abducted, tied up, thrown in a barn to his list of things he loathed.

He wasn't.

Dr. Moorehead was completely still.

Ivy checked his pulse for the hundredth time.

She couldn't believe it. The man she'd spoken to just hours ago—who had reamed her out—was dead.

Rebecca, too.

Her mind whirred, and she recalled what Vaughn had said in the car.

Or was it before that?

She didn't know.

Everything was just so fucked up.

Was it Zeke? Could he have set this all up?

A car parked behind Vaughn's, drawing her eyes, a reason to peel them away from Dr. Moorehead's blue-tinged face. It was that asshole cop who had pointed his gun at her and her father, and Kachinski, too.

"Delaney!" Vaughn waved a hand. "Put your mask on and bring that fucking detector thing."

Another vehicle—a black cube van—arrived behind the PPD squad car.

Delaney went to his trunk. Reappeared wearing a mask and holding a handheld gas detector. His footsteps faltered when he noticed Dr. Moorehead lying on the grass.

"Aw, shit—another game?" Delaney's voice was oddly high-pitched, resonant.

Ivy couldn't answer, even if she'd wanted to. She couldn't seem to catch her breath.

But it had been a game, hadn't it? The poem? Riddle?

Only Dr. Moorehead had no chance of winning this one.

It was on her.

This was all on her.

"We're going to have to cordon this area off for a bit. Levels are too high," Delaney said, his voice returning close to normal. His eyes were locked on the device in his hand. It was beeping incessantly. "Tell Landon—"

He looked up, noticed Ivy for the first time. Squinted at her, trying to make sure it really was Ivy behind the mask.

"Detective Ryan?"

Vaughn stared back.

"What?"

"Can I, *uh*, speak to you for a second?"

Delaney's dark eyes flicked from Vaughn to Ivy and back again.

About her, the look said.

"You can speak in front of her."

"You . . . *uh*, Captain Daniels . . ." His voice cracked.

"Just spit it the fuck out, Delaney."

The officer cleared his throat.

"He's on a warpath. Darnell mentioned Dr. Reeves at the last crime scene, and he lost it."

Captain Daniels.

That name . . .

Ivy had a flashback to the night of the fire.

The telephone call.

Her father was a lot of things, but until that night, she'd never seen or heard him scared. And Gene had been terrified.

The rapid-fire instructions. Her trying to get a word in, him not letting her.

Telling her that it was all over.

Later, after Ivy had dragged the body out of the still-burning house, Captain Daniels had arrived.

"Delaney, we've got a fucking dead body here! And you're worried that Daniels is pissed?" Vaughn shouted.

"I—I—I know . . . it's just . . . I thought . . . Darnell—"

"Why the fuck did Darnell mention Dr. Reeves?" Vaughn's face had turned scarlet.

"I—Vaughn, the kid—Zeke—his father is raising hell, too. Lawyers are barking shit about lawsuits. It's a fucking mess."

Ivy felt her hackles raise.

Delaney talking about a "fucking mess" back at the police station. Legalities, formalities, technicalities.

The *fucking mess* was right here.

The mess was Dr. Ben Moorehead dead on the grass.

That was the mess—none of the other bullshit mattered.

"What do you want me to do?" Delaney asked desperately.

Vaughn's reply came immediately.

"Call the captain, tell him to get his ass out here. I'll deal with him when he comes."

CHAPTER 63

Vaughn was fuming.

Darnell . . . after all the times he'd covered for his partner, Darnell had gone behind his back and mentioned Ivy.

It would have come out. Of course, it would have come out.

Zeke had attacked her, making her both a victim and a material witness in the murder of Rebecca Quinn. But Vaughn wanted to tell Daniels himself. Use the time to break it to him softly, explain the situation.

He was pissed at Delaney, too. If the man hadn't ratted them out initially, Darnell wouldn't have choked him.

Or maybe he would have.

Vaughn still wasn't sure what was going through his partner's skull. Cops fought a lot; detectives, too.

It was a high stress profession. Maybe the most stressful.

But if there was one golden rule, it was you don't put your hands on another member of law enforcement. The moment you did that, you were cooked.

Vaughn had heard many a story about cops who had

gotten into drunken fistfights after a dozen too many drinks at the local watering hole.

They eventually squashed the beef.

Or thought they did.

Then, when it came time to work together again, the animosity resurfaced. Only not in the form of a fistfight this time.

It was an accidental gun jam during a shootout.

Oops, sorry. Would have had your back, but my gun . . . you know how it is. This stuff happens. I feel bad that you now shit out of a bag and are stuck in a wheelchair for the rest of your life. But hey, at least we aren't fighting no more.

Vaughn pulled Delaney aside.

"Delaney, why the fuck did you tell the captain about Ivy that night in the field?"

The man immediately became defensive.

"I didn't."

"The fuck you didn't."

"No, I didn't. Vaughn, I swear, I didn't say anything."

"Who was it then? You were the only one—" Vaughn stopped. Delaney *wasn't* the only one standing outside the barn when he'd shown up.

Horowitz had also been present.

Shit.

Vaughn backpedaled. Attempted damage control. He knew this was second-tier in the grand scheme of things, but there was nothing they could do for Dr. Moorehead now.

Nothing they could do for any of the victims.

Too late, just like the note said.

"Look, Darnell's being going through some shit. He didn't mean to grab you."

Vaughn was still doing it. Still defending his degenerate partner. He just couldn't help it.

"He's been going through shit for *years*." Delaney's eyes narrowed. Not the response that Vaughn had been expecting. Thought the cop would back down, nod, say something along the lines of, *I understand, I get it.* But the man finally seemed to have grown some balls. Now, of all times. *Fuck.* "He shouldn't have grabbed me. Motherfucker grabbed my *throat*."

"I know, I know. But he's fucked up."

"He's a liability, that's what he is."

Vaughn couldn't argue with that.

"He's going to get help, Delaney. Cut him some slack."

"Too late for that. I didn't say nothin' to Daniels yet because this shit blew up, but I will when it's over. I'm going to report his ass. He thought I was gunning for his job before?"

Fuck.

Vaughn saw his partner in bed, his gun resting by the pillow.

It's all I've got, man . . .

"I'll tell you what, I'll *make* him get help."

"It's—"

—not enough.

"And when a spot opens up in the detective ranks, I'll go to bat for you. Tell them that when we catch this asshole, you helped. Invaluable, all that stuff."

"I want the collar."

Vaughn winced. He'd been fine with Delaney bringing in Perry partly because he didn't think the man was responsible. Even if Perry had been, things had changed since. Darnell needed the collar as much as anyone. Maybe even more. For

Delaney, catching the asshole behind these gassings meant a promotion. For Darnell, it meant keeping his job.

His *life*.

"I'll put a word in—I promise. Remember what you said about Darnell holding me back? I'll use that. I've got some sway with the captain, keeping Darnell in check for as long as I have. Please, Delaney."

Delaney was still on the fence, but Captain Daniels's arrival put an end to the discussion. And the cop was right. Daniels was pissed, his face so red it bordered on purple. He stomped his feet like some sort of granite golem.

Delaney's little meter indicated that the levels of H2S gas outside the barn had finally had dropped too low to do any damage, but Vaughn kept his mask on anyway—and instructed Ivy to do the same. Daniels didn't have one.

With all the smoke coming out of his nose and ears, no gas could enter his system.

"Detective Ryan, what the hell—"

Like Delaney, it took the captain a few seconds before he noticed Ivy.

"What the *hell*?" Same words, very different intonation. "I thought I told you that Dr. Reeves was not to be involved!"

"I know. But—"

"You disobeyed a direct—"

"I *am* involved," Ivy said, stepping forward.

The captain glared at her.

"You're a civilian, Dr. Reeves."

"I know that. But the note was addressed to me. I'm the one who reported Zeke to Dr. Moorehead. I'm the one who should have gone to the cops after he assaulted Rebecca the first time."

Vaughn didn't know how much Darnell had told Daniels, how much the captain knew. He couldn't read the man's scarlet face, either. The captain's lack of reaction to the mention of a note and the initial assault on Rebecca Quinn hinted that he was apprised of everything.

Vaughn wasn't sure if this was a good or bad thing. Either way, it saved him from explaining, which might make Ivy second-guess herself, repeat her claim that if she had worked faster, they might have been able to save her boss.

It's not your fault, Ivy. It's not.

"That's Dr. Moorehead?" The captain indicated the man on the ground. Unlike Delaney, the sight of the body seemed to have no effect on him. "The department head?"

There was familiarity to Daniels's voice, and Vaughn recalled the police report from the fire and Detective Howe's words. Howe saying that the PPD went to Princeton and they pressured them to close the case. Mark it as an accident. Suspicious, but still an accident.

"Yes," Ivy and Vaughn said at the same time.

"God damn it. When did this happen?"

"Just a few minutes ago," Vaughn said. "We got here as fast as we could. He was already DOA."

Daniels snarled, walked around the corpse toward the shed. Pointed at the canister.

"Same remote trigger?"

"Yeah," Vaughn confirmed.

"Could be Zeke Godfrey. You like him for this?"

"I don't know. He would have had to move quick—"

"One of my colleagues said that Moorehead was in the

office until about an hour ago—an hour and thirty minutes now. He left alone," Ivy interjected.

Daniels frowned, and Vaughn mentally went over the timeline.

Zeke had gone to Rebecca's house, killed her, then accosted Ivy. He didn't know exactly how long the kid had kept her hostage, but it couldn't have been more than a few minutes. Ten, tops. The door to her house was still open when he'd arrived. Vaughn had then apprehended Zeke, and Delaney had come to pick him up. Then the lawyers, Devon Godfrey, Ivy's truncated interview . . . how long had all that taken?

Definitely more than an hour and twenty-nine minutes.

Even if Zeke had set this all up beforehand—possible; Vaughn had no idea how often someone actually came to look in this small barn—he would have still had to kidnap Moorehead, leave the note for Ivy, bring Moorehead here, bind his wrists, and lock him in.

"There was a camera back in Dr. Moorehead's office," Ivy said. "Someone was watching me. Started a twenty-nine-minute timer as soon as I read the note," Ivy said. "Zeke was already in custody by then."

This was just a guess—Ivy couldn't have known if someone was actually monitoring the video feed. Vaughn assumed that the hiss they'd heard around the time Ivy's alarm went off was the gas starting to be released but it could just have likely been the end of the tank. And he had no idea how long it took to empty. Hadn't thought of asking Dr. McGill. The person who left the note could have just estimated when Ivy was going to read it and programmed the automatic release nozzle to go off around that time.

"Detective Ryan?" Daniels probed.

"If Zeke Godfrey is behind this, he's not working alone."

Daniels grunted.

"And there's one canister still missing?"

"Yes."

"Then I'm going live. No more deaths, Detective Ryan. No more *fucking* deaths."

CHAPTER 64

THEY WERE WRONG. It wasn't Zeke. Zeke couldn't complete a polynomial equation to save his life, let alone know the math behind any of the gas setups.

It wasn't him who had orchestrated this.

Then who the fuck was it? Who was doing this? And why the hell did they single me out?

Abby called again.

"Bitch, where the hell are you?"

"I'm sorry. Abs, this is so messed up. Dr. Moorehead is dead."

"*What*? Your boss?"

"Yeah."

"What the hell happened?"

"It's a long story." Ivy choked up. "Can you come get me? I need my car again."

"Where are you?"

"Thomas Clarke Historical House."

"The *what*?"

"Just put it in the GPS. Please—hurry."

Vaughn approached. The detective had just finished an

intense conversation—though "conversation" was probably too soft a word for the tongue-lashing he'd received—and looked spent.

"I'm going to need that note," he said. Ivy gladly handed over the letter she'd found on Dr. Moorehead's desk. "And the captain wants you to come back in and give another statement."

"Another?" Ivy's voice had degenerated into a whine.

"I'm sorry. I tried to convince the captain to let you give that statement tomorrow, but he's insisting."

"Now? My friend is on her way to pick me up."

Vaughn looked up. Squinted at her.

"The one from the bar?"

"Yeah."

"That's good . . . that's good." He nodded to himself. "She can give a statement, too."

"Vaughn, am I going to be okay?"

A loaded question.

Okay after all the fucked-up shit that had happened to her over the past two days? Or okay after the 'statement?' If it was anything like that last 'statement' she'd given, Ivy was beginning to consider the word a euphemism for interrogation.

"Yes."

Unsure.

For a moment, it appeared as if Vaughn wanted to hug her—which Ivy would have leaned into—but he pulled back. Probably for the best. She couldn't get involved with a cop, not in that way. Not in *any* way.

"Okay," Ivy said, mostly to herself.

"Just . . ." Vaughn trailed off.

"Just what?"

"Just tell them what happened. Keep it short, simple."

"I will."

Ivy was so tired that even offering a conciliatory smile proved impossible.

Captain Daniels, who had been speaking with a man in a black jacket bearing the letters "CSU," trampled over.

He was harder than she remembered.

Years ago at the hospital, Daniels had been curt, but he'd had at least a hint of compassion to him. That was long gone now.

"Press conference set up for half an hour from now back at PPD." The captain deliberately avoided looking at her. "You really think Zeke has a partner?"

The question was directed at Vaughn, but Ivy took it upon herself to answer.

"He doesn't know the math."

Daniels had no choice but to address her now.

"Who does?"

Ivy hesitated. Then said, "I do. Dr. Moorehead does—*did*, I mean. Shit. Anyone else in the math department, I guess."

Did—*Jesus Christ, I can't believe he's dead.*

Ivy stayed strong.

"What about another student? One of Zeke's friends?"

Ivy thought back to that night at the bar. She didn't recognize either of Zeke's buddies from her stats class, but they hadn't been the only ones there. Blake had been there, too. Blake, the handsome man in finance. Blake, who knew the obscure Penney's game but had let her win anyway.

Blake, who had come to her rescue when Zeke had confronted her.

"Dr. Reeves?" Daniels prompted.

Ivy shook her head, dismissing thoughts of Blake.

"I don't know everyone he hung out with. But if I had to guess? No, probably not."

Daniels frowned.

"I need your statement," he said to Ivy.

"I already told her, I—"

The captain interrupted Vaughn.

"Keep it short."

"I said that, too."

Daniels's frown became a scowl as he turned his attention to Vaughn.

"I'll do the interview with Darnell."

"I'll do it," Vaughn countered.

"No, you won't."

Vaughn squirmed. Daniels appeared to be tempting the detective to argue, and he fought hard against the urge.

"It's okay," Ivy said. "I'll be fine."

Probably the wrong thing to say. They'd gone for one drink, and everyone was acting as if they'd been married for fifteen years. Daniels even went as far as to shake his head in disapproval.

"Ten minutes," Daniels said, then walked off.

"Sorry about that," Vaughn said quietly. "He's a hard-ass."

"I know. I—"

There was a commotion behind them, and they both turned.

Abby had arrived. She'd parked at the end of the dirt road and was trying to get to them, but some dickhead cop was giving her trouble.

"Hey!" Vaughn shouted, realizing who Abby was. "Let her through."

The cop did, and Ivy met her halfway. Got the embrace she so desperately needed.

"You look like shit," Abby whispered in her ear. "Smell like shit, too."

"I feel like shit. Abs, they want us to give a statement."

Abby scrunched her nose as they disengaged.

"About what?"

"The kid at the bar."

A far-off look. CSU had thankfully covered the body, but Ivy had already told Abby that Dr. Moorehead was dead.

"That asshole? *He* did this?"

"Sort of."

"Fucking hell." Sigh. "Okay, let's go, then."

Ivy gave Vaughn a wistful look, to which he responded with a nod.

When they were alone in the car, Ivy said, "Abs, this is about Zeke. That's it."

Abby sucked her bottom lip into her mouth. Let it out with an audible *pop*.

"I'll just tell them what I saw. Nothing about—"

"No," Ivy cut her off. "Just about the kid at the bar."

"Got it. Let's go, bitch. Let's get this over with. Then we're heading back to my house for wine. Copious amounts of wine. Holy fuck, I can't believe this is happening."

Ivy couldn't either.

CHAPTER 65

Ivy was nervous. Would have been even more nervous if exhaustion didn't have a near monopoly on her emotions.

It didn't help that she felt like a suspect. For starters, Vaughn, who was waiting for both her and Abby at the station, led them through some back way. Explained that they were trying to keep them away from Devon Godfrey and his lawyer goons. And now she found herself in a dingy room that reeked of cigarettes and coffee. No offer of either.

Two big men—Darnell and Daniels—were seated across from her. They read her her rights and Ivy declined legal representation. She got the impression that the captain wanted this over with as quickly as possible. Suited Ivy just fine.

At least they were aligned on that.

"Dr. Reeves, tell us about Zeke Godfrey."

Ivy did. Ran through everything. The cheating, the bar, the threats in the hallway.

Rebecca Quinn.

Zeke breaking into her home and admitting to killing . . . someone.

It was painful, especially recounting the bit about Rebecca.

The poor woman. Ivy fought back tears and Daniels gave her a few seconds to collect herself.

Then, "So the first time that Zeke was aggressive toward you was at the bar, correct?"

"Yes. And like I told the detectives last time, there was this guy there. Blake something. He—he knows math. We were playing this coin flipping game and—"

Her mind kept coming back to Blake. The way he'd pretended not to know Penney's game. How smooth he'd been. How close Ivy had been to going back to his hotel with him.

"We'll look into it."

"He said that he was staying at the Marriott at Forrestal. Said he was only staying three days—"

"I said we'd look into it," Darnell repeated.

Ivy was reminded of what Vaughn had told her, which the captain had reiterated, "Keep it short."

But . . . three days?

This also triggered something in Ivy.

What?

She was just so damn tired, her thoughts a jumbled mess. An algebraic equation with so many variables that it was unsolvable.

"Tell us what happened when you went back to Dr. Moorehead's office. Start with *why* you went there."

"I . . ." She took a deep breath. Told the truth. "I was going to confront him. If he'd just gone to the cops like I told him to, Rebecca would still be alive."

"Let's keep this to things you did, Dr. Reeves. No need to speculate."

You asked me why *and I told you*, Ivy thought bitterly.

"So you found the note. Any idea why it was addressed to you?"

"No."

"And then you called Detective Ryan?"

"Yes."

Daniels pulled out the letter that he must have obtained from Vaughn. Read it out loud, likely for the benefit of the cameras.

"Did you understand the letter?"

"Not at first. I was too frazzled after seeing Rebecca. I didn't know what it meant."

"But then you did, right? You told Detective Ryan not to head to the Basin and instead to go to Princeton Battlefield?"

"Yes."

"How many dead bodies have you seen in your life, Dr. Reeves?" Darnell asked. Captain Daniels's expression soured.

"Three."

"Three . . . right. And two of those were today?"

"Correct."

"So you just saw two dead bodies, and you still managed to, " Darnell flicked the sheet of paper absently, "figure out this complex riddle?"

"One."

"Pardon?"

"You said I'd just seen two dead bodies. I'd only seen one up to that point—Dr. Moorehead was the second, which I didn't see until after."

Darnell didn't appreciate being corrected.

"Sure—fine. One, then. But you were also attacked by a

man with a knife. And despite all of this, you still managed to figure out the note? The correct location?"

Ivy didn't care for the insinuation.

"It's math. My brain went into math mode. It isn't that complicated once you understand what it's actually asking."

Darnell made a ridiculous face.

"Looks pretty damn complicated to me."

But you're not a math professor, a Clark Fellow, blah, blah, blah.

Not hearing a question, Ivy elected to remain silent.

"Why twenty-nine minutes?" Darnell asked abruptly. "Seems strange, doesn't it?"

"It's a prime number. Just like—" Ivy froze.

She realized why these—twenty-nine minutes and three days—had seemed familiar to her.

The email! That stupid spam email she received right before this all started. It had a rhyming scheme, just like the one that she'd found in Dr. Moorehead's office.

How did it go?

Ivy closed her eyes and it came to her.

1092 —three days to the date.

Twenty-nine minutes, why were you late?

Thirteen will fall, if their problem is unsolved,

Reduced to a constant, your death is involved.

By her count, there were thirteen dead: ten original victims, one in the second game, Rebecca, and Dr. Moorehead. Did that mean that this was finally over?

"Dr. Reeves?" Darnell probed.

Ivy's eyes snapped open.

Should I say something?

She would have, but Darnell was being such a dick, and Vaughn had told her to keep it simple.

"Sorry. I'm just tired."

Darnell grunted, but before he could speak, Daniels took over again.

"Dr. Reeves, I think that's enough for—"

Now, Darnell cut in.

"Tell us about your father, Ivy. Earlier you said that anyone in the math department could have set up these games or challenges or whatever they are. Your father could have done them, right?"

Captain Daniels tensed, but he didn't interrupt.

"No."

"No? But he's a professor, isn't he? Like you?"

"My father can't speak." Ivy's lips were so tight that she could barely get the words out.

"But he was a prof, right?"

Captain Daniels finally spoke up.

"That's enough, Detective Sacker."

"What? I'm just trying to figure out if—"

"I said that's enough."

Darnell clammed up.

"Dr. Reeves, thank you for coming in. We're going to need to do a follow-up interview with you at some point. Please don't leave the state."

Ivy stood, walked out of the room.

Vaughn was waiting, looked apologetic.

"Ivy—"

"No. Not now."

She walked right by him, tried to find her way out of the dungeon.

Why the fuck were they asking about Eugene? They think he did this? Impossible.

"Ivy?"

It was Abs.

She saw the look on Ivy's face. Hugged her again.

"How did yours go?" Ivy asked, only so that Abs didn't pose the same question to her.

"Fine. Some cute cop. Young. Delaney? Think he said his name was Delaney." She shook her head. "Doesn't matter. C'mon, let's get that wine."

They drove in silence back to Fine Hall. Stopped right next to Ivy's car.

"Ivy, you should give that therapist a call. Set something up. All those bodies . . . *Jesus*." Abs shuddered.

A suggestion veiled as a question.

After the fire, after her mom had left, Abby had put Ivy in touch with her therapist. Ivy wasn't a fan of therapy in general, but she had humored her friend. Actually didn't mind speaking to the dark-haired woman. Liked the fact that the therapist was bound by law never to repeat what she'd said. And Ivy had spilled everything.

Almost everything.

"Yeah, I think I should."

Abby nodded.

Things played out at Abby's apartment the way that her best friend said they would. Wine then bath. Ivy had even fallen asleep in the tub for a few minutes. When she got out, Abs was waiting for her. Refilled her glass.

"I need to go back to work for half an hour, okay? Still have Mrs. Brighton there waiting to get her lips done. Boss is pissed that I keep leaving during the middle of the workday. Then I'm coming straight home—took tomorrow off, too. We can just hang out. Take it easy."

Abby was rambling, clearly felt bad about everything that Ivy had been through. Ivy felt worse for getting her friend embroiled in another hot mess.

"It's okay—go."

Abby nodded.

"Lock the door behind me."

"I will."

"No, Ivy. Come with me. If that kid has a partner like the cops said . . ."

"Just go, Abs."

Abby's eyes drifted to the towel Ivy had wrapped herself in.

"Borrow something of mine to wear," Abby said. She opened the front door. Paused. "No going anywhere, okay?"

"Okay."

"Promise?"

"Pinky."

Abby hugged her. Ivy's towel slipped; she adjusted it.

"Love you, bitch."

"Love you, too."

Ivy locked the door and immediately went to her friend's computer to search for the spam email with the cryptic poem.

"What the fuck?"

It was gone.

Not in her trash folder, not anywhere. Ivy spent a good twenty minutes Googling how to recover deleted emails, but to no avail.

Her eyes blurred and she nearly fell asleep. Decided that if she stayed in front of her computer any longer, she would pass out. Almost convinced herself that she'd just made the whole thing up. She desperately needed to rest. Planned to crawl into Abby's bed and wake up in a week to the news that Vaughn had caught the man who had torn her life apart. Then she would see the therapist and start the long road to piecing her life back together, to going back to how things were before all this death and mayhem began.

But that never happened.

Ivy had promised not to leave the house and never intended to lie to her friend. But when she heard that familiar ring from her cell—*beep, beep . . . beep*—Ivy knew she'd done just that.

CHAPTER 66

"WHAT THE HELL is wrong with you, Darnell?"

Captain Daniels had already chewed the detective out for the way he'd handled the interview. Went as far as to pull him from the presser.

The room that Ivy had been in didn't have an adjacent viewing area behind one-way glass, but Vaughn had been close enough to the door to hear almost everything.

"Not the time, Vaughn."

"It wasn't the time for you to bring up Ivy's father. And it wasn't time to tell the captain that she was at the other crime scene."

"I brought up Ivy's father because I got a hunch. This whole 'can't speak, can't write' thing is a farce. He—"

"He's a fucking vegetable, Darnell!"

Darnell looked apathetic. Went so far as to shrug.

Ho hum, that's your *opinion.*

"I'm trying to figure this shit out, Vaughn. I got my hunches, you know that. Sorry if I hurt your girlfriend's feelings."

That was it.

Vaughn lost it.

"Fuck your hunches! Nothing you've fucking done is helping figure this out. *Nothing.* It's just been about you. How many times have I covered for you? Huh?"

Darnell balled his fists and Vaughn took notice.

"You gonna grab me by the throat, too? 'Cause I'll tell you what, I'm not Delaney. That shit won't fly with me."

It looked like Darnell would do just that, and Vaughn tensed. Then the man spread his fingers.

"Go home, Darnell. Go the fuck home. Get your shit together."

The senior detective bowed his head. Turned and left without another word.

Vaughn waited for him to disappear out the rear doors of the police station before finally exhaling.

Shit, that was intense.

Vaughn wanted to heed his own advice: Go home. It had been an insane day.

Night, week. *Whatever.*

He breathed again.

No—he still had to work. There was one tank of gas still out there.

Vaughn just had no idea where to look. He found himself back in his office staring at the murder board.

No help there.

Vaughn refused to follow Darnell's hunch and look into Eugene Reeves. Not yet, anyway. His mind turned to something Ivy had said during her interview about a man in the bar. An unlikely suspect, but somewhere to start, at least.

Vaughn called the Marriott at Forrestal, gave his

credentials, then asked if someone named Blake was staying there. The maître d', a slow-speaking Latino man, searched the database and told him that a Blake Lane had stayed at the hotel, but he'd checked out a day ago. Vaughn pressed his luck by asking if they had an address on file for Blake, but the maître d' informed him that he couldn't give out that information. He thanked the man and hung up.

Probably just a dead end anyway.

Vaughn had calmed down considerably when he approached Bowes, this time with his tech partner Caine, in the bullpen.

"Hey, Bowes, did Darnell give you some printer pages to compare?"

The man glanced up from his laptop.

"Sure did. Actually, I'm surprised that Darnell brought them to me. Didn't think you guys listened to anything I say."

"Not in the mood, Bowes."

Bowes eyed Vaughn.

"Right—shitty deal for that department head. Fuck, man, that whole Princeton math department is cursed or something. First those two math geniuses, then the student, now—"

"Bowes," Vaughn snapped.

"My bad. Yeah, I compared the two sheets." He produced the pieces of paper—one from the ad on Joshua Perry's windshield, the other some random shit that Darnell printed out from Gene's assisted living home—from a folder. "They're an exact match."

Vaughn was shocked, didn't think he'd heard correctly.

"What?"

Bowes nodded.

"Exact match. Same printer made the ad and this . . . whatever this is."

"Are you sure?"

Now it was Bowes's turn to give him the side eye.

"Sorry."

"Hey, Detective Ryan?"

Caine.

Ernie to Bowes's Burt. Heavyset, no glasses, but his thick eyebrows might very well have been trendy frames.

"Yeah?"

"I looked into that TikTok video, the one of Dr. Reeves."

Vaughn felt himself becoming defensive.

I didn't ask you to do that.

He let it go.

"And?"

"Did some digging. The account that posted it is new, and the guy who started it used a Proton email address to register—impossible to trace."

"Great."

"It's not all bad—found out that a lot of the initial reposts and likes are from a popular boosting service."

"What the hell does that mean?"

"Means that it initially went viral because someone paid a service to get the ball rolling. They *wanted* this to go viral."

"Can you track the payment made to the service? Credit card?"

"Naw, security's pretty good. Wouldn't matter anyway. They only accept crypto for payment, and that shit is completely untraceable."

"Huh."

Another dead end.

"*Buuuut* . . ." Caine continued. "New email account, but not a new phone. Tracked the embedded metadata to a specific device using the IEMI number. The phone is registered to a business called Impact Investing."

Or maybe not. Still, the name didn't ring a bell, and Vaughn felt his forehead crinkle.

"Majority owner is Devon Godfrey," Caine said with a grin.

"No shit." Vaughn scratched his chin. "Zeke posted the video."

"Sure looks that way."

"Anything else?"

"'Bout it," Caine said. "You not going to the presser?"

"No. Thanks, fellas."

The rest of the precinct was fairly quiet. Most officers were hovering on the ground floor or outside, watching Captain Daniels do his thing.

Vaughn returned to his office, addressed the murder board again. Added two more pieces of information: the printer and the cell phone.

Vaughn squinted. As much as he hated to admit it, maybe Darnell was right. Objectively, there were strong links between these crimes and the math department. And Gene Reeves specifically.

Did he know Zeke? Probably not. The fire took place three years ago.

Vaughn knew that Captain Daniels liked Zeke for this, for the gassings. The kid was not right in the head. But his crimes—killing Rebecca Quinn and assaulting Ivy—were crimes of passion. The gassings showed forethought, planning, patience.

In Vaughn's experience, unsubs usually fell into one camp or the other: plotters or impulsive. Even though crimes of this nature were plotted on a spectrum, and criminals often slid back and forth, they never went from one extreme to another this soon, this quickly.

Vaughn opened his computer, started looking into Zeke, then changed course. Dr. Moorehead. He linked both Zeke and Gene Reeves. The man had been the head of the Princeton mathematics and statistics department for eleven years. He'd been Eugene Reeves's boss.

Vaughn closed his eyes.

And now he was dead. This fucking case . . .

Darnell's face appeared out of the darkness. Vaughn saw his lips move.

This whole 'can't speak, can't write' thing is a farce.

When Vaughn had mentioned Ivy's name, he thought he saw Dr. Reeves cock his head. It had been subtle, but noticeable. Nothing else registered with the man, but that seemed to.

Was his mental deficiency all an act? Was Darnell right?

Despite his reservations, Vaughn found himself pulling up the police report from the fire. Read the part about the brain injury, the damage to Broca's area. Hesitated before firing off a text to Dr. Button, attaching Eugene Reeves' medical file from the case.

Then he stared off into space, wondering what in the fuck he was supposed to do next. If only he had a senior detective here to guide him . . .

Vaughn's head jerked.

Unbelievably, he'd fallen asleep in his fucking chair.

Have to move. Have to keep moving.

Maybe it was time to speak to Dr. Eugene Reeves again. Or at least try.

CHAPTER 67

Sarah Kachinski was standing outside the DAL when Ivy pulled up. Her doughy face was strained, and her hands were locked on her hips.

Ivy thought, *She spends more time waiting for me then she does waiting on my dad.*

She didn't get out of the car right away; she just sat and stared.

It was too much.

Too much death.

Too much murder.

Ivy was tempted to just drive away. And she almost did, too. After all, this was no longer her responsibility—Abby's words. Maybe it never was.

A shuddering sigh coursed through her, and Ivy finally opened the door.

"He's gone," Kachinski almost whined. "Slipped out during lunch. No one has seen him since."

Ivy felt for this woman.

"I'm sorry."

"It's not your fault," Kachinski said, shaking her head.

Ivy was sick of people saying that. It made her almost physically ill to hear those four words. People viewed the world, their lives, as this series of random events. Luck, chance.

Odds.

It wasn't like that. It was more like the Queen Anne's lace flower.

Fractal, predictable.

In essence, life was a math equation. A complex one, sure, but everything you experienced was part of this equation. Figure out all the variables, the terms, the operations, and you could predict the outcome with a fair degree of certainty.

This *was* her fault.

Gene had called her, not Wendy. She'd gone to the house first. Dialed 911 after.

"I couldn't—" Sarah sighed. "They know, Ivy. Management knows. They saw the cops last time and I managed to sneak Gene in, but—"

"I just want to find him."

Déjà vu—how's that for predictable?

"Me too. I already checked the field. He's not there."

"We need to spread out. I'll start with the field, just in case."

"Okay." Sarah hesitated.

"Sarah. If you want to stay, I'll—"

—understand.

"No." Sarah said. Ivy had misinterpreted the pause. "It's just that today is the anniversary of the fire."

This surprised Ivy.

She checked her phone.

June 5th. Three years to the day. That, too, in a way, was predictable. She'd just missed the pattern.

"I know," Ivy lied. She hadn't known.

"Do you want me to ask more people to help with the search? Call the police?"

Definitely not. Ivy pictured Darnell stomping around, getting everyone worked up, ruining any chance, however slim, that they'd accept the missing resident back.

"Not yet. I'm going to check the field, okay?"

Ivy hurried off before Sarah could convince her otherwise. Found the path, although it was more difficult today. Most of the bent stalks had recovered, their stems straightening.

The flowers were in full bloom. The size of dessert plates. Fractals. Repeating sequences from a central, radiating point.

Beautiful.

Ivy spent the next hour searching the field, softly calling her father's name. Kachinski was right; he wasn't here.

Where are you?

Ivy returned to her car, drove bleary-eyed to where she'd found the missing man in the middle of the night.

No sign of him.

She made her way to the barn.

After the events at the Thomas Clarke House, police had vacated the area. They'd left signs up, warning would-be hikers or nosy journalists that this was a crime scene. Trespassers would be prosecuted, *blah, blah, blah.*

Yellow tape surrounded the entire structure. A hint of egg smell still hung in the air.

Ivy ducked under the tape, stepped into the first room.

Her vision no longer distorted from the gas mask, it looked very different from the first time she'd been here.

The table and chairs were gone. The buttons and digital display also bagged and tagged and removed. A hole in the drywall.

The prisoner's dilemma.

Someone had built the interior precisely for the game.

No, it wasn't Zeke. Zeke couldn't plan for a simple quiz. He had . . . what did the kids call it? TikTok brain. Couldn't focus on any one thing for more than a few seconds. Swiping up—or sideways, or however the hell the app worked—to move onto the next fifteen-second dopamine-releasing video.

Next, Ivy found her way to the first crime scene. Recalled the approximate location from conversations she'd overheard between Vaughn and Darnell.

CiCi's Pizza. The Cedar Ridge Preserve.

It wasn't hard to find—the excessive use of yellow crime scene tape made it noticeable from a quarter mile away. This barn was larger than the first, and the interior was different from the photo that Vaughn had shown her, too. For one, there were no bodies on the ground.

The 100 prisoners problem.

No boxes, no numbers. But there had been numbers. *Prime* numbers.

Ivy peered through the hole that someone had crudely cut from the drywall. He wasn't there. She returned to her car and sat in the driver's seat.

Why prime numbers?

That wasn't part of the game. And Vaughn—or was it Darnell?—was right; using prime numbers made the game more complicated. They had to mean something. It was a message. Her mind went to the letter with her name on the envelope.

Neither 8001 nor 8128 were prime numbers. But the missing value—127—was.

Ivy took out her phone. Abby hadn't called yet—still at work.

Her eyes fell on the date again: June 5th. Five . . . a prime number. The anniversary of the fire. That *fucking* night.

Years ago, her father had taught her what it meant to learn something. Explained the process, the frustration. That's where Ivy had been lost for the past three days: in a state of frustration.

This vanished now, however. In a blink, a moment of clarity.

And Ivy Reeves knew exactly where the missing DAL resident was hiding.

CHAPTER 68

It finally happened.

PPD Detective Darnell Sacker's life had finally hit rock bottom. Amazing that it took this long, considering what he'd been through.

Darnell thought things couldn't get worse after his wife and daughter had been murdered, thought it impossible.

He'd been wrong.

The first thing Darnell did when he got home was head into his bedroom and grab a half-empty bottle of Jack. Took a massive haul.

Drank more.

The liquid burned all the way to the pit of his stomach.

Darnell relished the heat.

Following the murder of his family, the entire department had taken turns coming to visit. Brought him food and drink—too much of the latter. Over time, the number of visitors slowed.

Then they stopped completely—too soon. Everyone had their own lives to worry about, while his was effectively over.

And then he'd gone back to work. Tried to return to how things were before.

Met his new partner.

For a time, this had helped. He trained his partner, taught him about the job. A protégé, if you will. Detective Vaughn Ryan was a good kid, a great detective. Loyal, faithful.

Someone who stood by him, supported him every way he knew how. And Darnell had gone and fucked that all up.

Tears welling in his eyes, Darnell finished the bottle. It took him a minute or two to find another, this one only a quarter-full.

It would have been harder still had Vaughn not cleaned up the other day.

Darnell sat cross-legged on his bed, the bottle in his lap.

I'm sorry, Vaughn.

He closed his eyes as he gulped from the bottle. Didn't even realize that he'd taken his gun out of the holster and was now holding the heavy, PPD-issued pistol in his right hand.

He thought of his beautiful wife and daughter. About the sheer terror they must have felt when the masked men had kicked the door in.

Tied them up.

Tears streamed down Darnell's face. These burned nearly as much as the alcohol.

I should have been there.

But he wasn't.

Darnell was in the field, working a case that the captain had already pulled him off. Prioritizing the lives of others over the ones who meant the most to him.

Something metal clanged against his top teeth and made him shiver. Darnell thought it was the bottle.

It was his gun.

Darnell, fully weeping now, wrapped his lips around the cold barrel.

I'm sorry. I should have been there for you.

A great detective, a near perfect closing record. Moving up the ranks at a rapid clip. Some kind of man he was. Couldn't even protect his own family.

I'm sorry.

Darnell moved his index finger from the guard to the trigger.

His weapon was a Glock 19 semi-automatic pistol. Seventeen rounds in the magazine, one in the chamber. Darnell would only need the one. 5.3 lbf of pressure and it would all be over.

Darnell figured he was at just shy of 5 lbf—all this math had gone to his head—when he heard a knock on his front door.

CHAPTER 69

"SHE'S NOT HERE."

"Where did she go?" Vaughn asked the portly man named John—just John. Had an effeminate air about him, but also gave Vaughn the impression that he wasn't a pushover.

"Dr. Reeves wandered off again. Ms. Kachinski went to look for him, I presume."

"He's gone?"

"Yes. Second time this week. Management—"

Vaughn had heard all this before.

"When?"

"I don't know. An hour ago? Two?"

"Mind if I see his room?"

John's thick shoulders lifted. Fell.

"Won't be his room for long."

"Why do you say that?"

"Management's fed up. Insurance isn't going to cover him anymore—too many field trips, if you know what I mean."

Odd choice of words: "field trip." Delaney had come across Dr. Reeves in a field by the second murder scene.

This wasn't good.

"Can I see his room?" Vaughn asked again.

"Sure."

Vaughn knew the way. John unlocked the door.

"Suit yourself," he said, holding it open for him.

Vaughn looked around. It was identical to the last time he'd been here. The small chess board, this time the sole piece, the rook, lying on its side.

Nothing of interest.

Vaughn was desperate to find a link between Zeke and Gene Reeves. And there had to be one. Except . . . there wasn't.

Other than the chess board, the room was devoid of personal items. Made sense for a man in Gene Reeves's state. It did seem a little odd that Ivy wouldn't have put up something representative of the man her father used to be. One of his degrees, a photo of Gene receiving what was likely one of many prestigious awards.

Only, she hadn't. The walls were bare, save a motel quality oil painting. No signature.

"See?"

Yeah, Vaughn saw.

"Let me ask you something, John."

"Shoot."

"You ever see this kid before?"

Vaughn showed the man a photo of Zeke Godfrey. John took the phone, brought it close to his face. Rolled his head around.

"I don't . . . think so?"

Not exactly a firm 'no.'

"Take another look."

John did, spoke as he stared at the screen.

"It's the shaggy blond hair . . ." he trailed off.

"What about it?" Vaughn pressed.

"About two months ago, we had a break-in. I think someone came in through that window there." John, still focused on Vaughn's phone, raised a finger and pointed at the window leading to the outside. "Went through Gene's things while he was on an outing. Also went through the main office."

"Really?"

Vaughn thought that if something like this had been reported to the PPD, Darnell would have probably come across it while he was digging into Dr. Reeves. Only, Darnell was a loose cannon who could no longer be trusted.

"Yep."

Vaughn frowned.

"Anything stolen?"

"Don't think so. Management decided not to report it because—"

"Let me guess? Insurance?"

John pursed his lips.

"Yep. That and the fact that they passed it off as a resident snooping around, that no one came in from the window. They suggested that Dr. Reeves might have just left it open. Some of our residents have . . . issues. Once, we had this sex addict who made his rounds of the place. Slept with pretty much everyone. We had this one woman, Ms. Murphy, who had a colostomy bag. Right before management cut our resident nympho loose, she curiously developed a case of genital herpes . . . around the colostomy hole."

It took a few seconds for Vaughn to clue in to what the man was saying.

"That's disgusting."

"Yeah."

Vaughn shuddered at the thought.

"The thing is, one of our residents is a bit of a savant. A savant with a prostate the size of a grapefruit—no lie, the guy goes piss every hour. Also has a bit of OCD, doesn't like to piss in the same bathroom twice in a row. Don't ask me why. Anyway, he said he saw a young guy in a mask around the time of the break-in." John put air quotes around the final word. "Said he had blond hair coming out of the eye holes."

"Was it the guy on the phone?"

John rolled his eyes.

"He was wearing a mask."

"Right. Okay, thanks. Do me a favor?" Vaughn handed the man a card. This is what his job had come down to: handing out cards like candy at a carnival. For fuck's sake. "Give me a call when Gene comes back?"

"Sure."

Vaughn returned to his car, thinking about colostomy holes, grapefruit-sized prostates, a rook lying on its side on a miniature chess board.

The Bae-sian Prof.

Zeke posted the video of Ivy. Zeke paid bots to pump it up. Zeke drew attention to himself even though he was engrossed in a complex plan to murder people in the name of math?

Ugh, he didn't like it.

Vaughn pulled up the TikTok video on his phone.

It wasn't as popular as it had been when it was first posted—welcome to the new age where your fifteen minutes was cut down to mere seconds—but it had still amassed nearly two million views. Someone did call out during the lecture, as Ivy had told him, joking about Zeke maybe not having the clap after all. This, in turn, made him think of Ms. Murphy and her colostomy adventures.

Another shudder.

Vaughn was about to close his phone when he noticed something in the video. Ivy had told him that she always confiscated the students' cell phones before class. Only, on this particular day, she'd been late.

Vaughn had just assumed that no one had taken their phones. But while the video showed all of the students, he could only see three-quarters of Ivy. Vaughn had never been in the classroom that Ivy taught in, but could get the gist of it from the video.

Lower bowl, podium at the center, digital screen behind—barely visible. The angle was off. If a student had taken the video, he would have seen Ivy straight on. Vaughn paused the video.

There—*Zeke*. Clearly visible. Scowling, angry.

How was that possible? Vaughn thought back—thought hard.

The TA. If Ivy took the phones every day and she was late, it made sense that the TA would have done the same in her absence.

Vaughn immediately called Bowes.

"Detective Ryan, the captain was—"

"Bowes, I need you to do something for me. I need you to look into Dr. Reeves's TA. His name is Tristan something . . ."

CHAPTER 70

AFTER THE FIRE, Ivy had never gone back to her father's partner's house.

She found herself there now. Unlike her own house, which she'd inherited from her father, Steve Neely's place was—had been—a sprawling estate. Beautiful, worth seven figures, easy.

Eugene had been secretive about his work, as was to be expected. Gene and Steve had spent the better part of their adult lives investigating the Riemann hypothesis, a way to map out all known prime numbers. Solving the equation had widespread implications for everything from AI to cryptocurrency, to codebreaking, to financial markets.

The one million-dollar Clay Millennium Prize that was on permanent offer for the solution was a drop in the bucket, a mere hundred or thousand times less than the actual value. Governments, private investors, hedge funds, hell, even defense contractors would want the solution.

As Ivy pulled up to the burnt exterior of Steve Neely's home, she closed her eyes. Thought about that night. As usual, her fingers started to ache where she'd burned herself.

Ivy had been visiting town after wrapping up her PhD when she'd gotten the desperate call from her father.

"Ivy—"

"Dad? Everything okay?"

"I need you to listen."

Gene's tone was all business. More so than usual. Ivy listened. Couldn't believe what she was hearing. It was surreal. Like something out of a movie.

Two best friends, work colleagues, two of the smartest men on the planet, torn apart by the allure of money.

"I need you to come to me. I'm at Steve's place. He—" There was a shout, the specific words indecipherable. When Gene spoke again, he did so in a mere whisper. "If anything happens to me, you need to save the work."

"Dad? You're scaring me."

"Save the work, Ivy. Find Steve's laptop. Please. It's more important than either of us."

That was the last time she'd heard his voice. So much had changed that night.

Everything had changed.

Ivy got out of the car, walked toward the front door. She'd only been here twice before. That night and once about three months earlier.

They'd been on their way home from dinner out—one of the rare occasions that Gene had taken time off work to hang out with her—when he'd said he needed to stop at his partner's to drop something off.

Ivy had been in awe of Steve's house, so much larger and fancier than theirs. She'd made a comment to this effect, and Gene had replied by saying that his partner was less risk averse.

Steve had been an early crypto adopter, had made a shit ton of money.

The place was dark now, the night disguising the soot smears that marred the brick walls.

Ivy was on high alert. She looked upward. The windows had been boarded up with particle board. The house was silent—deathly silent.

Ivy reached for the door, not expecting to find it unlocked. Surprised that it was. She opened it a crack.

"Anyone here?"

No answer.

Ivy opened the door wider and put one foot inside. She remembered the house. Remembered the layout, even though the fire in the kitchen had been blazing at the time.

This was . . . different.

Ivy was so confused by the gray drywall in front of her, the three doors, pristine white, side by side, each with a large number written on them in Sharpie—one, two, three—that she didn't even realize she'd stepped all the way in. And when the door clicked closed behind her, following by a soft, mechanical whir of the digital lock engaging, Ivy knew that she'd made a mistake.

A fatal mistake.

"Hello, Ivy," a voice came from a speaker embedded behind her. "I'm surprised that it took you so long to come here."

CHAPTER 71

"Alright, I'll look into it, get back to you."

"Thanks, Bowes."

As soon as he'd hung up, Vaughn called Ivy. No answer. Tried Darnell next. Again, no answer.

Vaughn was starting to worry. Eugene missing was one thing. Ivy and Darnell not answering either? Not a good sign. He wracked his brain, tried to remember the name of Ivy's friend.

Abby, right? Abby . . . Granger. That was it.

He had no trouble finding the woman online. Abby liked to post selfies. Found one of her in a dark smock. On her right breast, a pumped-up breast, was a company name and logo. A cosmetic company. Found them online, too.

"Hi, my name is Detective Vaughn Ryan with the PPD. Is Abby Granger around?"

"I don't think so—let me check."

Vaughn listened to elevator music as he waited. The line clicked back.

"Abby had to leave to pick up a friend, I think? Do you want to leave a message?"

Vaughn had already hung up.

Dialed Delaney.

"Detective Ryan, the captain—"

"I know!" Vaughn said, his frustration bubbling over. "Don't care about that right now. You did the interview with Ivy's friend, right?"

"Abby Granger? Yeah. Hot—"

"You have her number on file? Address?"

"She filled out a report."

"Can I have her number and address, *please*?"

Fucking hell.

"Yeah, one sec."

No elevator music this time. Instead, Vaughn heard loud voices, one of which he recognized: Devon Godfrey. The man's baritone pitch was unmistakable. The sound faded, replaced by shuffling papers.

"Got it." Delaney sounded out of breath. He read off the phone number, which Vaughn immediately punched into the Notes app on his phone. Did the same with the address.

"Have you—"

Again, Vaughn hung up.

Abby didn't answer her phone either, and that creeping sense of dread grew. He couldn't stop thinking about that final tank of hydrogen sulfide gas.

Vaughn drove to Abby Granger's house, a small apartment in Trenton. Found her door and knocked, hoping that she was inside. Hoping that Ivy was with her.

"Abby Granger? Ivy? You in there? It's Detective Ryan."

Vaughn knocked again, then rang the bell. Wondered why he hadn't done that first.

A cop thing, he thought incomprehensibly.

"Ivy?"

He tested the door. It was locked. No warrant, no probable cause. And this wasn't Darnell Sacker's home. He would stretch the truth to acquire the information he needed, leverage suspects, apply pressure. Clean up his partner's messes. But breaking into Abby's home was taking things a step too far.

His phone rang and he looked up at the window. No movement from inside.

"Detective Ryan?"

It was Bowes.

"Yeah?"

"You're not going to believe it, but the TA? Tristan Coates?"

"What about him?"

"His name isn't Tristan Coates. I mean, it is *now*, but it wasn't always."

"What was his name?" Vaughn asked, his voice hoarse, throat dry.

"His name is Tristan Neely. He's Dr. Steve Neely's kid."

CHAPTER 72

THE VOICE FROM the speaker was distorted. Whoever was talking was using some sort of modulator. Ivy turned around and tried to open the front door. It was locked. She pulled, but the thing didn't budge.

"Only one way out, Ivy."

Ivy's entire body broke out in a cold sweat as she pulled even harder. All of the muscles in her hand and forearm ached.

"It won't open," the speaker informed her.

Ivy tried a third time, with both hands now.

"Turn around."

Ivy gave up and did as she was asked.

Three doors—one, two, three. All locked with a familiar sleek black device. The same one she'd seen at the barns that had hosted the prisoner's dilemma and the 100 prisoners problem.

"You recognize this, Ivy?"

Ivy wished she didn't. Wished she was more like Aaron Treadman, oblivious to the permutation approach. Looping. Wished she was more like Abby, too. Abby with the simple life. Conversely, everything Ivy did was calculated and measured—always had been. Even that night her father called, from inside this very house, her actions had been deliberate.

Heart-breaking, life-changing, but deliberate, nonetheless.

The three doors were from the Monty Hall problem, made famous on the 1963 television show *Let's Make a Deal.*

"I knew you would," the voice said, even though Ivy hadn't spoken. "I'm going to be honest with you, I thought you'd come here sooner. But oh, well—you're here now. Pick a door, Ivy."

Ivy shook her head.

"Pick a door, Ivy, or they all die."

"What?" Ivy gasped.

"You heard me. Pick a door or they all die."

"Why are you—"

"*Pick a door!*" the voice bellowed.

Ivy whimpered.

A door . . . *one* door.

In the show, the contestant was given three doors to choose from. Behind two of them was a goat. The last, a new car. The doors, like the ones before her now, were numbered one, two, three. Two of which were prime numbers. One wasn't.

"One," Ivy said, choosing the only non-prime number of the three. Her voice cracked. "I pick door number one."

There was a short pause, then she heard that familiar mechanical whir followed by a click. Door number two opened and Ivy gasped again.

It was the detective, Darnell Sacker.

He was gagged and bound, slumped on a stool, his back propped up against the drywall. The left side of his forehead was purple, a gash leaking blood into one closed eye.

"Why are you doing this?" Ivy said. She was trembling now.

"Because you have something I want."

"What? Who are you?" Desperate, begging.

"I'll answer after you play the game."

"I don't want to play your fucking games!"

Ivy's eyes roamed the retrofitted space. Spotted another one of those shitty cameras mounted in the corner. And an air vent.

The walls were made of drywall, just like at the crime other scenes. No mud, no tape. The vent . . . Ivy knew exactly what was hooked up on the other side.

Why did I come inside? Why?

"You know the game, Ivy, and you know what comes next."

She knew, all right.

"Would you like to switch doors or keep door number one, Dr. Reeves?"

CHAPTER 73

"STEVE NEELY'S KID," Vaughn repeated softly. This was for his own benefit, but Bowes confirmed it anyway.

"Yep. His only kid. Mom's not in the picture. Died of breast cancer nearly a decade ago."

What the actual fuck?

Tristan Coates, née Tristan Neely, was Steve's son.

Ivy's father and Steve worked together before a mysterious fire resulted in the latter's death and the former being burnt and turned into a living vegetable.

A fire that the retired detective who worked the case was convinced Gene had started.

Did Ivy know? Did she know that Tristan Coates was actually Tristan Neely?

No, she couldn't have; she would have said something.

Wouldn't she?

"How?"

"It's not hard to change your name. All you have to do is—"

"No, I mean how the hell did he become Ivy's TA?"

"Well, I did some digging. Tristan applied to be Dr. Reeves's TA at the end of last term."

"Okay, then *why*? Why did he change his name? Wouldn't letting everyone know he was Steve Neely's kid help him? I mean, his father was a legend in the math world."

"I'm guessing because he didn't want people to know."

He didn't want Ivy *to know*, Vaughn mentally corrected.

Vaughn blinked, shook his head. Tried to lock in.

He still didn't get it.

Zeke, Dr. Moorehead, now Tristan.

"There is something weird," Bowes said. *Colostomy hole weird?* "Weirder, I mean. Tristan's grades . . . they weren't great."

"Not great?" Stalling, trying to give himself time to figure this out.

"I don't know much about math," Bowes continued after a slurp of what was undoubtedly an energy drink of some sort, "but Princeton's math department is one of the best in the country, right?"

"Yeah, I guess so."

"Well, Tristan was a B+ student. So I did a little more digging."

Vaughn had no idea how Bowes had done all this in a matter of what? A half hour? Twenty minutes?

"And?"

"And he was the only applicant."

Vaughn wasn't following and asked Bowes to clarify.

"Tristan Coates was the only applicant for the TA position. I looked back at previous years and there were dozens of them. Top candidates had perfect 4.0 GPAs, awards, etc."

The VPNs. The remote nozzles for the gas that couldn't be traced. The cameras.

Speakers.

"He hacked in, didn't he?"

"Yep," Bowes said, a little too cheerily for Vaughn's taste. "Someone erased all other applicants, leaving Tristan as the only one. They were subtle, but not great. Wasn't as careful back then, I guess. I traced the delete actions back to a specific computer."

"Ivy's stolen laptop."

"Yeah, but here's the thing: it—"

"Bowes, I think Ivy's in trouble. You have an address for Tristan Coates?"

"I wasn't done—"

"Bowes, I need an address."

"Okay, hold on." Vaughn looked back at Abby's house, the dark windows, as he pulled onto the main road. "I've got it."

Vaughn punched it into his GPS.

It was close, less than fifteen minutes away. A townhouse on a winding road, relatively secluded. Nearest neighbor a couple hundred yards away.

"Thanks, Bowes."

Bowes tried to say something, but Vaughn had already ended the call. Bowes had done good work, but Bowes liked to talk.

This wasn't time for talking. This was time for acting.

Vaughn hadn't been willing to break into Abby Granger's place. But Tristan Coates/Neely?

Fuck a warrant.

The door gave inward with just a few mid-strength shoulder pops.

"Tristan?" Vaughn drew his gun.

Eyes trained ahead, he searched blindly with his hand for the light switch. Turned it on, squinting preemptively so as to not be blinded by the light.

"Tristan?"

The house was quiet. Sparsely decorated. Reminded Vaughn a little of Gene's room.

Vaughn swept the front hall, then the kitchen. Both were impeccably clean.

"Tristan!"

The house wasn't particularly large. One story. He cleared the two bedrooms, then the bathroom.

Vaughn found a door tucked on the other side of the kitchen. Probably a pantry. Only, no one he knew locked a pantry with both a digital padlock and an old-fashioned one. To be fair, no one he knew had an actual pantry, but still. Vaughn hadn't knocked on the exterior door, but he knocked on this one.

"Tristan! PPD! Open the fucking door!"

Impossible, not with the padlock on the outside.

"Ivy?"

Nothing.

He tried the door. It didn't budge. The locks were solid. But the thing about locked doors was that you could have a lock worthy of the Pentagon, but if your door and frame were shit . . .

Weakest link—*ha, ha*—and all that.

Another fucking game show.

Not as easy for Vaughn to break through this one—weak-ass shoulder pops didn't do the trick. But three solid, well-placed kicks and the frame split.

Two more and the lock portion that was bolted to the door broke free.

Vaughn found the lights.

He didn't even make it into the pantry—modified pantry, as it was—before he froze.

"Holy shit."

It wasn't the tools, the hammer, the boxes of drywall screws that made him stop. Nor the actual sheets of drywall, all different sizes, leaning up against one wall.

It was the photographs, the printouts, the red writing.

What Vaughn saw made his murder board back at PPD look like a children's science fair project.

The far wall was completely covered in pages.

A lot of text. Printouts of newspaper articles and what was most likely a series of text messages. Front and center was a photograph of two men, probably in their mid-forties. One was hunched over some sort of document, signing it with his left hand. The other standing behind him. Both smiling.

The caption revealed that the man signing the document was Eugene Reeves, the other, Steve Neely. Hard to believe that this was the same man as the one at the home, his face so scarred that he was forced to wear a mask so as to not disturb the other residents.

There were photos from the fire, too. Newspaper articles, actual printed photographs.

"Two esteemed math professors caught in deadly fire. One dead, one in critical condition."

The word "LAPTOP" was written in red ink across several sheets. Circled. "Riemann hypothesis," too.

One of shaggy-haired Zeke. Another of his father, Devon Godfrey. A printout of Impact Investing's prospectus.

And then Vaughn saw Ivy.

Photos of her receiving a degree of some sort. Another winning an award, following in her father's footsteps. Then there were the more intimate ones. Photos that wouldn't have appeared in any newspaper or university circulation. Images of her in class, unaware that her picture was being taken. Similar angle to the TikTok video. Another of her sleeping in her bed.

"Fucking hell."

Vaughn holstered his gun and clicked a contact on his phone as he continued to stare at the manic board.

"29 MINUTES."

That was written more than a dozen times, most with accompanied arrows pointing at the caption of a newspaper article from the fire.

"First on scene was Dr. Eugene Reeves's daughter, Ivy Reeves."

Another: the date of the fire. Three years ago, to the day. The location.

"Detective Ryan?"

"Delaney, I need you to come here. Document everything."

"What? Where?"

Vaughn gave Delaney Tristan's address. Repeated it twice, got him to say it back just to be sure. He didn't plan on being there when the cop arrived.

Vaughn ran out of the house.

With all of the shit pasted to the back wall, Vaughn hadn't

thought of looking behind him. If he had, he would have seen the small camera in the upper right-hand corner of the room, aimed directly at the door.

Would have seen the red indicator light glowing brightly.

CHAPTER 74

The math was simple: with three doors, the probability of the car being behind the initial door that you choose is one-third. The probability of it being behind one of the other two doors is two-thirds. When, in the show, Monty Hall opens one door, one of the two you didn't select, revealing a goat, the odds change. The door that you selected still has a one-third chance of containing the car. The remaining door, however, has a two-thirds chance.

From a statistical perspective, you should *always* change doors when Monty asks. But this wasn't a game show, and they weren't talking about goats and cars.

They were talking about people.

"I don't want to choose," Ivy said.

"If you don't choose, they all die." The voice sounded almost bored now. Repeating the same thing over and over again.

"I'm not picking. I'm not."

"Then *you* die."

"Why the fuck are you doing this?"

"Because of Twenty-nine minutes!"

Twenty-nine minutes? What the hell was he talking about?

Ivy thought of Dr. Moorehead and the note. The riddle.

"Twenty-nine minutes . . . the time that I had to save Dr. Moorehead."

"Twenty-nine minutes," the voice repeated, calm now, "was also the amount of time you spent in this house before calling 911."

Ivy squinted. Her brain worked.

"I know he called you, Ivy—I managed to get a record of your cell logs. Eugene called you at 9:52 p.m. Your cell phone signal pinged six miles away. Credit card statements confirm that you paid for your meal at Osaka's Sushi at 9:58 p.m. There was no traffic at that hour. Even if you were driving slowly, which I doubt you were, the drive takes at most twelve minutes. That brings us to 10:10. Except you didn't place the 911 call until 10:37. Twenty-nine minutes, Ivy!"

She was again transported back to that night. First the call, her father's ominous message. Then arriving on the scene, running into the burning building. Finding both men inside, charred, burnt. Ivy fought back tears.

"I know what you did."

No—no you don't. You have no idea.

It cost me everything. My mom. My dad.

"You took Eugene's laptop. Your father texted mine, told him that they were going to settle it once and for all. Eugene said he was going to bring his laptop. Except it wasn't here!"

Ivy didn't know if the voice modulator malfunctioned or if the man had shut it off on purpose, but the voice came through crystal clear when he'd shouted that last sentence. And of course, Ivy recognized it immediately. Didn't have to, though; "your father texted mine" was a dead giveaway.

"Tristan?"

A short pause. Accidental or not, Tristan didn't bother turning the voice modulator back on.

"Where is your father's laptop?"

"I don't—I don't know!"

"Twenty-nine minutes, Ivy!" the man screamed. "Where is Eugene's laptop?"

"I don't know! I swear, I don't know!"

"What were you doing in the house for Twenty-nine minutes!"

Ivy refused to let her mind go back there.

"Please! Let the detective go."

"Tell me where the laptop is and I'll let you all go. Or you can choose. Up to you."

"I'm a victim, too. My dad—"

"My dad is dead!"

"So is mine!"

"It's not the same."

It wasn't. But not in the way that Tristan thought.

Now, Ivy was transported back to three years ago. It was impossible to stop herself. The telephone call.

"We did it, Ivy. We did it! We solved the Riemann hypothesis. Steve has half on his laptop, I have half on mine. We're supposed to meet up, but . . . I don't trust him. He wants to go private, sell it to the highest bidder. I can't let him do that. If anything happens to me, you need to get the laptops."

Tristan's voice shattered the reverie.

"I see you, Ivy. You have the laptop."

Ivy's eyes darted from Darnell, still unconscious but

breathing, his thick chest rhythmically rising and falling, to the corners of the room.

Focused on the camera. Of course, he was watching. He was always watching. He'd been watching her in Dr. Moorehead's office and he was watching her now.

"Please, Tristan, just let the cop go. Let all of us go. I don't know where the laptop is. I have no idea what you're talking about."

"Pick a door."

"Tristan—"

"*Pick a door!*"

Ivy winced.

"I'm going to give you twenty-nine seconds—" Tristan paused. In the background, over the speaker, Ivy heard what sounded like an alarm. A sharp, piercing beep. Repeated. "Looks like the rules have changed, Ivy."

A resounding *click* and the two remaining doors opened.

Behind door number one: a man in a peach-colored face mask. Seated. Not moving.

Behind door number three: Abby Granger. Eyes wide, mouth taped.

"No!" Ivy screamed. "I switch doors! I want three! Please, I—"

With the alarm still going off and her own shouts echoing off the enclosed space, Abby didn't hear the door open behind her.

Didn't hear Tristan raise the thick burlap sack and yank it down over her head.

She did, however, hear the hiss of hydrogen sulfide gas being released.

CHAPTER 75

Vaughn grabbed a gas mask and his trusty crowbar from his trunk. Then he sprinted for the front door.

When he heard the sound of gas flowing somewhere inside, he pulled the mask over his head and wedged the crowbar between the door and the frame. He flexed; the door started to move. Now, he heard muffled cries from within. This was a good sign. Someone was still alive in there.

"Ivy!" He shouted, leaning all of his body weight on the crowbar.

There was a splinter and then a *pop* as the door opened. It struck something on the other side, and someone yelped.

A woman rushed at him, coughing, sneezing.

It wasn't Ivy.

"Out!" he screamed. "Get out!"

She ran outside.

Vaughn saw three doors in front of him, all open. In one of the small rooms beyond was a man in a mask.

"Move!" The man's eyes were closed. "Fucking *move!*"

Vaughn sprinted forward.

It was Eugene Reeves, and he was unconscious.

Vaughn cursed, bent down, and threw the man over his shoulder. He was thin, frail. Easy to carry. With a grunt, he rushed outside, did his best to lower the man as gently as possible onto the grass. Expected the woman to come over and help, but she seemed to be in shock.

He sprinted back in, went to the second door.

Darnell.

Holy fuck, it was Darnell.

And he wasn't moving.

The man was slumped on a stool that his girth almost completely enveloped. Vaughn grabbed his partner by the waist, lifted. Darnell barely rose half an inch.

"Darnell!"

The man coughed. A horrible wet sound behind the tape covering his mouth. Then his eyes snapped open, went impossibly wide.

"*Move!*"

Darnell was disoriented, maybe from the gas, maybe from the gash on his forehead.

Still didn't stand. And unlike Dr. Reeves, there was no chance he would be able to carry his partner.

Vaughn jabbed his thumb into the cut above Darnell's left eye. The man tried to scream and finally came fully to. With another yank, the man rose.

Darnell moved like a drunken sailor.

Apt.

He was a mere foot from the broken exterior door when he started to drop to one knee.

How long did Dr. Button say they had?

At high concentrations, hydrogen sulfide gas could kill in

less than a minute. If Darnell fell, it was over; Vaughn would never be able to drag the big man outside in time.

He did the only thing he could think of at that moment.

Vaughn placed both hands on the man's back and shoved as hard as he could.

It was a good push. Solid.

So good that Vaughn actually fell backward. Landed hard on his ass. His mask shifted but stayed on.

Vaughn quickly scrambled to his feet and ran out, having enough forethought to close the door behind him as best he could.

Darnell had made it. Barely. He was lying on his stomach, coughing so badly that his entire body was quaking.

The egg smell was potent, even with the mask. Some of the gas had leaked outside.

Fuck it.

Vaughn filled his lungs with air, then tore his mask off. Grabbed the back of Darnell's head, put it on him. Still not breathing, Vaughn hooked his arms beneath Darnell's and started to drag him backward away from the house.

Grunted with the effort.

It was easier on grass, would have been impossible on dirt.

Vaughn accidentally inhaled, coughed, spat. Kept dragging. They were ten feet from the door now, fifteen. The smell was no longer as powerful.

"Darnell!"

The man wasn't coughing anymore. Wasn't breathing.

The woman was beside him now, shouting into her gag. Vaughn ripped it off her mouth.

"Fuck!" she screamed.

It was Abby Granger.

"He took Ivy!" she yelled. Her lips were an angry red from where the tape had been stuck. "Tristan took Ivy!"

She turned around, and Vaughn unraveled half of the tape that kept her hands pinned behind her back. Abby wriggled out of the rest by herself.

"Help me flip him over," Vaughn said.

Abby grabbed Darnell's left side; Vaughn, too. They pushed and Darnell rolled. His eyes were closed; stagnant, pink-tinged foam plugged each nostril.

Vaughn laid one hand on top of the other and pushed down on the man's chest. His palms sunk into the man's fat.

"Breathe!" Vaughn pumped.

Abby went to remove Darnell's mask, but Vaughn told her to keep it on. With each chest compression, the foam in Darnell's nose bubbled. When he stopped, it went still.

"Breathe, you fat fuck!"

This time, Vaughn pushed with all of his waning strength. Darnell coughed. Vaughn pushed again.

Again.

When Darnell bucked, Vaughn finally got off him. Collapsed on the ground. Took a full breath of his own. Sputtered a little.

Darnell rolled over and Abby undid the tape from his wrists. As soon as he was free, Darnell took the mask off, tore the tape from his mouth. Hissed in pain.

"Jesus Christ, it I think you broke my ribs!"

Vaughn ignored him, caught his bearings.

Gene had also regained consciousness and was just lying there. Stunned. Seemingly unaffected by the fact that he'd nearly died.

That they'd *all* nearly died.

"Some asshole hit me on the head—"

"Tristan took Ivy!" Abby repeated.

Vaughn got on his phone. His eyes were watering so badly from the gas that he could barely see the screen. Didn't need to see all that well to dial 911.

"This is Detective Ryan with the PPD! I need EMS and police—"

"Badge number?"

"Fuck the badge number. I need EMS and police, now!"

Vaughn screamed the address, hung up. He swiped tears from his eyes. Found Bowes's number.

"Bowes, I need to know if Tristan owns any other properties."

"More—"

"Properties! Houses, apartments, anything! Him or his father!"

"I—I only found the one—I gave it to you earlier."

"Fuck. Put out an APB—" Vaughn stopped speaking as an image of the murder board flashed in his mind. Zeke was on that board. Devon Godfrey, too. "Impact Investing! Devon Godfrey's company . . . do they own any properties? Anything residential in Jersey?"

"Hold on . . . hold on . . ."

Vaughn gritted his teeth as he waited. He was shaking all over. Adrenaline or H2S gas?

"Hurry, Bowes!"

"I'm fucking trying! I'm fucking—okay, I've got something! Impact Investing has a place in Sea Bright. Want the address?"

"Yes! Fucking *yes!* Give me the address *now!*"

CHAPTER 76

Ivy was in the trunk of a car. She could feel the vehicle rolling, could hear the engine thrumming.

But she couldn't see anything.

The bag or sack or whatever it was that Tristan had put over her head was thick and heavy. Her own breath bounced back at her—sour, adrenaline-tinged, hot—making her sweat.

During the struggle, Tristan had somehow managed to bind her hands together in front of her.

Tight, thin. Zipties, most likely.

She tensed her wrists. Only ended up with more pain. Pain that numbed her hands.

"Help!" The sound was impossibly loud. Whatever leaked through the thick fabric rebounded off the trunk lid, echoed back at her. Ivy didn't care. "*Help!*"

She needed to get out.

Not for her.

For Abby.

Abby, who had been loyal, been by her side forever. Before everything. After everything. *Knew* everything.

"Help!"

She tried to kick, but the trunk was too small to extend her legs. Only managed to bang her knees.

"Help!"

Ivy screamed until her throat was raw and she was out of breath. She waited, then screamed some more.

She recalled a true crime podcast in which a young girl in a similar situation as her—bound, hooded, in the trunk of a car—remembered each turn the car made. Later, when the girl somehow managed to acquire a cell phone and call for help, she'd told the police exactly where to go.

This had saved her life.

It was also impossible.

Ivy didn't know if they were going left, right, up, or down. They could be in a goddamn spaceship heading toward the moon for all she knew.

Not that it would make a difference.

Tristan was going to kill her.

He was going to torture her for the information he wanted and then kill her. He'd planned all of this. The irony . . . *him* planning to capture *her*.

"You done?!"

Tristan had to shout from the front seat, and even then, Ivy barely heard him.

No, she wasn't done.

"Help!" She banged her knees. "*Help!*"

They made a turn—right?—and Tristan said, "You can still save yourself, Ivy. Just tell me where the laptop is."

All this for a laptop.

Sixteen dead for a fucking laptop, two more than the ominous email had threatened. Twenty-nine minutes, that was in the email, too, and she hadn't seen the pattern, hadn't recognized the significance.

The fucking laptop which contained Gene's half of the Riemann hypothesis. Did that mean that Tristan had his father's half all along? How? *Where?*

She shook her head.

It didn't matter. What mattered was that her dad was right; it was too dangerous.

If one man—one demented, fucked-up TA—killed sixteen innocent people for it, what lengths would government agencies go to?

Ivy thought back to when she was a kid. Gene just a young man back then. Excited, full of life. Took her out to the Queen Anne's lace field.

"Math is the key to everything, Ivy," Gene had told her. "It rules everything, from the way this flower grows to the way our DNA replicates."

"Is that what you're doing, Daddy? At work? DNA?"

Gene laughed. Twirled a flower.

"No, sweetie. I'm working on the Riemann hypothesis."

"What's that?"

Gene passed her the flower. She tried to twirl it like her dad, but couldn't.

"It's the greatest math problem in history. A way to understand the distribution of prime numbers. The applications are endless."

"I know prime numbers: two, three, five, seven . . ." Ivy got all the way to twenty-nine before stopping.

"You're right. But things get more difficult the larger the numbers get. Prime numbers run everything. They're critical in cryptography—in codes. Computer codes, cryptocurrency, the stock market. The larger the prime number, the harder the code is to crack. With huge prime numbers, even the best computers in the world can't determine if they're actually prime. But if I can solve the Riemann hypothesis, then the equation can be used to predict *all* prime numbers. Every single code can be broken in seconds."

The car suddenly lurched to a stop and Ivy blinked tears from her eyes.

Prepared herself to fight.

Never got a chance.

The trunk opened and Ivy thrust her arms upward. Cool air struck her from behind—she was facing the wrong way and hadn't even realized it.

An arm laced around her throat, and Tristan dragged her out of the trunk.

She fell on the ground.

Ivy tried to scramble to her feet, stopped when she felt something sharp poke into her back, right between her shoulder blades.

"Try anything and I'll sever your spinal cord. Your brain will still work, but you'll never be able to use your legs again."

To prove that he was serious, as if killing sixteen people wasn't evidence enough of his pathology, Tristan pushed the knife. It split the fabric of her shirt and pierced her skin just deep enough to draw blood.

"Get up. Slowly."

Ivy made it to her knees, then stood. Tristan shoved her left shoulder and she turned.

"Walk."

Ivy took a few tentative steps, half expecting to fall off a ledge.

"Keep going. There's a step. Another. One more."

Ivy mounted the stairs.

"Stop."

Tristan moved from behind her to in front, and Ivy thought about making a run for it. But which way? How far?

She couldn't see a damn thing. Would probably cripple herself on the steps, save Tristan from doing the act.

She heard a series of beeps, then what must have been a lock turning. A door opened and Tristan was behind her again.

A gentle push.

The door closed and the lock engaged.

"Move."

Ivy took another half dozen steps. Tristan grabbed a chair and shoved it against the back of her legs.

"Sit."

Ivy was already sitting.

Tristan grabbed the top of her hood, pulled it off. Took a clump of her hair with it.

"Now," Tristan said as she squinted and her eyes adjusted. "You're going to tell me what you did in those twenty-nine minutes. You're going to tell me where Eugene's laptop is, or I'm going to turn you into a vegetable just like your father."

CHAPTER 77

THE MAN STANDING before her wasn't the straight-edge TA that Ivy had hired. It wasn't Tristan Coates. Tristan Neely, neither.

It was a bleary-eyed, red-faced psychopath. A broken human being. A man without a father. A father who, like Gene, had prioritized work over everything. And when he'd died, his work incomplete, Tristan had nothing to live for.

"You can make this stop, Ivy. Just tell me where the laptop is."

"I don't know." Ivy took a deep, shuddering breath. Tears fell onto her lap. "I don't know."

They were in some sort of mansion. In the kitchen. Large bay windows behind Tristan, overlooking a series of bluffs. Sandy Hook? No, Highlands-Sea Bright. Yeah, that was it.

Ivy had no idea that Tristan had another place. Must have been Steve's, purchased with earnings from his early crypto investments. Hadn't shown up on any of the real estate documents that she'd spent hours combing through.

Tristan, knife still in hand, went to the table off to one side and picked up a laptop.

"This is my father's half—where's Gene's?"

Ivy stared at the laptop. Couldn't take her eyes off it. Thought of Abby, of the text she'd sent after their night out.

I couldn't find it.

No shit. It wasn't at his home. It was here. In this . . . place. Wherever the fuck this was.

And Tristan had it all along, just like she'd thought. Her father had entrusted her with his half, it made sense that Dr. Neely would entrust his only child with the other.

"Twenty-nine minutes . . . I know you were in that house for twenty-nine minutes. I know Eugene told you something before he hit his head. *I know.*"

Tristan was wrong about that. Both men had been unconscious when she'd arrived. Only one ever woke up, and he was never the same.

"I can't believe you gave him up . . ." Tristan was all over the place. Manic. Obsessed. "You wanted to switch—you wanted door number three." A tight laugh. "You were willing to sacrifice your own father for your bitch friend. You don't deserve a father."

"You don't understand." Ivy sobbed; her words were garbled.

"If my dad was still alive, *everything* would be different."

Tristan set the laptop down and came forward with the knife. He bared his teeth.

"Steve would still be alive . . . if your father hadn't killed him."

"That's not . . . that's not what happened."

"The fuck it isn't."

So sure of himself. So very wrong.

Tristan used the tip of the blade to lift Ivy's chin.

"You know what? Ivy, if you won't tell me where the laptop is, then you're going to sit here and do the work yourself. You're going to solve your father's half of the equation."

She couldn't. She'd tried to solve Steve's part, got nowhere. Even if Ivy had been smart enough, which she wasn't, the idea of sitting here and accomplishing what had taken their fathers more than twenty years was ludicrous.

"I can't."

"You can." The knife inched closer to her throat. "And you—" Tristan cocked his head as if he'd picked up a sound. He lowered his voice. "—will. Don't fucking move."

Ivy heard it now, too: a car. Approaching slowly.

Tristan put the bag back over her head.

"Don't fucking move."

1009 Ocean Boulevard. 1009 . . . a prime number.

Vaughn cut the lights and let the car coast. Spotted a vehicle in the driveway. Trunk open.

The house was incredible. Sprawling. Stunning. Overlooking a massive cliff.

Vaughn shut off the engine and watched the front windows. Shadows moved. He got out, gun clutched in his hand. Stayed low, hidden behind the car.

Ivy had to be alive in there; Tristan wouldn't kill her.

Vaughn pictured the wall of photographs in Tristan's locked pantry. The word "LAPTOP" in caps, circled multiple times. Ivy's photo. She was in there.

Had to be.

Ivy didn't need to see; all she had to do was remember.

In the same podcast featuring the girl who had mapped the car's route while locked in the trunk, she'd also explained how she'd gotten out of zip ties.

Ivy bent over and untied her shoes. Looped the long lace from one of them through the zip ties, worked her wrists before pinching it again between thumb and forefinger. She tied this to the lace of her other shoe. Then she pushed her feet down while pulling her wrists upward. She started slowly as Tristan mumbled to himself in disbelief. Alternated pushing one foot down, then the next, all the while keeping her elbows bent, the tension high.

"Fucking cop . . ."

Ivy worked faster now, sawing her legs back and forth. The shoelace rubbing against the tie made a *vrrp vrrp vrrp* sound. The plastic snapped in less than a minute, and the pain in her wrists instantly subsided.

Ivy ripped the hood off and ran, but not toward the rear doors—toward the laptop. Couldn't leave it. Not after everything she'd been through. Not after three years of searching. She grabbed it, looked for a place to hide it. Settled on the oven. Opened it and shoved it inside. The oven door closed loudly, alerting Tristan.

"Hey! Ivy, get back here!"

CHAPTER 78

VAUGHN SAW THE man come to the door, peer through the window. Saw another figure in the background, the outline of a woman.

Ivy.

The man turned and ran toward her.

Fuck this.

Vaughn broke from behind the car and went to the front door.

Locked.

Kicked it.

Didn't open.

Kicked again.

It was solid, more solid even than the door back at the firehouse or the pantry.

There was shouting from inside, and Vaughn knew he was running out of time. He backed up and took aim.

Squeezed off two shots. Both direct hits and the lock shattered.

Now when he kicked, the door buckled inward.

Stashing the laptop nearly cost Ivy—she barely made it to the door in time.

Tristan was right behind her.

She flicked the lock, threw the sliding door open, and sprinted into the night.

"Get back here! Ivy! *Ivy!*"

Ivy ran as hard and as fast as she could.

The sound of crashing water grew louder. The grass beneath her still-untied shoes a little longer.

Ivy didn't slow.

The back of the property was expensive, but not endless. Ivy knew she would eventually run out of space.

"*Ivy!*"

And Tristan was gaining on her.

The cliff emerged from the darkness so abruptly that Ivy nearly pitched right over the side. She skidded to a stop, moving her arms in comedic circles to maintain her balance.

Water roared.

"Ivy!" He was right behind her now. "Iv—"

Two gunshots broke the night.

Ivy swiveled.

Tristan was backlit by the moon, full and bright. The bluish light glinted off the blade.

"Just tell me." Tristan was out of breath. "Please, Ivy, tell me you have the laptop."

No longer furious—more sad than anything else.

Ivy felt a pang of guilt.

"Please . . ."

This wasn't about the laptop. Not for him, not for her. Probably never had been.

It was about a family legacy. It was about having something to definitely link to both of their lost childhoods. To their fathers. To justify them spending all of their time at work and not with them.

Then she remembered the bodies in the barn.

Thought of Abby.

Anger replaced the guilt.

"Please . . . my dad . . . my . . ." Tristan was crying now, too. "My dad . . ."

"He's not—"

"Drop the fucking knife!" A shadow appeared behind Tristan. "Drop the fucking knife, Tristan."

Ivy saw a gun, saw Vaughn's face.

Her eyes darted back to Tristan. He was crestfallen.

Broken.

Still clutched the knife, though.

"Tristan, it's over."

The blade finally slipped from Tristan's hand, landed harmlessly in the grass. He started to move to his left, away from Ivy, but toward the edge of the cliff.

"Your father took everything from me, Ivy." She could barely hear Tristan over the crashing waves.

"It's over, Tristan," Vaughn repeated. He, too, sounded defeated.

"It is over," Tristan admitted. Then he gave Ivy the saddest smile she'd ever seen. "I'm no longer a prisoner."

100 Prisoners problem. Prisoner's dilemma.

You're not the prisoner, Ivy thought. *Your dad is the prisoner.*

She realized Tristan's intentions a moment too late.

"No!"

Ivy reached for him, but missed.

Tristan jumped.

"*No!*"

He didn't scream. Didn't utter another word.

Ivy made it to the edge in time to see Tristan land. Only, his body didn't fall in the water.

The Shrewsbury River ran along the bluff, but there was a small embankment just below where Tristan had leapt, an outcropping of just a dozen feet of dry ground.

Tristan landed there.

A mist of blood coated the flowers that his mangled corpse hadn't crushed.

Queen Anne's lace, because of course it was.

Ivy felt an arm slip around her waist, gently ease her back from the cliff. She turned into Vaughn and cried against his chest as he hugged her.

"Abby?" she sobbed. "Is she—"

"Your friend's going to be alright. I got to her in time. I got to *you* in time."

Ivy cried harder.

CHAPTER 79

"WELL, THAT FUCKING sucked," Darnell said a week later as he collapsed in his chair.

Vaughn grinned.

"Hey, at least you went."

"Only thing AA is doing is making me fatter. Donuts are stale as hell, but even you would eat a dozen if you had to listen to Mr. Magoo whining about how he turned to alcohol because his cat died. His *cat.*" Darnell patted his belly. "You think the department will cover Ozempic?"

Vaughn chuckled, grabbed Darnell by the shoulder.

"Glad you're getting help."

"Hmm. What are you doing?"

"Taking down the board."

Vaughn reached up and removed a photo of Dr. Moorehead. Put it on the stack with the others. He was almost done. Took a moment to survey the remaining few photos on the board.

It reminded him of the wall in Tristan's house.

All those photos, the writing.

How many things did that psychopath put up on his wall? A thousand? Bowes and Caine were still working through it all, just to tie up loose ends. It was a moot point now that Tristan was dead.

All those photos, but one of them in particular bothered Vaughn. It should be the one of Ivy sleeping. Only, it wasn't.

It was the one of Steve Neely and Eugene Reeves, the latter signing a document at an award reception.

There was something about it that was off. Something that just didn't sit right.

Vaughn's phone rang and he answered, shooting a look at Darnell as he did.

"Delaney, what's up?"

"Found our boy Joshua Perry. He just walked out of a GMC dealership. Bought himself a brand new truck. You want me to pull him back in? Man's unemployed . . . only way he could get that truck is if he got that Bitcoin."

Vaughn thought about it.

"What's he saying?" No jokes from Darnell, no animosity toward Delaney.

"Hold on." Vaughn pressed the phone to his chest. "Josh Perry just bought a new car. Only way he could do that is if Tristan sent him the Bitcoin."

Darnell shrugged.

"So?"

"Wants to know if he should bring him in."

"Why?"

"I dunno. I guess the Bitcoin is evidence—"

"Let him go."

Vaughn's first thought was that Darnell was just saying this because it would fuck with Delaney. But he was inclined to agree with his partner.

Josh Perry had done nothing wrong. A little reckless, answering a shady ad for a fake TV show, but that was it. But being stupid and gullible wasn't a crime.

Besides, Perry had been through the wringer.

What had Ivy called the winning strategy? Tit-for-tat? Nice guy strat?

By all accounts, Perry was a nice guy.

Vaughn put the phone back to his ear.

"Let him go."

"You sure?" Delaney sounded surprised.

"Yep. Just forget about him. Actually, on second thought, is Horowitz with you?"

"He is."

"Have him follow Perry."

"Well, I drove, so—"

"Have Horowitz follow him on foot."

"On *foot*? Perry just bought a new—"

"On foot."

Darnell chuckled at this. A little petty, but Vaughn was still pissed at the cop for ratting on him to the captain.

"Okay. Hey, Detective Ryan, about that thing?"

"I already put a word in with the captain."

Vaughn had.

"Thanks. Owe you."

He hung up.

"So Tristan actually paid out the Bitcoin, huh?" Darnell mused.

"Seems that way."

"You think that's weird? Killing all those people and yet he pays out when someone beats one of his games?"

"Not really. I mean, he was a math guy. Had a set of rules."

"Rules that involved killing innocent people."

"He probably didn't see it that way. Probably thought he was giving them a chance—a chance his father never had. I dunno."

Darnell shook his head and poured himself a fresh cup of coffee. The man seemed to be replacing all of his alcohol intake with terrible coffee. Made him piss twenty times a day. Still, they were both better off for it.

"I still can't believe it. All this for a fucking math solution?"

It was more than that, though.

Ivy had tried to explain the Riemann hypothesis to him, but Vaughn didn't get it. Not even close. All he understood was that Gene and Steve's work was worth a lot of money.

"People have killed for less."

Vaughn went back to taking the photos off the board.

"You hear anything from the captain about Zeke?" Darnell asked.

His partner had only been gone a week, but it felt like a lifetime. Vaughn had done his best to keep Darnell apprised of developments in the case—both cases— but following Tristan's death, things had moved quickly.

They had Zeke cornered, had him dead to rights on Rebecca Quinn's murder. But like all rich criminals, Zeke had a card up his sleeve.

"They're working out a deal," Vaughn said.

"A deal?" Darnell scoffed. "Zeke's prints were on the knife, Rebecca Quinn's blood on his shirt. And with Dr. Reeves's testimony, the DA should—"

"He had information regarding Tristan Neely."

Darnell lifted an eyebrow.

"Go on."

"Zeke said that Tristan caught him cheating long before he was first reported. Offered him a proposition: 'I'll ignore the cheating if you find a laptop for me.'"

"Gene Reeves's laptop," Darnell said.

"Yep," Vaughn confirmed. "Gave him a tight timeline and when he failed, turned him in. Oh, and Zeke said that Tristan made him print out those flyers at the DAL, probably to redirect our focus to Gene. Zeke also let Tristan use his father's company mansion in Sea Bright."

"Convenient, no?"

"Yeah," Vaughn agreed. "I thought it was bullshit, and maybe Zeke's dad was using his connections in the PPD to feed him information that his son just gave right back to us. But then we found some of those flyers in Zeke's place."

"Huh. Bet that made the DA happy."

"Means that Zeke isn't going away for life."

"Also means that Devon's donations will keep flowing to the PPD. Maybe even Princeton." Darnell gave Vaughn a disgusted look.

"Yeah, my sentiments exactly."

Vaughn went back to taking down the photos and was on the last one when the door opened.

"Detective Ryan, there you are—finally managed to catch you."

It was Bowes, hopped up on caffeine and Adderall. Twitchy. Eyes darting.

"Well, I'm here—you found me."

"You like to hang up on people a lot, don't you?"

It took Vaughn a moment to realize that Bowes was just joking around.

"Have limited minutes and my cell phone bill is already hella expensive."

"I know a guy who can hook you up. Unlimited, untraceable—"

"What is it, Bowes?"

"Well, remember that whole thing about Tristan being the only TA applicant?"

"Yeah," Vaughn said. "He deleted the other applications, right? Using the laptop that Aaron had stolen from Dr. Reeves?" *The one Tristan thought Gene Reeves's half of the Riemann hypothesis was on?* "The laptop that Tristan likely paid him to steal for him?"

Just like he paid him for his security card?

They still hadn't found it yet—Tristan had probably ditched it after gaining access to the gas. Most of Vaughn's thoughts were assumptions, but they seemed to fit the narrative.

"Right . . . but not exactly."

"What do you mean?"

"The laptop that was stolen—Dr. Reeves's laptop—was the one that was used to delete the other applicants. But the applications were deleted *eight* months ago."

Bowes stared at Vaughn expectantly. He didn't get it. Was he that stupid?

"So?"

"So, the campus security report for the stolen laptop was *six* months ago."

Now he understood.

Oh, shit.

It clicked and Vaughn's heart skipped a beat. Not just the laptop, but the reason why the photo of Dr. Reeves and Dr. Neely, the former signing the award, felt so strange to him.

All the jokes with Darnell and Bowes were back of mind now.

"Bowes, did you put this in your report?"

Bowes picked up on Vaughn's change in both tone and attitude. He, too, grew serious.

"Not yet."

"Lifetime supply of Red Bull in it for you if you keep it to yourself."

Bowes removed his glasses and cleaned them on his shirt.

"Make it Celsius and you got a deal."

"Done. And thanks for everything."

"No prob."

Bowes left and Vaughn turned to Darnell. The man mimed zipping his lips and tossing away an invisible key. Seemed fair after all the secrets that Vaughn had kept regarding Darnell during their time together.

Vaughn finished with the board, closed the folder containing all but one of the images. Kept that one for himself.

"You wanna grab a bite after work today?" Darnell asked. "Boring-ass non-alcoholic dinner with a friend who owes you? My treat?"

"Wish I could, Darnell, but I have a date."

"Let me guess, Bae-sian Prof?"

"You nailed it."

Darnell's lips curled downward slightly.

"You be careful with that one, Vaughn."

You and your fucking hunches, Darnell.

Vaughn hated that his partner had been right.

Again.

"Whatever." Vaughn dragged out the word.

"I'm serious. She's smarter than all of us combined."

Oh, of that, I have no doubt.

The entire time, Dr. Ivy Reeves had been playing chess while they were all engaged in a simple game of checkers.

CHAPTER 80

"You look nice," Vaughn said.

"Better than last time you saw me, that's for sure."

Ivy hugged him.

"Neither of us were at our best," Vaughn admitted.

They entered the small restaurant. A sushi joint, Ivy's choice. Dark. Intimate.

They ordered drinks. Vaughn was quiet.

"So they promoted me to interim department head."

"Really? That was fast."

"No kidding. I think they just want to keep me happy. Squashed that bullshit breach of code of conduct case. It's only temporary, but the higher-ups said that it would likely become permanent at the start of next year, if . . ." Ivy trailed off.

"If?"

"If I keep my mouth shut."

"And will you?"

"Never liked to gossip."

"Congrats, then."

Vaughn raised his glass of beer. Ivy clinked hers against his. No Guinness this time. A lager.

They didn't talk much. And when their trays of sushi arrived, they talked even less.

Ivy was beginning to think that this was a mistake. She knew the odds. Relationships born during times of high stress had a low probability of success. Nothing ever lived up to the intensity of the initial interactions.

This seemed different, though. Ivy didn't know all that much about the handsome detective, but she was good at reading people.

There was something on the man's mind.

"Vaughn?"

He swallowed a piece of tuna sashimi.

"Yeah?"

"You wanna ask me something?"

Vaughn screwed up his face. Opened his mouth, closed it again.

"Vaughn . . ."

"Actually, yes."

The man's phone had remained in his pocket up to this point—a good sign on a first date—but now he pulled it out.

Flicked his thumb across the screen, held it up for her to see.

"You recognize this man?"

Of course she did.

"Yeah, that's Blake. The guy from the bar."

Vaughn shook his head.

"It's not. I mean, we're pretty sure it's him—your friend Abby confirmed it—but his name isn't Blake."

"Really?"

Ivy wasn't terribly surprised; "Blake" wouldn't be the first man to make up a persona to try and pick up a woman at a bar. She was confused why Vaughn was telling her this, however.

"Really. His name is Henry Lane. Hard as hell to track down, but we found him."

Ivy shrugged, not sure where this was going.

"He works for Devon Godfrey."

"Okay. And?"

"And Devon's son, Zeke, who you are familiar with, was being blackmailed by Tristan to do his bidding."

Ivy pressed her chin to her chest.

"*What?*"

Vaughn nodded.

"Yep. Just not sure how Henry Lane fits into all of this."

Ivy was still stuck on the idea of Tristan blackmailing Zeke. She relived the moment when Zeke had been threatening her in the hall and Tristan had approached. Zeke had immediately backed down. He'd done the same thing when Blake—no, not Blake, Henry—had saved her at the club. But Henry was much bigger than Zeke.

Tristan wasn't.

Something had felt off about the interaction, but Ivy had been too preoccupied to put much thought into it.

Now she realized why: Zeke had been terrified of her TA, a hundred-fifty-pound math graduate student because he had dirt on him.

The cheating. It had to be the cheating. Tristan knew about it before he told Ivy. Blackmailing Zeke for what, though?

"Henry's not saying anything," Vaughn continued. Ivy was only half listening now, trying to put this all together. "I guess it *could* be a coincidence, but I just don't like coincidences. It did get me thinking . . . Tristan was staying in a home owned by Impact Investing, which is, in turn, owned by Devon. What if Devon wanted the laptop, too? Which, by the way, we never found. It's possible that Devon was also working with Tristan."

Two murderous psychopaths working together, financed by a third—maybe unfair to Devon, but Ivy had read once that all major business leaders had at least some psychopathic and sociopathic tendencies.

What were the odds?

"Anyway, food for thought. And all of this," Vaughn swirled his finger in a small circle, "for a laptop." He swiped his finger across his phone screen. "Speaking of which, do you know this picture, Ivy?"

She expected to see "Blake's" friend Tony, perhaps with an accompanying comment about how he was a registered sex offender or had some other equally nefarious past, but instead, she was surprised to recognize the image.

"Of course, that's Steve and my dad. They'd just jointly won the Bôcher Memorial Prize. Why?"

"That's your dad signing the paper, right?"

"The acceptance—yeah."

Ivy had no idea why Vaughn was showing her this photo, either.

"With his left hand. Your dad, he was—sorry, is—a lefty, right?"

Ivy clammed up. This wasn't trending in the right direction.

Vaughn nodded to himself, put the phone away. Ate another piece of sushi.

"So . . . I did a little research in my spare time."

Nope, not trending well at all.

"Found out that after the fire, the ME used two things to identify the body of the unfortunate man who died. One was your claim that you recognized your father from his wedding band—Steve didn't wear one, his wife died years ago—and you dragged him out of the fire. Saved his life. The second was dental records for the deceased. A positive match to Steve Neely."

Ivy pressed her lips together so tightly that small vertical creases formed in her upper lip.

"I got to wondering, how difficult would it be for someone who was pretty good with computers—good enough to, say, delete all applicants but one for a TA position—to switch the dental records of two individuals? I mean, you wouldn't have to even copy or paste the images. You could just change the names in the main database." Vaughn swirled his glass. The beer spun a miniature vortex—exactly what Ivy's life suddenly felt like. "You know, this whole time, I thought that Tristan deleted the other applications to get close to you. But that wasn't right, was it? It was you who made sure he became your TA so that you could get close to *him*."

Ivy felt sweat break out on her forehead.

Vaughn drank the rest of his beer. Then he surprised her by raising his hand and calling the waitress over.

"Can I get another, please?"

"Sure. And for you?"

Ivy hesitated. She still had three-quarters of a pint left. She downed it all, but her throat remained parched.

"Please."

The drinks came a few minutes later. Ivy hadn't touched

her food in the interim. She took a heavy gulp. Set her glass down. Stared at the condensation on the side.

"And then," Vaughn finally continued after what seemed like an age, "I went to Dr. Reeves's room at the DAL residence. Found it strange that you visited him every week, but never put up a single photo of your father on the walls. Not of you and him, not of him at work. Definitely not the . . . what did you call it? Boucher Award signing?"

"Bôcher Memorial Prize," Ivy said dryly.

"Right. The one where he's signing with his *left* hand. The thing is, Ivy, when I saw your dad the first time, he was fiddling with this chest piece—the rook. And he was using his *right* hand."

Ivy lowered her eyes. Her own hand was burning. No, not her hand—not exactly.

Her thumb and right index finger.

CHAPTER 81

Three Years Ago

Ivy drove as fast as she dared, her father's ominous words repeating over and over in her head.

The work . . . the work is what matters . . . Dr. Neely . . . he's going to do something . . . find his laptop . . . the laptop, Ivy . . . the laptop . . .

She didn't notice the fire, not at first; it wasn't visible from outside. But, to be fair, she hadn't really been looking.

Ivy opened the front door and immediately felt the heat. It was like a wall. Her eyes watered; her skin immediately became slick.

"Dad! *Dad!*"

She saw the flames now. Mostly white and yellow. High heat.

The kitchen.

Jesus, it was hot. So fucking hot.

"*Dad!*"

She found him. Ran to his crumpled body. Inhaled smoke, broke into a coughing fit. Dropped down.

"No . . ."

He was gone. Face was practically melted off. Blood dripping from his forehead. Boiling. Blood on a rook paperweight off to one side.

Sobbing, she checked for a pulse. Pulled her hand back. Her father's skin was as hot as a stove element.

"No! Please . . ."

Her own flesh was starting to crisp.

From somewhere above, she heard a thump. Eyes shot up. It came from the second floor.

The laptop, Ivy. Find Steve's laptop.

The words so vivid that it was like the dead man in her lap was saying those words rather than her remembering them.

Ivy reluctantly lowered her father's head to the hardwood and went up the stairs. The flames that engulfed the kitchen had yet to reach the top floor, but the smoke was thick.

She covered her nose and mouth with the neck of her shirt, but this didn't do much. Every breath was like inhaling acid. Put her on the verge of a coughing fit.

Steve was on the upper landing.

Like Gene, he was face down. His skin was even more scorched than the man's downstairs. But he was still alive. Unbelievable.

The thump she'd heard was Steve collapsing on his stomach.

"Where's the laptop?" Ivy demanded. "Where's your laptop?"

The man couldn't answer. Was barely breathing. But he'd come upstairs. There'd been a confrontation on the floor below, and then Steve, instead of running out, had come *here*.

The laptop.

Ivy left the man where he lay and went to the first room she found. A bedroom.

No laptop.

She went to the next room. Black smoke everywhere.

Moved her hands around blindly, knew she was accomplishing nothing other than getting closer to asphyxiation.

If the laptop was here, she'd never find it. *If* it was here.

Her father's laptop wasn't—he'd told her as much on the phone. Told her where he'd stashed it. Trusted her with it. No one else. Not even his wife.

Hid it in plain sight.

Ivy retreated back to the man in the hall.

Steve's skin . . . it was so bad. Like crispy pork. Nose completely black.

The laptop . . . the laptop . . . find Steve's laptop . . .

Ivy did her best to drag Steve carefully down the stairs without hurting him too badly. But when she started coughing and horking up thick strings of phlegm, she gave up. Just pulled.

Somehow managed to get him onto the front lawn—no idea how.

She put her hands on her knees, tried to clear the tears from her eyes. Tried to stop coughing.

Find Steve's laptop . . . save the work . . .

Steve was still alive. Barely. Might not make it.

Gene's laptop wasn't here. Ivy would bet her life that Steve's wasn't either. Steve was the only one who knew where it was.

If he stayed alive . . . he wouldn't tell her. Why would he? The man had already killed Gene—her father had warned her about him, about what he might do—and Gene's head had been bleeding. Steve would probably kill Ivy too, if he thought she had her father's laptop.

Ivy's mind was swimming. Inhaling all that smoke had cut the oxygen to her brain.

If Steve wakes up . . . if Steve wakes up . . .

He was likely to be as confused as she was now. And if she was the first person he saw, she might be able to take advantage of this.

An insane idea. But that's how Ivy felt right now—insane. One minute, her father had been yelling at her over the phone. The next, she found him dead.

Ivy gagged and vomited. This stripped her of more oxygen. Didn't make the idea that had popped into her head go away, though. Did the opposite.

Made it real.

But how would she be by Steve's side if he woke up? The police would investigate, keep her away from the man who killed her father.

Unless . . .

There was no denying the resemblance between Steve and Gene—both tall and thin. Steve's hair had gone salt-and-pepper; Gene's was pure salt. But now, neither had any.

The laptop . . . Steve's laptop . . . save the work . . . promise me . . .

Ivy wasn't thinking straight.

She ran back inside. Found her dad. Grabbed his left hand. Touched his gold wedding band. Cried out. It melted the skin on her fingers. Grabbed it again, took some of Gene's flesh with it. Some of her own, too. Hurried out. Placed it on Steve's finger, weeping the entire time.

Ivy Reeves called 911 twenty-nine minutes after her father had interrupted her dinner. After she reported the fire, she called Abby.

"Hey, bitch? What's up?"

"I need you to listen to me—there's something I need you to do. You can't ask questions, but I promise to fill you in later. It has to be quick. Like, *now* quick."

"Everything alright?"

"No, definitely not."

And Ivy Reeves doubted things would ever be 'alright' ever again.

CHAPTER 82

"Right before I came to you on the bluff, Tristan was saying something . . . he was saying, 'Please, my dad . . . my dad,' something like that?"

Ivy's hand was shaking when she tried to pick up her beer. Decided it wasn't worth the risk of soaking the dress that Abby had loaned her and opted to leave it where it was.

"You said, 'He's not,' and then I showed up. I thought a lot about that. About what you were about to say before I arrived. I think I finally figured it out." Vaughn paused, then raised his eyes, leveled them directly at hers. "You were going to say, 'He's not dead.'"

The final sentence hung in the air.

Ivy hadn't thought the detective was stupid, despite him pretending but clearly not understanding the prisoner games or the Riemann hypothesis. But she hadn't thought that he was *this* smart, either. This good.

A photo, a rook, half a sentence. Deleted TA applications. That was all it took for this detective to blow apart a secret that Ivy had been keeping for three years.

"It was your dad who died in that fire, wasn't it? Not Steve."

Ivy started to cry.

"I think you kept this from everyone. Even your mom. Maybe you meant to tell her, maybe not. But when Steve woke up, even though he couldn't speak, she knew. That's why she left, isn't it, Ivy? Not because she couldn't handle looking after her husband, but because she couldn't handle looking after Steve." Another pregnant pause and then, "How much do you know about Broca's area? The part of Steve's brain that was affected by the fire?'

Ivy didn't answer.

"Well, I didn't know anything, so I asked the ME. Here, this is what he said." Vaughn was reading off his phone now. "Broca's area is critical for both spoken and written language. In the image you sent me I see severe degeneration. I asked him if it could recover and he said, no, the brain cannot regenerate. He did say, and I'm paraphrasing here, that the brain has a certain degree of neuroplasticity. Stupid me, I didn't know what that meant either. Apparently, other structures in the brain can rewire themselves so that healthy portions can take over for damaged regions. That's what you thought might happen, right? You thought that, eventually, he might recover enough to tell you, or at least write, where he hid his laptop."

Ivy didn't know what to say. Couldn't say anything.

Vaughn steepled his hands over his drink.

"I'm not going to sit here and pretend to know what you went through that night or to understand why you did it. I can't possibly . . . seeing your father dead like that, making the decision to switch their identities. You know Detective Howe? The one who worked your father's case? He almost figured it out. He said that your father started the fire and that he killed

Steve. He was right, just had the roles reversed. Steve killed your dad, not the other way around."

Ivy's fingertips, where she'd burned them removing Gene's scalding wedding ring, were beyond aching now. It was as if they were on fire.

"Ivy, I only want to know one thing: *how*? How did you go this long looking after the man who murdered your dad?"

Vaughn had been speaking for more than half an hour now, during which Ivy hadn't said a single word. She didn't want to talk. Vaughn saying these things made it all the more real.

And it wasn't real. It was a farce. A lie.

"I don't know." Ivy's voice barely topped a whisper. Truth was, she didn't think about it much.

At first, yeah—she'd spent hours thinking about how insane everything she'd done was.

How, if her blood oxygen saturation hadn't dropped to 81 percent—a level the paramedic said was fatal to most—she wouldn't have even considered it.

It would have never crossed her mind.

But Vaughn expected an answer. In some ways, he deserved one, too.

"I guess I just fell into a routine," Ivy said softly. "When it became apparent that he was never going to regain his faculties, I could have told someone. But by then—"

"It was too late."

Ivy nodded. Wiped tears from her eyes.

"I actually began thinking of him as my father. He didn't speak, obviously. So, I got comfortable talking to him about things. After my mom left, my friend recommended her therapist. I was skeptical, but gave it a shot. Didn't mind it so much.

The issue was that she was professionally obligated to speak. I didn't want someone to speak. You know, people don't listen anymore. They pretend to listen, but in their heads, they're just working out what to say next. That's what my fath—I mean, Steve—is for me. Someone who just listens."

Vaughn opened his mouth, but when he didn't say anything, Ivy surprised herself by chuckling.

"See? You're doing it now, aren't you?"

"I'm not."

"But you want to ask me something else?"

"I do."

"Might as well spit out it."

"Did you know?" Vaughn said flatly.

Ivy didn't understand.

"Know what?"

"Did you know that Tristan was behind all these murders?"

"No," Ivy said immediately. "I had no idea."

Vaughn stared at Ivy. Probably tried to use his cop instincts or whatever to try and figure out if she was lying.

Ivy didn't break her gaze, and Vaughn was the one who averted his eyes first.

Ivy drank. So did Vaughn. She still wasn't hungry, so Ivy just picked at her food.

"What are you going to do, Vaughn?" The words just came out, unplanned.

The detective took his time before answering.

"Never liked gossip."

Ivy finally felt her face relax.

Maybe relationships borne out of high-pressure situations could work after all.

CHAPTER 83

Sarah Kachinski met Ivy in the doorway. No hands on hips this time, no dour expression. The woman was actually smiling. This was so unusual that Ivy found it slightly alarming.

"How is he?" she asked.

"He's good—fine. Adjusting well to the new surroundings."

Ivy waited.

But he ran away again? He's missing?

She held her tongue.

"Great. How about you?"

"I'm fine, too. Much easier looking after one person than a whole building's worth." Kachinski suddenly grew uncomfortable. "About my salary—"

"It won't be a problem."

"You sure? Because it's—"

Ivy smiled weakly.

"I'm sure. I just got promoted."

"Congratulations, Dr. Reeves. And, again, if the salary becomes—"

"Please, Sarah. It's fine."

The woman's smile returned.

"You want me to stick around? Help put him to bed?"

"No, I'll be okay. Have a friend coming over later."

"I'll see you in the morning then."

"You know what? Take the morning off. Come in around noon."

"Really?"

"Yeah, you deserve a little break. These past few days . . ." Ivy trailed off.

Sarah's smile became strained.

"Thank you."

Ivy watched Sarah get into her car and drive away.

She entered her home. Found the man in the mask seated at the kitchen table. The small chess table was in front of him. He was clutching the rook in his right hand.

Ivy walked over and gently unfurled his mangled fingers. Set the chess piece down.

"Come on, let's get you ready for bed."

It took a good half hour to get the man's teeth brushed and into bed. Sarah had already helped him into his pajamas.

The last thing Ivy did was carefully removed his mask and set it on the nightstand.

"You're not going to need this anymore."

Ivy kissed him on the forehead, said goodnight, and went back downstairs.

Grabbed two beers out of the fridge, opened one, set the other on the table beside the chess board.

Sat and sipped.

Despite what Vaughn Ryan had surprised her with tonight, and the subsequent tears and raw emotions, things had been easier for Ivy over the past few days. It was hard to believe that after three years, it was over.

There was a knock at the door.

It opened.

"Hey, bitch! I'm home!"

"Hey, Abs."

Ivy didn't get up.

Her feet hurt. Back, too. Wrists were still a little red, even though it had been a week since Tristan had bound her and thrown her in the trunk.

In time, these, too, would fade.

Abby was wearing all black. Her blond hair was pulled up in a ponytail, and she kept one arm hidden behind her back.

"Got you a beer. Did you—"

Abby grinned as she moved her hand out in front of her.

"Right where you said it would be, cooking in the oven. Cops did a number on the place. But they never looked in the oven . . . they were probably men, never seen the inside of one before."

Abby placed Tristan's laptop on the table, swapped it for the beer. Collapsed in a chair.

"Weird how it's easier to break into a crime scene than to gain access to a private residence, huh? I mean, breaking into Tristan's house was easy enough, but he had this pantry. It was locked up like Fort Knox."

Ivy stared at the laptop.

"You didn't say anything about a locked pantry," she muttered absently.

"I know. I was planning on going back—with more time, I probably would have gotten in. And I thought the laptop was in there. It had to be. I wanted to surprise you. Guess I was wrong. But, hey, it's here now. It's all yours."

Ivy's thoughts drowned out her friend completely now.

Three years. Three *long* years.

First, searching the house, causing severe burns in her throat for the effort. Forever scarring her fingers. Then reviewing everything the cops had pulled from the rubble. Having Abby break into Tristan's dorm. Steve's old office.

It wasn't there.

For three years, Ivy had been looking for the laptop. And when she'd found out that Steve had a son—which her father had never mentioned before—she'd gone as far as to ensure Tristan was hired as her TA with the hope of getting closer. But while she'd been searching for Steve's laptop, Ivy had had no idea that Tristan was looking for Gene's.

And his approach had been more . . . visceral. Visceral and desperate.

She should have known. Should have seen the pattern.

Steve had killed for the laptop; Tristan had done the same.

Like father, like son.

So much death . . .

That had never been part of the plan. Ivy wanted to find the laptop to prevent any more deaths.

"What are you going to do with you know who?" Abby asked, her eyes flicking upward. "He's not your responsibility."

He never was, not really.

Despite the rather simple way Vaughn had framed her relationship with her surrogate father, Ivy knew that what she had with Steve was more complex.

Vaughn didn't understand the math. Didn't know the true

value of their work, the value of the solution to the Riemann hypothesis. He didn't know how hard things had been for her.

One day, she was a math protégée, daughter to one of the most brilliant minds the country had seen in decades.

The next, everything had been ripped from her grasp. Adopting Steve had been the only thing that had kept her sane. The only person who could understand her problems, her questions, even though he could never answer her.

"I know," she said simply.

Abs knew better than to press.

"By the way, they finally took that TikTok video down," her friend said as she continued to drink her beer.

Ivy had forgotten all about it.

A video of her, taken by Zeke's cell phone but orchestrated by Tristan. He'd planted the seed of the lecture in her mind, knowing that the cops would eventually need help with the crime scene. Paid to boost the video so that her name came to the top of every search list.

Too many variables for her liking, too many unknowns, but it had worked out for Tristan.

Until it hadn't.

Ivy pictured him lying on the blood-spattered Queen Anne's lace.

The only thing that had bothered Ivy was the fact that Tristan had used Zeke's cell phone.

Acquiring the phone had been easy enough—he had access to all the students' cells before class. But to take the video, Tristan would have had to have known the man's passcode.

Tristan was good with computers, knew how to hide his tracks. To break into a cell, though?

Ivy was skeptical that her TA had that sort of skill.

What Vaughn had told her at dinner solidified her theory. Tristan and Zeke had been working together. Henry Lane, too. Probably Devon Godfrey. Everyone wanted the goddamn laptops. And now she had Dr. Neely's, with his half of the Riemann hypothesis, which her father wanted to give away while Steve intended to sell it to the highest bidder.

That was the reason for the fight that night, when they'd finally solved it. Opposites attract.

Ivy set down her beer and swapped it for the chess board she'd taken from the DAL residence. Flipped it over. Picked at the sticker of the 8x8 alternating black and white squares. Peeled it off in one piece.

Tristan had broken into the DAL looking for the laptop, probably broke into her home, too. But it had been there all along, right before his eyes.

Ivy lifted the lid of her father's laptop.

Save the work . . . save the laptop, Ivy . . . it's more important than any of us.

Ivy opened Steve's laptop next, set them side by side. Finally, both pieces of the puzzle. The Riemann hypothesis solved. Thought impossible.

Abby got out of her chair and put her arm around Ivy's neck from behind. Squeezed her. Ivy patted her friend's hand.

"What are you going to do with it?"

Ivy continued to stare at the two computers in reverence, in awe.

"I don't know," she said honestly.

"Well, whatever you decide, I'll always have your back, bitch."

CHAPTER 84

Ivy felt refreshed. For the first time in a week, her sleep had been sound and dreamless.

She awoke just after ten.

When was the last time she'd slept in past ten o'clock?

Couldn't remember.

Not even as a kid. Her late father had always touted the importance of getting up early, having a routine.

Ivy yawned, stretched a little. Laid in bed for a good five minutes before finally getting up.

She took her time in the shower. Finished with a blast of cold water.

It wasn't until she was making her way downstairs that she remembered that she no longer lived alone.

Ivy had a roommate.

Abs had said that Steve Neely was no longer her responsibility. True. But she still felt obligated to look after the man.

And despite his inability to communicate, their relationship was far from one-sided.

For three years, Steve Neely had acted as a stand-in father

to her. And before he'd started wandering, the predictability of the man's routine had offered her comfort.

He couldn't talk, but Ivy could still speak to him. And when they were alone, she did just that. Shared things with him, things that only Abby knew. About that night, sure, but about other stuff, too. Her struggles with her work, with balancing everything on her ever-widening plate.

"Gene?"

It felt good to call her father's name, even knowing that he was gone.

"Gene?"

Ivy ducked into her father's room. Found the bed not just empty, but made.

This made her brow crinkle. Confused, Ivy headed downstairs next.

"Gene?"

Had Sarah showed up? She'd told the woman to take the morning off. Come in around noon or whenever she felt like it. Sarah Kachinski had been through a lot, too. The woman was kind. Kind and caring.

"Sarah?"

No answer to that, either.

Now Ivy's brow was so creased that it nearly folded over. The lines on her forehead and at the corners of her eyes felt thick.

Maybe I'll speak to Abs after all. Get a little Botox.

Yeah, things were different this morning.

"Gene?"

He wasn't in the kitchen. Wasn't on the back porch, either. Where the hell was he?

Ivy knew Abby thought that her looking after the man who had killed her father was odd. And it was a little off base. But Ivy never looked at it that way; she came at it differently.

Steve Neely was part of an equation, a means to an end . . . no, not an end, a means to a *solution*.

A piece—

Ivy froze. Only her heart continued to beat.

A *piece*.

There was a chess piece on the kitchen counter. A rook.

A smaller version of the paperweight that Steve Neely had used to cave her father's head in.

Ivy finally managed to move. She picked up the chess piece, felt the strange texture in her fingers that had long since lost most of their feeling. Ivy squeezed the rook in her palm. The pain of the sharp edges digging into her skin brought some of her senses back.

Her eyes scanned the kitchen counter. Saw nothing.

Saw . . . *nothing*.

The laptops!

Gene and Steve's laptops. She'd left them there last night.

Where the hell are they?

Still gripping the rook, Ivy rushed out the front door. The sun was bright, and she squinted as she looked up and down the empty street. Continued to search until a car made its way into her driveway and parked. Sarah Kachinski got out, a big smile on her bigger face.

"Morning!" She took two steps. Halted. "Ivy? What's wrong? Is Gene wandering again?"

Oh, he was wandering, all right. But it wasn't Gene.

Ivy cleared her throat. The rook fell from her hand, landed

on the porch. Bounced once before resting on its side, a miniature version of the one she'd seen at the fire. It even had a dot of blood on it from where the sharp edges had cut into her skin.

For three years, Ivy had kept a terrible secret.

Turns out, she wasn't the only one.

Neuroplasticity—Vaughn teaching her something for once.

Ivy had used Steve, told him everything. And in return, he'd used her. Waited for her to do all the legwork.

Find the laptops.

Both of them, together.

And then, the moment she let her guard down—for one *fucking* night—he'd stolen them both.

Ivy thought she was smart, but Steve Neely, like her real father, was smarter.

Always had been.

"Ivy?"

"He's gone," she whispered. "Steve's gone."

It was the first time she'd called the man by his real name, but if Sarah noticed, it didn't register with the woman.

"He's gone, Sarah."

And Ivy knew, deep down, that this time, they'd never find him again.

Him or the laptops.

END